'Lee's story celebrates the power of poetry, of book, reading, to lend us a "sixth sense" that can heal and transform even in the harshest times. In this hellish jail, poetry both subverts and redeems, and "Only the purest language could testify about the most brutal era" . . . this Korean bestseller deserves to fly across our own prison walls'
*Independent*

'Gripping . . . Not just a whodunnit that provides the relief of a clear resolution. The book also tells the story of Japan's wartime history and is inspired by the real-life jailed Korean poet and dissident Yun Dong-ju, whose work is quoted throughout'
*Financial Times*

'Lee's extraordinary *The Investigation* is set in a period of Korean history that isn't widely known in the West . . . this is a heart-wrenching novel with many unexpected twists'
*Sunday Times*

'I was gripped by *The Investigation*. It came at me from nowhere and consumed me. It's a thriller, and a war story, and so much more besides. I tore through the last 100 pages, my heart literally racing at times. An intense, captivating achievement, inspired by reality'
Matt Haig, bestselling author of *The Humans*

'This novel mesmerizes the readers with its prison setting, complex characters, solid structure, and foreshadowing through a wide range of literary devices. Readers who have enjoyed Marcus Zusak's *The Book Thief* or Stephen King's *Shawshank Redemption* will also like *The Investigation*' List

# THE INVESTIGATION

J. M. Lee has sold hundreds of thousands
of copies of his books in his native Korea. One, *Deep
Rooted Tree*, was made into a popular TV series.

Chi-Young Kim is the celebrated translator of the
Man Asian Literary Prize-winning international
bestseller *Please Look After Mother*.

# THE INVESTIGATION

## J. M. LEE

TRANSLATED FROM THE KOREAN
BY CHI-YOUNG KIM

PAN BOOKS

First published 2014 by Mantle

This paperback edition published 2015 by Pan Books
an imprint of Pan Macmillan, a division of Macmillan Publishers Limited
Pan Macmillan, 20 New Wharf Road, London N1 9RR
Basingstoke and Oxford
Associated companies throughout the world
www.panmacmillan.com

ISBN 978-1-4472-2825-7

Originally published in Korean in 2012 as *Byureul Seuchineun Baram* by EunTlaeng NaMu Publishing Co.

The Daesan Foundation supported the translation and publication of this book.

Typeset by Palimpsest Book Production Limited, Falkirk, Stirlingshire
Printed and bound by CPI Group (UK) Ltd, Croydon, CR0 4YY

Visit **www.panmacmillan.com** to read more about all our books
and to buy them. You will also find features, author interviews and
news of any author events, and you can sign up for e-newsletters
so that you're always first to hear about our new releases.

# THE INVESTIGATION

# THINGS LONG GONE
# FLICKER LIKE FIREFLIES

Life may not have a purpose. But death requires clarity – not to prove that death occurred, but for the benefit of those who survive. This lesson, which I learned this past winter, made me who I am now. War had whipped me like a sandstorm. Somehow, even as I was worn down, eroded, I grew up, little by little. One might be congratulated for maturing, for the body becomes stronger and one accumulates experience; but to get here I'd lost so much. I am unable to return to who I'd been before, when I was unaware of the world's cruelty, the evil among us or the power inherent in a written line.

The war ended on 15 August 1945. The prisoners were freed, but I'm still here. The only thing that's changed is that now I am behind bars, my brown guard uniform exchanged for this red prisoner's garb. Dark numbers are printed clearly on my chest: D29745. I don't entirely understand why I'm here. During the war I was stationed as a soldier-guard at Fukuoka Prison. Now the Americans have classified me as a low-level war criminal. I am incarcerated in the very cell I once patrolled, in this immense prison of tall brick walls, sharp barbed wire, thick bars and the brick rooms that swallowed the lives of thousands.

Pale sunlight falls on the dark wooden floor, which not long ago was soaked with blood and pus. With a finger, I scrawl down some words in the rectangular patch of light, as though I were writing on paper. My muscles are firm, my skin is smooth, my blood is red, but my eyes have seen too much brutality. I'm only twenty.

The American military has charged me with the abuse of prisoners. I suppose it's a logical accusation; even I wouldn't say I'm innocent. I've abused prisoners, sometimes on purpose, at other times without even realizing it. I've yelled at them and beaten them. I have to accept responsibility for that. But I'm guiltier still of something else: the crime of doing nothing. I didn't prevent the unnecessary deaths of innocent people. I was silent in the face of the insanity. I closed my ears to the screams of the innocent.

The story I'm about to tell isn't about me; it's about the war's destruction of the human race. This story is about both the people who lacked humanity and the purest of men. And it's about a bright star that crossed our dark universe 10,000 years ago. I don't really know where this story will start or how it will end, or whether I can even finish it. I will just write it all down. My story is about two people who met at Fukuoka Prison. In my narrow cell I remember their lives behind the tall, firm brick wall, on the sun-soaked yard and under the shadows of the tall poplars. One prisoner and one guard; one poet and one censor.

# PART ONE

# AS A STRANGER I ARRIVED, AS A STRANGER AGAIN I LEAVE

The bell clanged, ripping through the dawn air. What happened? Had there been a prison break? I sprang up from the hard bed in the guardroom. It was still dark outside. I tightened my boot laces as the lights flickered on in the long corridor.

An urgent voice rang out over the crackling speakers. 'All guards report to your cells and begin roll call. Report anything unusual immediately. The guard on patrol duty for Ward Three, stand by at the entrance to the main corridor!'

Two guards manned the overnight rounds, which began at exactly 10 p.m. It took an hour and fifty minutes to check each cell on both sides of the long corridor and to inspect the locks. Shift change was at midnight, two and four in the morning. Sugiyama Dozan, with whom I worked, was a veteran over forty years old. When I'd returned to the guardroom after the 2 a.m. rounds, he was perched on the bed, tightening his gaiters. He'd left the room without a word, his club fastened to his hip. As he disappeared into the darkness, his back looked indistinct, ghostly. My eyelids, heavy with fatigue, had tugged me down into the black swamp of sleep – sleep that was now shattered.

I forced my tired eyes open and sprinted down the main

corridor leading to the guard offices. Big dogs were barking in the darkness beyond the red-brick walls. The spotlight from the watchtower sliced through the night like a sharp blade. The urgent shouts of the guards outside reached my ears. On either side of the narrow corridor prisoners looked out through the bars of their cells, bleary eyes ripe with annoyance and resentment. The guards threw open the cell doors to conduct the roll call. Voices calling out prisoner numbers and the prisoners' responses swirled with the alarm. I ran, chased by the thudding of my own boots. I skidded to a stop in the main corridor of Ward Three. What I saw made me want to escape into a dream. It was worse than a nightmare. Reddish-black blood was splattered on the main corridor, making a sunburst pattern. It was still falling from the second-floor railing. The body was hanging naked from a rope wrapped around a crossbeam on the ceiling. His arms were open at his sides and tied to the railing. Blood dripped from the left side of his chest, down his stomach and thigh, and hung for a moment on the tip of his big toe before falling to the ground. His head was bowed. He was staring down at me. Sugiyama Dozan.

Goosebumps pricked my body. Death was something I'd never thought about; it wasn't a becoming topic for a nineteen-year-old. Although I was in uniform, I was still only a boy. I gagged a few times and wiped my wet eyes. Other guards were milling around in confusion, unable to decide whether to leave the corpse hanging over the main corridor or cut it down. I approached again and shone my torch on his face. His lips had been sealed. Seven neat, delicate stitches led from the lower to the upper lip and back. I forced myself to lock my rattling knees.

Head guard Maeda arrived, and the blood drained from

his face. He stuttered an urgent order: 'Take the body down, cover it and move it to the infirmary!'

Several guards ran up to the second floor to undo the knot and eased the corpse slowly to the ground. Two others brought a stretcher and quickly disappeared with the body.

'Who's the alternate patrol?' Maeda asked, looking around.

I stiffened to attention. 'Watanabe Yuichi! Patrol on duty.'

Maeda threw me a sharp glance and shouted at me. Overwhelmed by the sour odour of vomit and the bright searchlight slicing the darkness, I couldn't hear anything other than the siren from the outer watchtower and the barking of the guard dogs.

The guard who had been searching the building entrance ran back in. 'About half a foot of snow fell overnight, but there isn't a single footprint anywhere; nobody has entered or left this building.'

That much was obvious. There were no puddles of melted snow or wet footprints around the crime scene. Where did the murderer come from? Where did he go?

A senior guard tapped me on the shoulder. I came to my senses. He relayed Maeda's order to gather Sugiyama's belongings and prepare an incident report. I ran up the stairs to the second floor. Flung to the ground next to the railing was his uniform. Sugiyama always had every button fastened. The uniform was his skin; without the uniform he was nothing. Now the arms and legs were inside out, the buttons were missing. I noticed that his uniform top didn't have any cuts in it. The murderer had taken off his uniform before hanging him. Only then had he driven a long, steel stake into Sugiyama's heart. His trousers, with worn, baggy knees, had been tossed carelessly aside, but crisp pleats still ran down the middle of each leg. Sugiyama had stitched his pockets closed to ensure that he didn't slide his hand into them; the neat needlework was the secret to his composed gait.

I reached into the inner pocket of the uniform top and trembled like a boy reaching into a warm bird's nest. My fingertips touched something like a baby bird's feather – a piece of coarse paper folded twice over. I unfolded it. The words, nestled together to create small villages, whispered to me:

## GOOD NIGHT

*As a stranger I arrived,*
*As a stranger again I leave.*
*May was kind to me*
*With many bunches of flowers.*
*The girl spoke of love,*
*Her mother even of marriage,*
*Now the world is bleak,*
*The path covered by snow.*

*I cannot choose the time*
*Of my departure;*
*I must find my own way*
*In this darkness.*
*With a shadow cast by the moonlight*
*As my travelling companion*
*I'll search for animal tracks*
*On the white fields.*

*Why should I linger, waiting*
*Until I am driven out?*

*Let stray dogs howl*
*Outside their master's house;*
*Love loves to wander*
*God has made her so*
*From one to the other.*
*Dear love, good night!*

*I will not disturb you in your dreaming,*
*It would be a pity to disturb your rest;*
*You shall not hear my footsteps*
*Softly, softly shut the door!*
*On my way out I'll write*
*'Good Night' on the gate,*
*So that you may see*
*That I have thought of you.*

Each line exuded grief and despair, and an intense love; each stanza recalled a sad man walking away on a snow-covered night road. I examined the note carefully – the spot of ink that had spread where the pen had stopped, hesitating; the shape of the clumsy, rapid or slow strokes; the small changes of indentation from pen pressing against paper. Did he write this poem or did he simply copy someone else's? If this hand wasn't his, whose was it? Did someone plant this note, and why was this poem in Sugiyama's inner pocket?

Before I speak about Sugiyama Dozan's death again, I should talk about his life. I had spent three months in Ward Four before being transferred to Ward Three a mere three days prior to his death. I knew next to nothing about him. He didn't become a ghost in death; to me, he'd been one when he was alive. He would pace the corridor in Ward Three under the incandescent lights, his footsteps measured, holding the register in one hand. When he did so, the prisoners quieted and studied his back from the safety of their cells. His pale skin was almost transparent and his face was as cold as a plaster bust. He never spoke, his mouth like Ali Baba's cave that had forgotten how to open. Once in a blue moon a flat, hoarse voice would leak out through his dry lips. He didn't need to yell; he knew how to strike fear into someone with his soft voice. His cleanly shaven chin was dark blue under his crooked nose. The guards gossiped about who could possibly have crushed his nose – a legendary left-handed *yakuza*, a tall Soviet soldier he'd encountered at Nomonhan, or perhaps shrapnel from a shell that exploded right next to him or the butt of a Soviet Type-99 Arisaka rifle. But nobody knew the truth. His cap settled low on his brow, hiding his eyes. A reddish scar ran down his face to his lips and glistened in the sunlight. Not many people knew where the scar began; it might have stretched past his eye all the way up to his forehead.

Sugiyama was omnipresent. He was where he had to be and he did what he had to do. He was so skilful that it was as if nothing ever happened. Everyone knew his name – guards and prisoners, Japanese and Korean – and feared and scorned it. I don't mean to repeat tall tales simply to cast him in a more interesting light. But if I had to say anything about him, I think it would be best to start with those stories.

Sugiyama was assigned to Fukuoka Prison in the summer of 1939. The warden had high expectations for the Manchurian

Front hero; he hoped the arrival of a proper military mindset would remedy the chaos in the prison. According to hearsay, Sugiyama was a sergeant in the Kwantung Army in Manchuria – the 64 Brigade of the 28th Infantry Regiment. He fought without understanding why, and witnessed his comrades dying. At one point his company was surrounded by the Soviet 9th Mechanized Corps. The Imperial Japanese Army's Division Headquarters gave orders to each unit to break through the siege and retreat eastwards. Sugiyama lay in ambush all day with thirty men and, when the shelling stopped at night, launched an attack on the Soviet tank division. After two weeks of isolation they managed to break through the siege and retreat. He was practically the sole survivor to emerge from the fire pit that saw the demise of thirty tanks, 180 aeroplanes and 20,000 troops.

Nobody knew if that story was true. All that could be confirmed was that the Kwantung Army's 28th Infantry Regiment battled with Soviet-Mongolian forces in Nomonhan. Facts stood here and there throughout the story to give plausible support to his heroic exploits. The guards talked about the battle as though they had actually witnessed it. There was a guard who said he had seen seven bullet wounds on Sugiyama's body. One guard claimed that Sugiyama was completely deaf in his left ear because a bomb had exploded right next to him. Another insisted that there was a fist-sized piece of shrapnel embedded in Sugiyama's torso. These rumours were laid over his reticence, creating a sheen of truth.

A few guards were actual witnesses to another story. When Sugiyama arrived at the prison, he had a slight limp from a gunshot wound to his right leg. His beard was unkempt and his eyes glinted like those of a wild animal.

He seemed to view this isolated prison as a new battlefield; though there was no enemy, he regarded everyone as the foe. He brandished his club freely, not letting a single action or word by a prisoner go unchecked. He was vicious and crafty. The prisoners feared him and the guards avoided him. Overnight he gained even more notoriety, thanks to the way he addressed a Korean prisoner riot.

Three Korean prisoners had locked themselves in the prison workshop, convinced some student draft-dodgers to join them and gone on a rampage. They took three Japanese prisoners hostage and demanded that the warden grant all the rioters prisoner-of-war status. Although such incidents were to be reported to the Special Higher Police, the warden chose not to; he considered the confines of the red-brick walls to be his territory. Calling the Special Higher Police to the prison would be a humiliation. He opened the armoury and distributed rifles to the guards. That was when Sugiyama stepped up, offering to enter the workshop to subdue the rioters. The warden just stared at him. Sugiyama took off his uniform top and told the warden to storm the doors with armed guards if he didn't re-emerge in ten minutes. He stepped inside as though he were being sucked in. The doors closed quietly behind him. The warden kept his eyes locked on the clock; the long, thin second hand sliced his heart with fine strokes. Five minutes passed. The guards' sweaty palms began to slip against their rifles. The warden prepared to enter, bracing himself for the loss of life. At that moment they heard a crash emanating from inside, along with faint screams. The guards pushed through the doors. Sugiyama was standing on a tall worktable with his club by his side. On the floor were men with bleeding heads, torn lips and swelling eyes, squirming like insects.

This story might be an exaggeration, too, but it was true that Sugiyama had gone alone into the rioters' den, and an undeniable fact that he came out without a scratch. After that incident, he resumed his shadowy existence. He was someone who existed through rumours alone. Only after he died did I explicitly feel his presence. And only then did I realize I really knew nothing about him.

Giant steel doors and a looming brick wall guarded the main entrance to Fukuoka Prison. The central facilities looked like a person prone, with the head facing the north and both arms outstretched. Fukuoka Prison had been a regional prison until three years before, when it was elevated to national status. With the Pacific War the country fell into chaos. Anti-war intellectuals and criminals ran wild, beyond the reach of the police. The prison was extended repeatedly, but still it couldn't handle the massive influx of prisoners. But the authorities had deemed it necessary to have internment facilities to isolate the anti-Japanese Koreans, who were quick to erupt with complaints, and decided on Fukuoka Prison, away from the heart of the country.

The administrative offices, including the warden's office, were sited in the central facilities. Japanese prisoners who were accorded special treatment were held in Ward One. Wards Two and Three split off at the end of the administrative wing. In Ward Two were vicious murderers or robbers, and long-term prisoners. Ward Three was reserved for anti-Japanese Korean rebels and death-row inmates. Lesser Japanese criminals were held in Wards Four and Five, which were added onto Ward Three to the west.

Despite the additions, the prison still overflowed with inmates. Ward Three in particular teemed with incidents, accidents and trouble. Prisoners went on hunger strikes, violence was frequent and executions were common. These Koreans were determined to be the most vicious, dangerous inmates and they were treated accordingly. The most robust and strongest guards were assigned there and every order was given with the swing of a club. Countless prisoners were beaten to death.

The dark scent of tobacco and mahogany washed over me as I stood at attention in the warden's office. The bracing morning air came through the open window. An award certificate stamped with the Emperor's royal seal was hanging on the wall and underneath it, side by side, were the crest of the samurai and the Rising Sun. A long military knife and a gleaming rifle were displayed on a solid-wood cabinet. Warden Hasegawa, whose balding pate was ringed with a thatch of hair, waved a long baton as though it were an extension of his body, his eyes closed. His chestnut-brown trousers were sharply creased and badges flashed on his chest. A man's powerful, elegant singing, edged with sadness, reverberated in the room. A record was spinning on the phonograph, which stood on a table draped with red velvet. The warden's office, complete with elegant floor-to-ceiling windows, sonorous singing and blinding morning sun, was a sanctuary. I had no idea that such a plush space existed in this drab brick building. Hasegawa picked up the needle and the phonograph's crackling halted. Stroking his neatly trimmed moustache, he seemed to revel in the music's lingering resonance.

'Watanabe Yuichi, Ward Three, sir!'

Hasegawa moved the baton to his other hand and stood up. The thoughtful middle-aged man enjoying a mellifluous song quickly transformed into a cold prison warden, his smile stiffening and his eyes emitting a chill. 'I already heard all about the dead guard, from Maeda.'

I wondered why he'd called me in. That was when it dawned on me – I was the last person who had seen Sugiyama alive. I clenched my molars to still my trembling lips.

'Are you a student-soldier?' His voice, as sharp as a hawk's talons, sank into me as if I were a field mouse.

Was I a suspect? 'Yes, sir. I was a liberal-arts student at the Third High School in Kyoto.'

'Lucky fellow. Your friends who were conscripted at the same time would have been sent to the Southern Front. You were assigned in Japan – to a prison, at that – not even to a military battalion.' His eyes glinted as he appraised me. 'You'll take this incident.'

Did he mean I should take care of the funeral? Or was he accusing me of the murder? It would have been preferable to go to the Southern Front. 'I will report the murder to the Special Higher Police,' I managed to squeak.

Hasegawa nodded and looked at me with his piercing gaze. 'Right. That would be the standard procedure. But here in Fukuoka Prison we can't follow standard procedures. We have the most dangerous elements of the archipelago here – men who need to be eliminated from society, people who shouldn't have been born to begin with. You can't employ common sense with them. The military can't do anything with them, let alone the Special Higher Police. Everything that happens here is a battle, and we're the only ones equipped to deal with what goes on in here. So don't bring up the goddamn police again!'

There was nothing I could say in reply.

'Take over this investigation. Find out which criminal element killed Sugiyama Dozan and why. Get yourself immediately to the head guard's office and request assistance. He'll see to it that you don't have any difficulty with this investigation. He'll get you the documents you need and set up interrogations with the prisoners. I want to know immediately if anything new is revealed!'

I clacked my heels together and froze at attention, feeling lost. I gave him a military salute, turned around and left.

The guard office was at the end of the administrative ward, where Wards Two and Three split off. Behind the wooden door were the guardroom and the holding cell, a neutral space between the prisoners and the guards. At one end of the guardroom was a shabby office, sectioned off by temporary walls. I opened the crooked door. Water was boiling in the kettle on top of the rusty stove, tended to by Maeda, his dress-uniform cap pressed firmly over his eyebrows. He never took off that cap; it made him taller, covered his balding head, and cast an authoritative shadow over his close-set eyes, drooping eyebrows and flat nose. Nearing fifty, Maeda looked much older than his years; he'd spent his entire life trapped in the brown uniform, surrounded by people who'd reached the end of their lives. He nodded to me and murmured, 'So it's finally come to this.'

I wasn't sure if he was addressing me. 'Did you know Sugiyama-*san* would be killed?'

His face became impassive, as though a curtain had been drawn. He tossed a file onto his desk, the Ward Three shift report. He licked his finger and flipped through the document. 'I'm not the only one who thought something would happen to him. I didn't know it would be in this horrible way . . .'

'What kind of shit was Sugiyama involved in?' I deliberately chose to call him by name, without the polite -*san*. That removed any suggestion of sympathy.

Maeda softened. 'When he came back from Nomonhan, he couldn't rid himself of his wartime habits. He treated prisoners as if they were enemies. He acted as if he were waging battle. I mean, someone had to. The prisoners here look submissive, but don't be fooled. They'll rip you apart if you give them the chance. Sugiyama became an animal, too.'

Outside, the wind blew through the gaunt spindle trees, creating a piping sound. The kettle on top of the stove stopped boiling; the fire was dying down.

'This isn't just a guard's death!' Maeda shouted suddenly. 'This is war. They've declared war! The murderer is here, somewhere. Let me tell you, Ward Three is a different beast. It's where the worst of the criminals go, the most vicious – Koreans, traitors and Communists. This place stinks of blood. They bare their fangs and rip into each other. If you aren't careful, you could end up just like Sugiyama.' His words dripped with hatred and derision.

The coal in the furnace crackled. I didn't know what he was talking about. I felt like a pilot who'd made an emergency landing in enemy territory, unsure of which direction I was facing. But I had to do my job. I picked up the file Maeda had tossed aside. I opened its worn, glossy cover. I inhaled the scent of sweet paper, losing myself for a moment in delicious ink and fragrant trees. The last entry was dated 22 December.

Guards usually scribbled 'nothing out of the ordinary'

instead of a detailed record of the day or, if even that proved too difficult, they wrote: 'N/A'. But Sugiyama's reports were notable for their detail. Even almost-identical events from the previous day were recorded slightly differently. On the night before he died he'd written: '349 prisoners sleeping in a total of 48 cells. Patrol time 2–6 a.m. 348 steps round-trip along Ward Three corridor. Many patients with colds. Slow recovery of one patient with contusions and fractures.' The previous day he'd written: 'From 2 to 6 a.m. checked 346 prisoners in 48 cells through the surveillance window. More patients with colds, one patient with fractures and contusions.' The patient with contusions and fractures was mentioned daily; I became curious about his identity and the source of his injuries. I flipped back, page by page. The first clue I found was in the 13 December report. 'Prisoner 331 in Cell 28: repressed with club for refusal of orders and inappropriate actions. Moved to infirmary after collapse, took emergency measures. Contusions all over the body including the head, suspected fracture to shoulder and ribs.' I was a little surprised that he'd faithfully recorded the conditions of the men he'd personally clubbed. I looked up 331's records. Name: Choi Chi-su. Crime: study of Communism and overthrow of the government, assassination attempt of a key government figure, rebellion plot. He was a long-term prisoner.

I stood up and adjusted my uniform. I wondered whether this man could illuminate the mystery of Sugiyama's death. But when Sugiyama was killed, all the prisoners were in their cells. Only guards and rats were awake and mobile. Still, 331 was the only person I could think of to question.

\*

Later, under the faint shadow of the tall brick wall lining the yard, I studied the piece of paper I'd found in Sugiyama's uniform. Its worn corners were disintegrating, but it seemed to retain his body heat. I turned the paper over; it was a ledger of incoming and outgoing post for Ward Three. *27 March 1942. Incoming: 14; Outgoing: 5*. At the bottom the sender's name, address and the prisoner number of the recipient were written in black ink. The first hesitant stroke revealed a careful personality, while the following clumsy but sure strokes suggested a strong sense of purpose.

I believed handwriting revealed one's soul. The shape and position of the script announced not only a person's character and desires, but also his mood and feelings at the time he was writing, as did the space between the letters and lines and the speed with which he scrawled. Even a blank piece of paper tells the reader something about the person who chose not to write. As for the content – I was well aware of the magic of consonants as they ruptured in my mouth; of the elegance of vowels as they tumbled out fluidly; and of the way they created pitch and meaning and feeling as they mixed and crashed into each other. I recalled characters from novels I'd read long ago. The bleak prison yard became the snow-covered Siberia in Tolstoy's *Resurrection*; if I were to love someone, I would love a woman like Katyusha. If words could explain lives, why couldn't they illuminate death? I searched for Sugiyama's core in his strokes and punctuation, but I soon grew confused. I glimpsed two very different people. The exact same writing was on the shift report and the post ledger; the writer was confident and fearless, like the Sugiyama I was familiar with. Though the poem seemed written by the same hand, the strokes seemed bashful and hesitant. Did

Sugiyama write both the official reports and the poem, too? Or did someone copy Sugiyama's handwriting? And, most importantly, why was that piece of paper in his pocket?

# THINGS THAT POOL IN THE HEART
# BEFORE TRICKLING DOWN

Darkness began to descend over the prison walls. Every afternoon at this time I heard the same seductive piano melody playing somewhere; I hummed along automatically. A light was on in the infirmary. Drawn by the music, I started walking towards it. I stopped at the auditorium window and looked in; a grand piano stood imposingly, as confident as a boat with expanded sails voyaging through the red sunset. Its colonnades, curves and the fine, elaborate carvings — it created an otherworldly effect. A woman was sitting at the piano, which let out a clear, delicate sound each time her fingers caressed the keys; I felt as though I'd seen the source of a majestic river, a small spring deep in the mountains. Her white fingers undulated like waves, scurried like mice and flitted like curious birds. In a trance, I gazed at this forbidding world from the other side of the clear glass. Time passed ever so slowly. She was like an exotic bird flying into the sunset, into darkness, into silence. As the air absorbed the last melodies, she straightened and looked out the window. Was she looking at me? I stared at her, bewitched; she was indeed real. She was wearing a neat white nurse's uniform; her slender face was as smooth as a ceramic pot; her hair glistened in the amber light of the waning sun. Her high forehead, slender eyebrows and the corners of her almond-shaped eyes were enchanting, her cheeks were flushed, and her slightly parted lips prodded my curiosity.

I wanted to introduce myself, but my shabby appearance made me hesitate. I watched as she held a hairpin in her mouth before securing her nurse's cap. She glanced down at her reflection on the piano lid before taking her files and hurrying across the auditorium. With each step, her white skirt flapped at her calves. Before I realized what I was doing, I stepped into the building. I walked down the pristine corridor to the auditorium. The doors opened silently as though they had been waiting for me. I approached the glistening piano, awed by its black-and-white keys, the vibrant grain of the wood, its sturdy tendon-like strings. I looked down at the back of my cracked, rough hands, at my fingernails rimmed with grime. Could fingers this dirty make a melody? I pressed a key; a clear note rang out, thawing my heart. I closed my eyes.

'That's soh.' A voice twinkled like the scales of sweetfish swimming upstream. Hundreds of bells tolled in my ears.

I looked behind me. Her lips were pursed, but she didn't seem reproachful. She held black files against her chest, creating a vivid contrast against her white uniform. Her fingers were pale and long and delicate; her pinkish nails had a transparent lustre. How long had she been watching me?

'It's also called G. It's the fifth note. For your little finger. It's the arbiter of sound that harmonizes with all notes, a bridge that links the ponderous dark low notes and delicate high notes.' She looked me over.

I shrank. I was bedraggled; my uniform was covered in

dirt, my skin had been pummelled by dusty winds, my lips were blistered, I hadn't bathed in a while. She smiled slightly. Was she jeering silently at me? Or was it compassion?

'I'm sorry,' I said, stiffly. 'Coming in here without permission and touching this object . . .' I searched for a way to end the sentence. I wanted to bite my clumsy tongue for calling this enchanting, captivating instrument an object.

She said it was fine, that it wasn't her piano, and reached over to pick up the sheet music she'd left on the rack.

I mustered up the courage to speak to her again. 'The piece you just played – what is it called? I think I've heard it before, but I don't remember the title.'

Instead of answering, she opened the sheet music. The title was written on the top. *Die Winterreise*. 'It's German. Winter Journey.'

'Winter Journey . . .' I echoed.

'Schubert composed these lieder for Wilhelm Müller's poems. It's a total of twenty-four songs published as Opus 89. The singer tells of the loneliness of life and the pain of love, but even played with just the piano, it's truly beautiful. The piano in *Die Winterreise* doesn't merely accompany the singer. It sets the tone of the whole piece. I would say it's a duet of a pianist and a singer.'

'It makes me wonder which singer would be able to hold his own.'

'Professor Marui Yasujiro. He's the foremost tenor in Japan. He teaches at Tokyo Imperial University Music School and has made several records. He's renowned worldwide, especially for performing Schubert. To really express the loneliness and gloom of this piece, he sang it as a baritone. His performances are some of the best interpretations of Schubert's work.'

I was sufficiently awed, and it must have shown on my face.

'Professor Marui is planning to give a concert, wishing for peace in Asia, here next February,' the nurse told me. 'He decided not to use his usual accompanist for this concert; he wants someone working here. He thought that was more fitting with the themes of hope and peace. That's why I've been practising so hard.' She smiled, revealing her even teeth, which resembled the piano's white keys. 'I'm Iwanami Midori,' she said. Her words rippled like water and pooled in my heart.

'Watanabe – Yuichi . . .' I stammered, disgusted with myself that I couldn't utter my own name without stuttering.

She nodded before walking across the wooden floor.

'Iwanami Midori . . .' I murmured. Her name sounded like a melody.

It was snowing outside. The snow fell through the darkness, crackling like thin ice. The night air was heavy with ice and cold and heartlessness and conspiracies and secrets and other unknowable things. Our barracks formed a makeshift structure on the west side of the central facilities. By the time I returned, the lights were out and the other conscripted guards were deep in slumber. The coal stove glowed in the middle. I stumbled into my sleeping bag, which smelled of other people. It had been a long day. Sugiyama's death, searching for clues but learning nothing, the mysterious poem. I wasn't Sherlock Holmes or a Special Higher Police detective. I didn't have the skills to solve a gruesome murder, let alone the means to catch the perpetrator.

The wind swept the snow off the galvanized iron roof

above my head. The amber light, the warm air, the elegant piano, the girl in white . . . I folded my hands on my chest and felt the piece of paper that I'd retrieved from Sugiyama's uniform:

> *As a stranger I arrived,*
> *As a stranger again I leave.*
> *May was kind to me*
> *With many bunches of flowers.*
> *The girl spoke of love,*
> *Her mother even of marriage,*
> *Now the world is bleak,*
> *The path covered by snow.*

That violent guard wrote such poetry? It didn't match up. Was it a clue, or a sign left by the murderer? Why would a criminal leave a mysterious poem in the victim's pocket? I was as puzzled as ever, but grew convinced that the poem contained the key. The song I'd heard Midori playing earlier circled in my head – the song of one man's despair, of painful love. Melody embraced poetry, and poetry was laid over melody. The harmony of sounds layered over the verse; the tinkling of the piano sparkled in the golden light of the furnace. Three faces hovered in my mind – Sugiyama, Hasegawa, Midori. Poetry, melody, piano.

Before the war tore my life into pieces, my days began in a single-storey house topped with an attic in the outskirts of Kyoto, and proceeded to a small used bookshop run by my mother. I spent hours among the old wooden bookshelves piled with dust, surrounded by paper. Walls of books protected us from the ominous news of the war. Nothing could filter in through the hundreds of thousands of pages; not the brawling of merchants or the clomping of marching soldiers or the cold of the winter night. The books protected me from the era's rebellions and from my anxiety about the future. I snuggled deeper in my prison-issue sleeping bag, recalling forgotten names, their faces as vivid as a new photograph – Fyodor Dostoyevsky, André Gide, Lord Byron, Rainer Maria Rilke.

We opened the bookshop the year I went into middle school. Three years earlier my father had applied to the Manchurian military academy, but he was too old. He was finally able to enrol after audaciously demonstrating his sincerity with a letter written in his blood and sent to the Army Minister. Early in the morning on the day of departure, my mother and I followed him to Kyoto Station. From behind, amid the plump flitting snowflakes, he looked like a wooden toy soldier, weighed down with gear. Thick, solid icicles clung to the dark wheels of the train that was puffing out white steam. Father's scratchy beard was caked with frost. His eyelashes were long, like mine.

'Yuichi, be good to your mother.' Father's frozen words mixed with his white breath, the whistle of the black train and the stomping of military boots. The crying of women fell away, buried by military song, as Father walked slowly into the black steel monster.

Mother rented a small shop front, installed bookshelves and hung up a white tin sign. A few strands of hair kept falling across her forehead. I bought her a butterfly pin as a fulfilment of Father's last request. At the front of the shop Mother repaired torn covers with thick paste, replaced missing covers with stiff strawboard, restitched unravelled bindings and re-created ripped spines with silk cloth. Books ruined beyond salvation ended their lives there, becoming kindling or a sack containing warm roasted sweet potatoes on a winter night, or the paper with which to wipe a young child's nose. Even after the books died, their sentences lived and breathed. Plato's wisdom printed across a sack of sweet potatoes might attract the attention of a poor student; Dumas's words might move the father who wiped his young son's nose, prompting him to unfold the sticky sheet.

Our days began and ended in that small bookshop. Every day at dawn we went there, stepping through the chilly air. When we opened the locked glass door, the stale smell of books rushed at us in greeting. After school I returned to the cradle of books. Mother was at the front counter greeting customers while at the back, among the narrow bookshelves, I stamped the inside of each book with our shop's seal, like a cowboy branding a calf, to welcome the books into our family. I sneezed from the dust, sliced my fingers on the sharp pages and bruised myself with the heavy corners, but I was happy. I organized the books by field and subject and displayed popular books at the front; each and every book became a world of its own. Universes were organized on the shelves according to my will. I exerted absolute control according to my own order and rules, putting Tolstoy's essays on the same shelf as Dostoyevsky's *Crime and Punishment* and a yellowed copy of *Othello* next to *King Lear*. Soon I could guess the age of a book just by its scent and understand a book's core from a quick glance at the table of contents, like a farmer who could tell the maturity and sweetness of a fruit from just its colour and the texture of its skin. I could conjure up people's interests by taking in their expressions as they entered through the glass door. Most of the time I handed them the books they asked for, but sometimes, when they sought books I wanted to keep forever, I didn't – *The Notebooks of Malte Laurids Brigge*; a book of Van Gogh's paintings in colour; *The Hunchback of Notre-Dame*. When the customers turned away in disappointment, I felt both guilty and secretly thrilled.

A maze of books beckoned at me from the back of the shop. I hid in the sewers of Paris on the eve of revolution and met a woman in snowy, frigid Siberia. I ventured into the world of heroes and gods and visited a lone island where a dethroned prince was imprisoned. Books were cities I'd never visited, filled with pillars of great thoughts and streets of phrases, mazes of abstruse sentence structures and alleys of complicated syllables. They were stores that displayed a wide range of things, punctuation twinkling like the crest of a venerable family, sentences breathing peacefully, words whispering. I returned to reality when the roof of the Temple of the Golden Pavilion shimmered from far away and the sky turned orange. As darkness descended, Mother closed the doors. The world of sentences sank into the night, the heroes and kings and ladies mourning lost love falling asleep. On our way home Mother looked lonely; I would make endless conversation, asking about the books that had been sold that day, who bought them and what they were about. I was always pleasantly surprised when Mother gave me detailed answers about what she'd read long ago, or books she'd wanted to read but hadn't got round to. Mother sometimes laughed, although her laughter was always hollow. I knew I couldn't take on her loneliness or her exhaustion; I could almost smell Father's cigarettes and sweat and faint sorrow. Like a drawing in sand, Father's face eroded with time. We didn't receive a single letter from him. Eventually I found myself no longer waiting for him to write, no longer pining for his return. I forgot him; I had to forget him first, so as not to be forgotten myself. I didn't want to waste my whole life hoping for a miracle.

Mother was lonely and I was withdrawn, but we weren't unhappy. That fortress of books was our refuge. I discovered this only a long time later, but it was also the price of my father's life, what he'd given us when he walked into the war zone in Manchuria. I might have been a little less sad if I'd never known that. But the timing of everything is always off. Man is in pain because he finds love too early, because he hasn't seen someone for too long and because he discovers the truth too late.

# I SEE THE BACK OF A SAD MAN
# WALKING ALONE UNDER A METEOR

The next morning, Maeda greeted me in his office with a smile. He poured me a cup of tea. 'What have you discovered?'

My voice as hard as a log, I answered that I didn't have anything special to report.

He fiddled with the brim of his cap. 'No, it won't be easy for a young student-soldier like you. But make it your business and see it to the end.'

I took out the piece of paper from my inner pocket and unfolded it. 'I discovered this note in the dead guard's pocket. There's a mysterious verse written on one side of it.'

Maeda looked at me, then at the note I placed on his desk. He laughed. 'Of course. You can't get rid of your habits that easily. He couldn't help himself.'

My curiosity was piqued.

'Sugiyama Dozan was a bookworm, but he was like a lost dog among the sentences.' Maeda smiled slyly. 'He was also the censor of Ward Three.'

The role of censor sounded important, but I knew that all he had to do was sit in a back room. When I was in Ward Four the censor there was an old guard. It was a position given to him out of respect because he found it difficult to manage the prisoners. He sat in his small office and dozed all day, reading letters. How could a top-notch guard like Sugiyama have been the censor?

'Ward Three is a separate entity within the prison,' Maeda explained, noting my surprise. 'The most evil criminals are kept there. Compared to these Koreans, the prisoners you're used to in Ward Four are gentlemen. To inspect their correspondence, the censor has to be just as vicious and unmerciful. Sugiyama was not just an excellent guard, he was also the best censor in the prison.'

'But he seemed not to care for words . . .' I said, unbelieving.

'Quite. Since he was new to reading and writing, he could be an excellent censor.'

'How?'

The water boiling on the stove melded with his voice. Maeda cleared his throat. 'When those Koreans poured into Ward Three, we found that we needed a different censorship method, because they think differently from us Japanese. First we banned all correspondence not written in Japanese. So, to inspect their Japanese, we wanted someone new to literacy. A novice would read and write the language the same way as Koreans who aren't used to Japanese. So he would be able to pinpoint suspicious expressions.'

'So Sugiyama was the perfect man.'

'He'd never even crossed the threshold of an elementary school, but his capabilities of comprehension and learning were amazing. Instead of reading like a normal person, he instinctively zeroed in on forbidden words and expressions. His eyes caught every expression with an ambiguous meaning.' Maeda shook his head in awe.

I knew that censorship was essential. After we bombed

Pearl Harbor, the war had intensified and daily life had grown more chaotic. Thugs and subversives, armed with knives and petrol, roamed the streets. All anti-Japanese Koreans were arrested, but subversive activities continued. The delusion of independence floated hazily over the streets and universities of Tokyo, infecting other Koreans. Every time a Korean political offender was arrested, all their writings, books and documents, including personal promissory notes, were confiscated to disarm them of vicious ideas. Upon sentencing, the boxes of confiscated documents and a list of their contents accompanied the prisoners into prison.

Maeda explained that Sugiyama was given special orders to act as censor for Ward Three; consequently he had to learn to read and write. Sugiyama protested at first; he despised literacy. To him, writing was merely a tool with which to corrupt the world, applying various -isms to set fire to the hearts of the weak and prey upon them. But in the end he was a soldier; orders weren't for him to understand, they were to be followed. He began his education by writing down words he didn't know on a sheet of paper. The inspection office was a makeshift structure at one end of Ward Three and was once used as an interrogation and execution room until a large-scale execution area was built, complete with gallows and a place for fusillades. Sugiyama spent all day in that office, studying diligently like a silkworm gnawing through green mulberry leaves. That office was his solitary battlefield, his enemy the Korean prisoners – Communists hell-bent on destruction, terrorists eager to assassinate high-ranking officials, anarchists trying to overthrow the government, thieves, robbers and swindlers. Sugiyama pawed through papers, ferreting out seditious meanings from each phrase and sniffing out forbidden expressions. No suspicious phrase ever got past his prying eyes. He sorted boxes of confiscated material, assigned them unique numbers, organized them in the storage area and incinerated them. His red pen slashed the page. He paid no heed to the use of a word, the length of a sentence, the strength or weakness of an expression; if it didn't fit his strict standards, he marked it with his red stamp: *To Be Incinerated*.

Sugiyama had come home alive from the war zone. For seven years and three months he'd experienced trench warfare in the rain, gun battles in snow-covered fields, sieges and bayonet fights in the heavy darkness. But according to Maeda, Sugiyama considered this silent war in his quiet office the most valuable of them all. Books and records marched forward like enemy soldiers, and within them he found the enemy that gnawed through our healthy empire like a swarm of moths. He would look up when he noticed the setting sun dyeing the small westward window red, only to leap back into the world of paper and ink. When he raised his eyes again, it would be dawn. Only then would he rest. When day broke he moved the seditious books and letters he had uncovered to the new incinerator that had been built in the empty lot next to the inspection office. Watching the flames quietly swallow the forbidden documents, Sugiyama would feel relief, as though he were burning a rebel village or executing a traitor.

Maeda paused and rifled through his pockets. He pulled out a lighter, shining in his heavy palm, and lit a cigarette. 'This was Sugiyama's. Take it. You'll need it.' He took a deep drag. 'Without Sugiyama, there's nobody to act as censor. There's already a backlog. For the time being, you're it.' He flicked white ash from the tip of his cigarette.

I was horrified. I felt like Abraham having to kill his own son. 'There are well-qualified guards with more experience than I. And I don't know what censorship entails.'

'As far as I'm aware, you're the right man. You have skills they don't have.'

'What are they?'

'I looked at your records. You were not only a liberal-arts student, but you'd won a prize in the Emperor's national essay contest. You can find subversive ideas between the lines.'

I understood what Maeda wasn't saying. There was a hierarchy in the world of guards; exchanges and vigilant competition, surveillance and jealousy, plots and conspiracies helped a guard rise through the ranks. Nobody wanted to sit in a back room like an old man and flip through prisoners' letters all day. Maeda was boosting my ego to force me to do work nobody else wanted to do. But I didn't want this, either. I tightened my grip on the lighter. 'But I'm supposed to settle Sugiyama's affairs and investigate his death.'

'Nobody told you to find the murderer,' Maeda scoffed. 'That would be impossible. You just have to tie up any loose ends before this gets out. We can't have detectives from the Special Higher Police poking around. But censorship is different. You can do it.'

Maeda didn't really seem to want me to conduct a thorough investigation; he was tying me down with censorship duties so that I wouldn't have enough time even to think about the murder. They must be trying to hush the whole thing up. Why else would the warden entrust me with this investigation?

'The censorship rules are simple,' Maeda explained. 'I don't have to tell you to burn letters not written in Japanese, right? If you're not sure, just burn everything. Every last page. Understood? Now, get yourself to the inspection office.'

I realized I didn't have a choice. I suddenly resented Sugiyama; if he hadn't died, this wouldn't be my problem.

The inspection ward was at the end of the corridor. I opened the heavy, squat door to step into Sugiyama's isolated world. I ducked to go through; a narrow hallway was on the other side. I took a few steps into the darkness, then saw a door to the left. I unlocked the padlock and pushed it open. It was an interrogation room, fitted out with an old wooden desk and two chairs. Sugiyama must have interrogated the authors of seditious writings and the owners of banned books here. At one end was a leather-covered metal chair – a torture rack. I closed the door and locked it. Another door led to the library, filled with wartime citizen-action guides, manuals on how to increase industrial production, educational books emphasizing the duties of the Emperor's subjects. The inspection office was at the end of the hallway. When I unlocked the big, heavy padlock and opened the door, the scent of paper and dried ink seeped out. I was suddenly overcome. I'd yearned for this musty old smell of dust hovering in the air; I'd been desperate to fall asleep over print. I walked dreamily between the narrow book-shelves. A wooden desk stained with blue ink held the tools of censorship: knife and scissors, magnifying glass and tweezers, red pens and an assortment of dictionaries – Japanese, English, Chinese characters and Korean.

I noticed a shelf lined with files marked 'File Room Log', 'Prohibited Writings Log', 'Censor Report', 'Log of Documents to Incinerate'. I opened the censor report. Sugiyama had written down the details, pinpointing problematic sections in the prisoners' writings. The titles of books that had met their deaths were listed on the log of documents to incinerate. Ivan Turgenev's *First Love* and *Fathers and Sons*, a collection of short stories by Nathaniel Hawthorne, Dante's *Inferno* . . . Sugiyama had slashed through the titles in red ink; it looked as though the dead books were bleeding. The list was expansive, even including a Korean rice-dealer's credit ledger, and the reason for incineration was given as 'Infinite repetition of meaningless numbers that cannot be decoded'.

There were two mailbags next to the desk, one with outgoing and the other with incoming post. Prisoners' postcards mostly requested various goods and necessities from loved ones. They were fated to receive unsatisfactory answers in this time of government rationing. I blacked out troublesome expressions with a thick pen and returned them to the bags. I opened the shallow desk drawer and found a stack of files – the previous year's duty report, with the cover and steel tie removed. A thought flitted through my head. I took out Sugiyama's ratty paper from my pocket. The back of the crumpled sheet was dated; it was from an earlier date than the files in the drawer. I flipped a page in the top file and discovered something written on the other side in blue ink:

### CONFESSION

*In the bronze mirror stained with blue rust*
*My face remains so disgraced*
*A relic of which dynasty?*

*I reduce my confession to one line –*
*What happiness did I wish for during my twenty-four*
*years and one month?*

*Tomorrow or the day after, on some happy day*
*I must write another line of confession*
*— At that young age back then*
*Why did I make such a shameful one?*

*Night after night*
*With my palm, with the bottom of my foot*
*I polish my mirror.*

*In the mirror*
*I see the back of a sad man*
*Walking alone under a meteor.*

I felt as though I'd been stabbed. The powerful symbolism amplified the anguish running through the poem. The poet's introspection reminded me of Rilke; his pure, poetic language was reminiscent of Francis Jammes. My head was roiling, fearful and confused, like the ocean on a stormy night. Who wrote this? What did he have to do with Sugiyama? I knew Sugiyama wasn't the author, from the expression 'twenty-four years and one month'. After all, Sugiyama had learned to read and write only after his arrival at Fukuoka. Why did he copy this poem and keep it in his drawer? Did this poem have anything to do with the one I had found in his pocket? I examined it again from the beginning, but despite its perfect structure it didn't allow for easy analysis. Whoever the poet was, he wrote it when he was twenty-four years and one month old. And he'd committed a humiliating act at that time. That was all I could glean. I looked up. The hallway beyond the bookshelves had sunken into black darkness. I rubbed my tired, dry eyes.

*

The next day I continued with my censor duties, culling books to make room for the next batch to be reviewed. I picked ten books and piled them into a wheelbarrow. *Romeo and Juliet*, a novel by Stendhal, two volumes of Communist ideology and six Korean books. The incinerator was about fifty metres from the inspection room. I compared the log of confiscated materials with Sugiyama's list of documents to be incinerated. There was no discrepancy. The incinerator was an altar awaiting offerings. My feet dragged; I felt as reluctant as I imagined an executioner might feel as he climbed up to the gallows. I yanked the door open – the smell of paper, smoke and ash poured out, sending me into a coughing fit. I pulled out the lighter. Flame, not poison and dagger, would kill Romeo and Juliet. A small spark would fell Stendhal. And the Korean authors whose names I couldn't read – I peered at the faded title on the cover of a Korean book; the author's name trembled under the bluish light. How would I atone for annihilating the soul of a poet condensed on these pages? It was a good thing I didn't know Korean; if I did, I doubt I would have been able to burn that book. I squeezed my eyes shut, ripped out the first page and lit it. I threw the whole thing into the incinerator. The flame licked the edges of the book and erupted when it reached the middle. Korean letters, round as well as hard-edged, shrivelled in the fire. Into the blaze I shoved the rest, all of which had once comforted me. All ten books disappeared; only a line of smoke and a fistful of ash remained. I reached out, my hand hovering over the ash blinking with embers. I felt the heat of the dying books. My breath came out ragged, like a whale spouting after a long-held breath; I reminded myself that incineration was a part of my duties as censor, that I'd burned seditious literature confiscated from unwholesome elements. These had to disappear from the world. Although, deep down, I wanted to keep guard over sleeping words and sentences, really I had become an executioner of literature.

# INTERROGATION

In the small, dark interrogation room I nodded at Prisoner 331, Choi Chi-su, directing him to sit on the icy wooden chair. Dampness and the sour smell of mould surrounded us. I sat across from him, the old wooden desk between us. His eyes were calm; he seemed at ease in this room. He reminded me of the Koreans I'd seen in my youth in Kyoto. They'd coolly glared at everyone, or else they'd looked around as though they were searching for something. I found out only later why their eyes were empty and accusatory; they'd lost their entire reason to be.

'331!' My voice was sharp, frightening even myself.

He replied gruffly. 'My name isn't 331. It's Choi Chi-su.'

'Not your Korean name. Give me your Japanese name!'

'I don't have one,' he said, a jeer staining his lips. 'I don't care what you call me. How's this? Since my prisoner number ends with 1, call me Ichiro. It's not inaccurate, since I'm the leader of the prisoners.' He was right, since Ichiro meant first-born son.

'Tell me how you got injured on 13 December.'

He glanced at me, trying to figure out why I was asking about that. 'It's no big deal. My wrist was broken and my forehead was bashed. So I bled a little, that's all.'

'It's a big deal for me. Because the guard who beat you died.'

'13 December? Let's see. That day, as usual, we went to our work areas. I dawdled and stayed behind in my cell. That bastard opened the surveillance window and shouted at me for still being there. I told him I had a cold. He came into my cell and clubbed me over the head. But it turned out fine for me, since I was sent to solitary for ten days instead of having to work.'

'I just told you that he died, but you're not surprised.'

'Should I be surprised? Or afraid? Why? I didn't kill him.'

That much was clear. He had a watertight alibi. Between 2 and 4 a.m., when Sugiyama was murdered, he was locked in a cell. In fact, he was locked in solitary, which was always under strict surveillance, away from the regular wards. To ask him about what happened on 22 December was to be suspicious of Fukuoka Prison's ironclad security system. I felt aimless, like a hunting dog that had lost his prey. '331! I'm not asking you about that. I want to know about you.'

He clasped his hands together and tucked them inside his sleeves. He leaned back on the chair. The cuffs on his wrists glittered. He gave me a cold smile. 'I forgot who I was a long time ago.' He shot me an intense gaze.

I felt cowed. I opened his file and rattled off the facts. 'Name: Choi Chi-su. Forty-two. From Gaeseong on the Korean peninsula. At age seventeen, attacked a police sub-station, assaulted a Japanese merchant and attempted arson of a Japanese-owned shop. At age twenty-two, firebombed Gaeseong Police Station and immediately fled to Manchuria. You reappeared nine years ago in the middle of Tokyo. You were arrested on the scene for throwing a bomb at the

41

celebration of the Emperor's birthday in Ueno Park. You were lucky; you were sentenced to life in prison because that bomb didn't detonate. You were serving your sentence in Tokyo Prison when the Home Ministry proclaimed that Korean convicts were to be sent to Fukuoka. You were transferred here. You attempted escape sixteen times in seven years, and spent 348 days in solitary for a total of twenty-seven incidents.'

He glared at me. 'I was locked up when he was killed.'

'That's no excuse. You've been here longer than anyone else. So you know this place better than anyone. You might know of a way to escape from solitary. You also have a motive. Sugiyama clubbed you.'

'Sugiyama? Should I tell you what I know about him?' Choi smiled mysteriously.

What did he know? What was he hiding? I leaned forward swiftly, like a fish taking bait.

'Sugiyama Dozan lived as a soldier his whole life. But in the end he died a weak man.'

I was sparring with a powerful, cunning bastard. But I refused to yield. 'Careful. I'm going to figure out whatever it is that you're plotting.'

He smiled. 'How?'

'I'm – I'm going to figure *you* out.'

He arched an eyebrow. 'Yet another guy who says ridiculous shit. I thought it was only Hiranuma who went on about figuring people out.'

My ears perked. I etched those four syllables in my head. *Hiranuma.*

The log of incoming materials had prisoner numbers, book titles and arrival dates recorded in tiny print. The books were behind bars, just like the prisoners – Hugo, Tolstoy, Stendhal, Cervantes – but their souls shimmered, alive between the pages. The paper was their skin, the ink their blood and the binding their ligaments. I'd got to know them in our bookshop; I'd grown up revelling in their reassuring presence. I was orphaned when I was taken away from them. My soul had lost its way and my dreams stumbled around in the dark.

I flipped a few pages of the log to find Hiranuma Tochu's records. Prisoner 645. I approached the shelves. A prisoner number marked each dusty box. The sides of box 645 were slick with grime – someone had accessed it frequently. The censor was the only one who could freely look through confiscated documents. Heat shot up my spine. Was Hiranuma involved in Sugiyama's death? I opened the box and spotted a file containing his biographical information:

Hiranuma Tochu. Born in 1917 in Mingdong village, Helong Prefecture, Jiandao Province, Manchuria. In 1932 enrolled in Eunjin Secondary School in Manchuria and in 1935 transferred to Sungshil Secondary School in Pyongyang, northern Korea. Returned to Longjing, Manchuria after Sungshil Secondary School was shut due to its refusal to worship at a Japanese Shinto shrine. In 1938 enrolled in Yonhi College in Seoul. In 1942 moved to Japan and enrolled in the English Literature department of Rikkyo University. In the autumn of that same year transferred to the English Literature department of Doshisha University in Kyoto. In July 1943 was arrested as a political offender by the Special Higher Police and incarcerated in Shimogamo Police Station. Indicted on 22 February 1944 and given a two-year sentence for the violation of the Maintenance of Public Order Act.

His criminal record was similar to most of the others. I opened the log of confiscated documents. *Crime and Punishment* by Dostoyevsky, *Strait is the Gate* by André Gide, *Les Fleurs du mal* by Baudelaire, poetry by Paul Valéry, Francis Jammes and Rainer Maria Rilke. I haltingly sounded out those familiar names. The names twinkled like stars inside me; my heart hammered furiously. Hiranuma's box contained fifteen or sixteen worn books, tattered from frequent handling. The book on top was *The Notebooks of Malte Laurids Brigge* by Rainer Maria Rilke. I could feel the blood coursing through my veins. I'd hoped to read Rilke again after the war. Instead of granting my wish, God had given me a different opportunity: I could read Rilke now, but in this prison. Something fluttered down from the pages. I carefully picked up the yellowed piece of paper:

### SELF-PORTRAIT

*Alone, I round the bend of the mountain to the solitary*
*well by the rice paddy and look quietly down.*

*In the well the moon is bright and clouds drift and the*
*sky is vast and blue wind blows and it is autumn.*

*And there is a man.*
*I leave, disliking him for some unknown reason.*

*On second thought I pity him.*
*I return and look down; he is still there.*

*Again I leave, disliking him.*
*On second thought I start to miss him.*

*In the well the moon is bright and clouds drift and the*
*sky is vast and the blue wind blows and it is autumn*
*and there is a man, like a memory.*

This poem was perfect, just like a Swiss-made watch, though made not of screws and springs and saw-toothed gears, but of nouns and verbs and adjectives. I'd always been awed by the grandeur of machines, how, when well made, they serve the soul of humanity. Fabric pours out of a roaring textile mill to allow mankind to luxuriate; a compass, a gun, a steam engine, a car and an aeroplane fire up a man's will, boost his courage, and each transforms life. This intricate apparatus of words filled a part of my soul with satisfaction. Another poem leaped into my mind: *Confession. Self-Portrait* and *Confession*. The two smelled the same; they were like twins. They both featured calm self-examination, melancholy and a tiny whiff of hope. They began with despair, but soon transformed into ardent optimism. Though I'd read only these two poems, I felt that I knew the poet. Did Hiranuma write these poems? To find out, I had to meet him.

The door to the interrogation room opened without a sound and Hiranuma entered. His handsome face glowed in the dim interior. His shaved head and neat eyebrows accentuated his round forehead. He had almond-shaped eyes and a delicate but strong nose. A smile hung from his blistered lips. He looked as though he were dreaming. How could someone like this, with such gentle eyes and a peaceful smile, end up in this place? I checked his file to remind myself of his crime: involvement in the Korean independence movement.

Hiranuma spoke first. 'I see you, too, were dragged here for no reason.'

Was he proclaiming his innocence? He'd said 'you, *too*'. It didn't matter. I wasn't a judge; I was only a lowly guard. 'Every prisoner says he's innocent,' I told him. 'Even a cold-blooded murderer. But if you're in prison it means you committed a crime of some sort. Unless you're Edmond Dantès.'

His eyes gleamed in recognition. 'What about Prometheus, chained to a rock in the Caucasus?'

I started. We'd read the same books, knew the same authors and shared the same memories. 'Prometheus stole fire. No matter what you steal or for whom, theft must be punished.'

'Is it a crime to be powerless and naive? Like Edmond Dantès, who loved Mercédès but couldn't stop the conspiracy of Mondego, Danglars and Villefort?' Hiranuma wasn't really asking a question. He seemed to want to talk about the fictional characters confined in his head, just as I did.

'To be innocent and powerless isn't itself a crime, but it could be the cause of a crime. Because nobody can protect someone who won't first protect himself,' I said.

He nodded, acknowledging my oblique argument that Koreans were criminals for being unable to hold onto their own country; that being Korean was a crime in itself.

I took out the two pieces of paper from my shirt pocket and spread them on the desk. *Self-Portrait. Confession.*

Surprise and fear flashed across his face.

'*Self-Portrait* was written on paper torn out of Rilke's *Malte Laurids Brigge*. That book was in your box of confiscated documents. This is something you wrote, isn't it?' I asked.

'Yes, the Special Higher Police confiscated that book. But I bought it at a used bookshop. How can you be so sure that I wrote that poem?'

'Language is a person's signature, like his fingerprints. It contains his birth and growth, memories and past. *Self-Portrait* and *Confession* are twins. If you wrote *Self-Portrait*, it's obvious that you wrote *Confession* too.'

'Prove it!'

'This person is used to loneliness. He's taciturn – he reduces his confession to one line and he wordlessly goes back and forth to the well. He hates and pities himself, but misses himself. He accepts the weight of life. The man who uses his entire body to polish the rusted artefact of a fallen dynasty in *Confession* is despairing but tenacious. That expression, "a relic of which dynasty?", refers to his identity. As in: he's Korean.'

Hiranuma looked at me with an odd expression. After a while he raised his shield. 'I'm just a prisoner. None of that is proof that I wrote those poems.'

I was waiting for this opportunity. 'There's decisive evidence that you wrote *Confession*. Twenty-four years and one month, that's how old the poet was when he wrote it. Why would he have written a poem called *Confession* at such a young age? What would he have to confess?' I wasn't looking for an answer; I already knew it. According to the sentencing records, Hiranuma had come to Japan in the spring of 1942 to enrol at Rikkyo University. He had turned twenty-four that past December; he must have written that poem a few months before coming to Japan.

I continued: 'A Korean needs a certificate to come to Japan legally. You could enter illegally by stowing away on a ship, but not if you were officially enrolling in a university. In order to receive that certificate you are required to have a Japanese name. Your Korean name is the artefact of the fallen dynasty. The "disgraced face" reflected on the rusted bronze mirror refers to your name change. That's what distressed you. That's what you were confessing to, as you stared at the person you had to discard in order to come here.'

Hiranuma looked tired. His voice was hoarse when he spoke. 'It's just a poem I wrote before coming to Japan. Is that a crime? It's never even been published.'

'No, that's not a crime.'

*Then why am I here?* his eyes asked.

'This poem is linked to a murder case. I found *Confession* in the desk drawer of the guard who was killed three days ago. The same poet wrote *Self-Portrait*. Now, why did that guard copy down your poem? What do these poems have to do with his death? That's what I want to find out.'

His eyes were neither guarded nor tense as a smile lingered on his lips.

# HOW A BOY BECOMES A SOLDIER

The stove in Maeda's office was still emitting heat. My blood warmed, making me tired and lethargic. Maeda barely glared at the censor log I handed him before stamping it. I wasn't sure what to say and what to keep to myself. 'Regarding Sugiyama's case,' I said hoarsely.

'What about him?' Maeda asked with a bored expression. 'Did he rise from the dead?' He shoved a finger in his ear as though to dig out what I'd just said.

'I think I'm starting to understand the significance of the poem I found in his uniform.'

He removed some earwax and wiped it off his finger, looking puzzled. I couldn't blame him; a few anonymous scribbles couldn't be evidence of anything much, let alone murder. 'There's nothing of note about that case. Just focus on your censorship duties.'

'Yes, sir. I won't neglect my duties because of the case. If you look at the log you'll see that I've been on the task. But I would still like to investigate the cause of death and the situation surrounding Sugiyama's murder.'

'That's all in the autopsy report the infirmary sent over.'

'There are certain facts I can't determine from that document. I think it would be a good idea for me to go to the infirmary and talk to the doctor who performed the autopsy to find out more about—'

Maeda flung aside the newspaper he'd begun to read. 'You're in over your head, boy. Do you realize what the infirmary is? It's solely for Kyushu Imperial University Medical School researchers. It's a first-tier security zone where guards aren't even allowed! You can't just waltz in whenever you want.'

I persisted. 'I'm conducting the murder investigation according to the warden's express orders. Something caught my eye on the daily-duties log and that led me to interrogate Prisoner 331. Sugiyama had beaten him so badly that he suffered broken bones.'

Maeda's wrinkled face showed a glimmer of curiosity. 'Are you telling me that he killed Sugiyama because of a grudge?'

'To confirm that I have to interview the doctor who performed the autopsy and take a look at the corpse.'

'All right. I'll write you a note. But be careful.' He stamped a form granting me permission to enter the infirmary. 'Just do what you need to do and leave. Be invisible!' Strangely, his order sounded more like a plea.

The infirmary was a two-storey building to the right of the central facilities. From the outside it looked like a single structure, because a long corridor linked the two. Inside, however, it was a different story. The tart smell of disinfectant floated around the infirmary corridor, in stark contrast to the stench of sweat and bodily waste in the central facilities. The clean scent made me faintly dizzy, but it was a small price to pay. The infirmary was built when Fukuoka Prison became a national long-term prison. Before then, nobody gave a second thought to the health of criminals and traitors. So instead of an infirmary, there was a makeshift ward in the administrative wing, without adequate medical equipment and staffed by a doctor pushing sixty and a nurse in her forties. They dealt mostly with corpses fresh from execution, illness and riots. There was no need for medicine, as there was no saving the dying or curing the sick. The situation changed thanks to Professor Morioka of the Kyushu Imperial University Medical School, the country's foremost medical expert. A charming, sociable man with a deep appreciation for the arts, Morioka was well known in Kyoto as a philanthropist and intellectual. His decision to leave the university for the prison system was therefore a shocking event, and the media covered the move with a tinge of hysteria. Morioka, explaining his decision as a strict adherence to the Hippocratic Oath, said that prisoners, too, had the right to receive medical treatment. As university hospitals were overflowing with good doctors, he would serve those who needed him most. He emphasized that he would continue to conduct research in the prison. The head of the university hospital was flummoxed, and even the mayor tried to persuade him to stay. Morioka recruited a medical staff of ten specialists, a dozen interns, twenty researchers and twenty-odd nurses. When he arrived at the prison, everyone greeted him expectantly. The prisoners were elated that their health, ruined from the cold, starvation and harsh beatings, would now be monitored by Imperial University doctors.

I floated by the patients' rooms, nurses' station and treatment rooms. Bright lights cast everything in sparkling white. Doctors and nurses wearing dazzlingly white coats rushed about. In my mind, a uniform represented one's soul – the prisoners were washed out, the guards were dark, the doctors were clean and the nurses were pure. The autopsy room was in the basement, at the far end of the corridor. Sugiyama's body was lying on a metal gurney in the middle of the empty room. Bruises — blue, black and red — covered his body. I noticed his knees were scratched, and darkly calloused. Dried blood tattooed his smashed forehead. Meticulous stitches sealed his pale, dry lips.

Eguchi Shinsuke, the head researcher who oversaw autopsies, stood behind the gurney, his face obscured by a surgical mask. I saluted. He held out a dry hand and removed his mask. He smiled broadly. In every way a gentleman, he looked to be in his forties. Men at war aged quickly, but he seemed to have avoided the harsh reality of the times. He guided me out of the door and led me into an observation room reserved for those viewing an execution or coming to collect a body. He placed the autopsy file on the desk and opened it. 'The primary cause of death was cranial rupture and cerebral haemorrhage, due to a blow to the back of the head. The bruises all over his body are consistent with being hit with a blunt weapon while unconscious.'

I felt intimidated. The doctor gave me a kind look, then went back to the gurney and covered the corpse with a white cloth. He returned and washed his hands. I smelled something faintly fishy in the cool air. 'Can you tell me what the blunt weapon was?'

'It's probably one of the clubs you guards have. The bruises are shaped like the tip of the club. The lacerations on the cranium have the same circumference. The long metallic weapon thrust into his chest caused some real damage. That sharp object punctured the heart.'

I knew that metal shafts were easy to come by in the prison. Whenever a prisoner came upon a piece of metal he plotted how he would use it to kill someone. Prisoners shaved down spoons into makeshift knives, or they took the mesh netting that kept them at bay, made it stronger by twisting it around itself, filed down the tip and walked around with it hidden in their sleeves. 'The body was hanging from the second-floor banister,' I reminded Eguchi.

'Hanging was not a direct cause of death.'

'You mean he was already dead?'

Eguchi gazed at me over his glasses and shook his head, indicating that he didn't know.

I tried another angle. 'What does it mean that his lips were sewn shut?'

He shook his head again.

It was left to me to discover the truth. The results of the autopsy were clear, but the pieces of evidence it scattered failed to create a complete picture. I left and walked down the corridor. I couldn't wait to leave that white, shining ward. I was more suited to a damp, dark, grey space.

8 December 1941 dawned the same way as any other morning. The tram clanged its bell and rattled along the street, kimono-clad women rushed past and men glared with angry expressions. That afternoon a university student stepped into the bookshop to tell us that the same important breaking news was being continuously broadcast on the radio. I ran over to the radio shop next door. People were milling around outside the glass doors. I heard an impassioned voice burst through static: 'At six this morning the Japanese Imperial General Headquarters, comprising the army and the navy, entered into battle in the Pacific

against American and British forces. The navy air fleet bombed Pearl Harbor, Hawaii, causing massive damage to American battleships.'

By the time I stepped out of the radio shop I was a boy no more. Men were standing in the streets, intently reading special editions of the paper. Fist-sized letters leaped off the page to punch me in the face: 'Empire Declares War Against America and Britain'; 'Navy Attacks Honolulu: Two American Ships Sink in Pearl Harbor'. War had been raging during my entire life; one war began before another was completed, in Manchuria, in China, in the Pacific. But this new war was different; it squeezed the life out of my fellow citizens. The elementary schools were renamed National Schools. Men altered the lapels on their suits, converting them into nationalist uniforms. Private gatherings were proscribed and goods were rationed. The *oden* plant began to produce food only for the military, and the suit factory began to make military uniforms. Children, taught that even a small nail would become a bullet and pierce the heart of an enemy soldier, scoured their houses for any scrap of metal to donate at school. Air-raid shelters were constructed from sandbags on street corners, though trams continued to run from one sandbag-piled shelter to another as if nothing had changed. Like a parrot, the radio continuously spat out news of victory from various places in the Pacific – Rangoon, Surabaya, the Dutch East Indies. The slogan 'Wait for what you want until the day of victory' burned in my ears. I desperately waited for victory, looking forward to the special food distribution that came with good news: sugar, beans and sweets, which would paint our grey hearts with colour. Drill instructors barked terse commands at us as they marched around the school yard. We began with close-order drills and first aid; by the end of the term we'd learned bayonet skills and marksmanship, how to identify American bombers, as well as different evacuation plans depending on the sound and smoke colour of various bombs. We never loosened the gaiters around our ankles; with the fiery belief that we were suffering along with soldiers on the front and in honour of the dead, we resolved that we would dash to the front if called. Our school uniforms could serve as military uniforms at a moment's notice, but we didn't think that would actually happen. Although we gathered at Kyoto Station Square to send off with cheers upper-classmen entering the military, we didn't believe that would ever be us. We still thought of war as unreal, something far away.

But fate is fair in its dealings.

One summer day before the end of the term, when I had just turned seventeen, a red note flew in like an air raid and combusted my life. I was in our bookshop, immersed in *Oliver Twist*, when I heard the glass door slide open and a man call my name: 'Watanabe Yuichi!'

His low, gloomy voice shattered my daydreams. I closed my book and came out to the front of the shop, staggering a little in a dream-like trance. The postman, in a nationalist uniform, glanced at me before sticking his face into his mailbag. He flipped through his bundles of letters. I could tell he was trying to avoid my eyes. How many boys' gazes had he had to avoid? Boys who trembled, as though they were awaiting execution, as though they were young deer caught in a trap. After a long interval he looked up, his face expressionless, and held out a sealed letter and an inkpad. I pressed my thumb on the inkpad and stamped his mail-receipt log. He didn't meet my mother's eyes, either. He turned around woodenly. On the envelope were the words 'Japanese Imperial General Headquarters'. They reached out, grabbed me by the throat and throttled me. I found a red note inside.

Time of assembly: 6.30, 27 March, Showa 18
Place of assembly: East side of Kyoto Station Square

I couldn't breathe. That was when I realized that words, not bullets or bombs, were killing the soldiers dying in battle. One line of text was powerful enough to turn the world upside down and destroy lives; boys became soldiers, were shipped to the front and were thrown into battle. I dropped the Dickens novel, not because I was afraid of death, but because I was suddenly afraid of words. My mother, who had been sewing up bindings, let out an almost imperceptible sound; red droplets of blood spotted her thumb. She was trying her hardest not to collapse in the face of despair.

Months later, early on the morning I was to enlist in the army, I rubbed my newly shaved head and thought about my father, who had walked along this path before me. Just like that day when my father went off many years ago, a black train puffed out steam and a military band played a martial song. I wasn't afraid. Nor did I feel it was unfair that I was to become a soldier. I just worried about my mother, who was too small to open the heavy gate over our shop front by herself every morning.

After training I was assigned to be a guard at Fukuoka Prison. High walls, sharp barbed wire and cold bars enclosed my future. My youth was incarcerated in a brown uniform. I was strictly isolated from books. No text was allowed. Staid directives were the only things to read, and the only words I wrote were in the log detailing my rounds.

Hungry for words, I read everything I could lay my hands on. I devoured incarceration logs, punishment records, directives and administrative documents, even the entrance and exit signs. But they were merely dead words that couldn't move me. My soul was perpetually malnourished. I wanted to encounter a living, vibrant line of prose. But that was a luxury not afforded a soldier in wartime.

That was how I walked into war – as though entering dreamland. I wanted to return to my former life. I wanted desperately for the war to end so that I could toss my military uniform aside, replace it with a school uniform and read Stendhal. But I didn't know when that would happen, or whether the war would ever end. I didn't know that, instead of the school uniform, I'd be wearing prisoner's garb when the war was finally over.

# CONSPIRACY

The inside of the workroom was damp with sweat. Together the prisoners repaired and dyed military uniforms and clothes. This indoor workroom was reserved for skilled long-term prisoners. The less fortunate suffered outdoors in the cold, willing their frozen bodies to make bricks, haul materials on their backs, push wheelbarrows and shovel the cold earth. Any talk during working hours was forbidden; if caught, the prisoners would be beaten within an inch of their lives. Even a brief pause caused work to pile up and invited beatings from the guards. They died from torture, the cold and disease. Families were given ten days to claim the corpses. If nobody showed up, their bodies were donated for research. The squat hill outside sprouted a cemetery for those unclaimed bodies; as the war grew intense and the number of prisoners increased, the cemetery grew in tandem.

The prisoners tasted their only freedom during outdoor break time from four to five in the afternoon. Exhausted Koreans grouped together near the wall, seeking the wan rays of the sun. They murmured endlessly among themselves, secretively, turning the yard into a noisy marketplace. This ruckus always made the guards tense; those manning the checkpoints made sure to keep their machine guns loaded.

These prisoners insisted on their innocence, telling stories to each other. Although they were thieves and thugs and crooks and spies, they had a visceral understanding of each other's sense of injustice; they all believed that they'd been caught in cunning Japanese traps and falsely accused. They raged in despair.

I walked along the wall, watching the group clustered together. They were all troublemakers; quick fists were a source of power within the prison. I was well aware that prisoners frequently attacked guards. When unpopular guards were on duty, they purposefully picked fights and disabled machines in their work unit, despite the certainty of beatings and solitary confinement. They quietened down when I approached, gripping the hilt of my club. 'I'm Watanabe Yuichi! I am the investigator assigned to uncover Sugiyama's murder. You better cooperate.'

The men looked me up and down. Prisoner 156, a balding former dockworker, mocked me. 'I thought the special investigator was from the Special Higher Police. But a brand-new student-soldier? Well, sir, we haven't done a thing.'

I'd heard about him. Prisoner 156 had stowed away ten years ago to Shimonoseki, and three years ago he'd received a seven-year sentence for leading a dockworker riot in Tokyo. The Japanese workers were the ones who'd plotted and instigated it, but 156 had been made a scapegoat. I studied each man carefully. One of them spat on the ground and another feigned disinterest, picking dirt from under his nails. I could tell they were hiding something. Then again, everyone in this prison was hiding something.

'I didn't say you did,' I snapped. 'But you might in the future. Your talents lie in fighting, ostracizing, violating the rules and getting sent to solitary, no?'

'A student-soldier? Then you can't even be twenty,' Prisoner 945 mocked. 'A snot-nosed kid investigating a murder?'

Prisoner 397 turned to him. 'The warden knows that if this incident gets out, he's done for. That's why he's not calling the Special Higher Police. He's trying to hush it up.'

They were all playing with me. My cheeks burned. I wanted to pull my club out and hit them.

'It's too bad that the guard died, but it has nothing to do with us. Just leave us alone,' said Prisoner 945 soothingly.

'I'm not going to bother you. But I'm going to uncover who did it.' I met each person's eyes as though I were stamping a seal.

Prisoner 156 frowned. 'Don't even think about blaming us. You don't have any proof. I don't know anything about how that arsehole died, but I know one thing. He got what was coming to him. So watch out, if you don't want that to happen to you.'

I swallowed. 'Is that a threat?'

'I guess so, if it scares you.'

'Don't you talk back to me. I can send you to solitary.' My flinty words didn't have any effect.

'Go ahead, put me in solitary. I can spend a week there – easy. Wanna beat me up? Be my guest. Any wound will heal in a week.' 156 pounded his chest with his fist and shoved his head towards me, taunting me to club him.

I glared at him, my hand trembling on the club. I knew I would lose, the moment I pulled it out. I wasn't Sugiyama. The club wasn't the solution.

Prisoner 543 glanced at the watchtower. 'It's stupid to kill a guard,' he commented slyly. 'Who could have done such a ridiculous thing?'

Not caring that I was right there, Prisoner 156 snapped

impatiently, 'Why is it stupid to kill an evil guard? Comrade, you know he deserved it!'

They all turned to look at a man standing far away, whose wide chest bore clear numbers: 331. He continued walking around the yard, oblivious to the men. Then he turned and came closer.

'Comrade Choi!' 156 called loudly. 'You tell us. Who do you think killed that son-of-a-bitch?'

'It doesn't matter who killed him,' Choi answered as he rubbed the tip of his reddened nose. 'What's important is who survives.'

He was clearly addressing me. He looked up at the sky, then at the watchtower with its two guards, a loaded machine gun and a 2,000-watt searchlight that illuminated the prison at night, tracing automatic arcs.

The waning sun faded. The men's voices became heated, ignoring my presence, as they argued with one another. A long bugle sounded, signalling the end of outdoor break.

'Disperse!' I shouted.

The men slowly parted ways, shuffling their feet. Their toes were poking out of their worn shoes; their yellowed toenails were split and their heels were chapped and cracked. The guards quickly finished the head count. Grousing in Korean, the prisoners went back into the work areas like a herd of sheep. Choi and his men walked along together. I noticed that the fabric on their knees was baggy and thread-bare. They must have habitually knelt before someone. Who had brought them all to their knees?

Back in the guardroom I searched through files, looking for the log listing the names of inmates sentenced to solitary and the length of their stay. The solitary wing was a makeshift cement building in the knoll between the prison wards and the cemetery. It consisted of small rectangular cells, one metre wide by two metres long, closed off by thick steel doors. A prisoner lying on the floor would touch each wall with each shoulder. It was as stuffy as a furnace in the summer and froze like a block of ice in the winter. Being sent to solitary during a heatwave or a cold snap was, for all intents and purposes, a death-sentence. All you got to eat was half a rice ball and half a bowl of miso soup, once a day. Countless men left wrapped up in straw mats, and even if one managed to walk out on his own two feet, his life often hung by a thread.

Maeda looked over my shoulder. 'The murderer's name isn't written in the log, you foolish boy! It doesn't matter who it is. Just hang those Koreans upside down and beat them, and they'll talk. There's no harm in giving them a little tap on the hand.' His eyes creased in a smile.

Was he actually urging me to force someone to give a false confession? But then that prisoner wouldn't be the murderer, he would merely be a pitiful liar. I flipped through the solitary log. Even if I did end up interrogating someone, I still had to be prepared.

'There's nothing useful there,' Maeda said. 'It's filled with Koreans. They're all troublemakers: 397, 156, 331, 543, 954, 645.' He smirked. 'I know all of them, each and every one. Kang Myeong-u, Lee Man-o, Choi Chi-su, Choi Cheol-gu, Kim Gwing-pil, Hiranuma Tochu! Those dirty pig-names are fouling my mouth.'

I paid no attention to him as I started to scan the records from six months ago.

Maeda spat on the floor. 'They love it in there. Those dumb monkeys don't even keel over.'

I pointed at the numbers. 'But last August all the solitary cells were empty for two whole weeks, as if they planned it!'

Maeda was indifferent. 'Obviously. It was during the worst heatwave.'

'Why do such aggressive men become so docile during a heatwave?'

'Because they know being in solitary during a heatwave is the express train to the graveyard. They were probably more careful.'

'If they're able to avoid solitary because of a heatwave, why wouldn't they behave all the time? Isn't that odd?'

'What's so odd about that?'

'They kept going to solitary at other times, as if they wanted to.'

'You wouldn't think that, if you saw those cells. The fittest person couldn't survive a week. It's next to the cemetery. Even the guards are spooked. It's actually a problem. They keep making up fake reports and skipping their rounds. Anyway, why would those imbeciles choose to go? It's not like they've hidden a pot of honey there!'

'They might be hiding something, though. I'll have to take a look.'

The solitary wing was a shabby building of eight cells and a small guard post. The wind raced around the ridge of the hill, causing the dark fir trees to howl like wolves. Maeda jerked open the door to the guard post. An old guard wearing thick, padded clothes was hunched by the extinguished furnace, his face blue from the cold, awaiting the end of his shift.

'Rounds of the solitary cells! Open the doors!' Maeda shouted.

The old guard scampered off, his bundle of keys clanging. The steel doors of the solitary wing were secured by a thick metal bar and by two large locks. With clumsy hands, the old guard unfastened the locks and removed the bars. Four cells lined either side of the hallway. When the old guard opened the door to a cell, a terrible stench assaulted my nose.

The old guard explained, 'The prisoners come here with broken bones or festering wounds. The infected wounds smell so awful that we can't open the cell doors in the summer.'

I pressed my sleeve against my nose and stepped into the first cell. From the outside it looked to be somewhat roomy, but when I stepped in I realized it was only half the width I thought it was, because of the thick retaining walls, filled with pebbles and sand. It was so cramped it couldn't hold a single piece of furniture. It wasn't a prison cell; it was a trap. The spotted walls weren't even lime-washed and the blackened floor was marinated in sweat, vomit and pus. Everywhere there were fingernail scratches and spots of blood, along with Chinese characters of common Korean girls' names, some Korean words, and numbers counting down to the day of release. At the far end of the cell there was a waist-high wooden partition. I peeked over it, but had to grab my nose and jump back.

The old guard, jangling his bundle of keys, laughed. 'That's the can, my friend. They all bring their own commodes and put them there. When they're released from solitary they remove them. We don't clean up those dirty Koreans' shit, you know.'

I held my breath and looked behind the partition again. A wooden lid was on the floor. I flipped it up to discover a round hole with a handle on the front. I plugged my nose with one hand and with the other lifted the contraption by the handle. Two feet below the hole was a wooden plank soaked in excrement. It was where the prisoner placed his personal latrine. Down there, on the wall, a small ventilation window was covered in inch-thick metal bars.

I walked through the steel doors of the solitary wing and was instantly blinded by the sun. Prisoners 331, 645 and the others who frequented solitary were somehow connected. I was sure of it. I rounded the back of the building and a gust of wind buffeted my face. Coarse grains of sand blew into my eye. 'This is a year-long problem,' the old guard said. 'That shit-storm coming from the mountain, I mean. All the sand and dust pile up under the walls of the buildings. So much so that the prisoners have to shovel it into sacks every month and clear it away.'

A thought darted through my mind, so quickly that it almost slipped by. I whipped around and cried out, 'Open the cell doors!'

Befuddled, the old guard ran down the corridor. The doors to the solitary wing screeched open again. I ran into the cell I'd just left. I jumped down into the latrine hole and hit the ground with a hollow thud that trembled up through the tips of my toes. I pulled my club out and scraped at the edge of the wooden plank. It caught on a small notch. I squeezed closed my eyes and stuck the tip of my finger in it and pulled. Damp, lukewarm air came rushing up at me, carrying the smell of dirt and tree roots and rocks. An empty hole opened its dark maw between my feet.

The siren blared. Maeda rushed into the solitary wing, looking as hollow as the hole beneath my feet. I shone my torch into the long, narrow tunnel that reeked of excrement, before crawling in. I couldn't breathe. I crawled along for about five minutes. At the end of the tunnel I discovered worn wooden spoons, flat rocks, broken bowls and bits of china.

'Fucking moles!' Maeda said angrily, crawling behind me.

We crawled backwards out to the cell. When Maeda and I emerged from the tunnel, we were relayed the warden's order to prepare a report. The sun had set. Searchlights scanned the main wing, the outer wall and the roof of the central facilities. They'd increased the number of guards on rounds.

In the warden's office, standing in front of Hasegawa, Maeda mopped his damp forehead with his sleeve. 'We did a cell check and everyone is accounted for. The man who dug the tunnel is still inside the prison.'

Hasegawa glared at him. 'That isn't the issue, is it? The problem is that there's a tunnel at all! Don't you know what will happen if this leaks out?'

'Yes, sir!' Maeda said. 'We'll find out who did it and fill up the tunnel at once.'

'And how will you find him?' Hasegawa grabbed his military sword in fury.

Maeda shot me a panicked look. 'This one's young, but very determined. He's the one who discovered the tunnel in the first place.'

Hasegawa glared at me, waiting for me to explain.

'During my investigation of the murder I began to observe Prisoner 331, who'd been severely beaten by Sugiyama. I thought that might be motive enough for murder. I saw that his gang wore uniforms that had unusually worn and baggy knees. I thought maybe they frequently kneeled before him, but 331's trousers were like that too. When I checked the solitary-wing log, I found that they were often sent there. They were practically volunteering to go. Because it's quiet there and they were left alone, it's the best place to plot something. And surveillance over there is lax, because the wing is remote and has thick double-layer walls.'

Hasegawa raised his eyebrows. 'How did you know they dug a tunnel?'

'The solitary wing is in the path of a strong mountain wind. The guard there said the wind carries dirt and piles it under the walls. In each solitary cell there's a small barred window. Each time the wind blew they'd toss the dirt they dug out through it to get rid of the evidence. The piles of dirt and sand weren't really from the mountain. The prisoners had dug it up.'

'And how did you know that the tunnel was under the latrine?'

'It's the only place we don't inspect. Even if the cell was searched, nobody would look there. A filthy place is safe from prying eyes.'

By now, Maeda had regained his confidence. 'Sir, the murder of the guard and the escape attempt are not separate incidents. We will catch these barbarians and punish them accordingly.' He turned to me, encouraging me to explain.

I continued in a louder voice to chase away my fears: 'The prisoners harboured deep animosity towards Sugiyama's excessive violence. He had focused his surveillance on a few people. Prisoner 331 was one of them. Sugiyama discovered his escape plot, so 331 got rid of him.'

'So this 331 is the murderer?' Hasegawa asked.

'That's still only a hypothesis. We'll have to interrogate him and get him to confess.'

Hasegawa gripped the hilt of his sword. 'Well, what are you waiting for? Hurry up! Get him to spill!'

# THE RECONSTRUCTION OF DEATH

The floor of the interrogation room was soaked through. One side of the room was filled with pincers large and small, bars, chains and sharp tools. On the other side were a cement tub filled with water, a rack and a wooden stool. The smell of rusted metal and blood permeated the stale air. Prisoner 331 was naked, tied to the crossbeam with his arms outstretched. Blood trickled down from his swelling eye, and his ankles were scabbed, rubbed raw by his shackles. A guard, wearing rubber gloves up to his elbows, repeatedly threw water on him. The guard smiled, flashing his yellow teeth. But the guard was no different from the man he had broken. He must be a father who embraced his young son when he returned home, a gentle husband who fixed a broken shelf in the kitchen, a friendly neighbour who was now beating a helpless man to a bloody pulp.

'Good luck,' he said to me as he fastened the buttons on his coat. 'I loosened him up, so he should start talking soon.' He went up the stairs to leave.

It was a common manoeuvre: the prisoner would be relieved at the departure of the brutal guard and would tell his replacement everything. My role was to appear at the appropriate time and write the report. After the other guard left, I undid the pulley block attached to the cross-beam and Prisoner 331 collapsed on the floor like a pile of sand. I dragged him to a chair and seated him, and he squinted, slowly focusing his swollen eyes on me. I draped his uniform on his shoulders. His eyes betrayed complicated feelings.

I opened the report file and sharpened my stubby pencil. '331! How long have you been digging that underground tunnel?' I knew I wouldn't get an answer. He had withstood twenty-four hours of beatings so far. I got up, shovelled some peat into the furnace and lit it. The light from the weak fire danced on his blood-soaked face.

'It's all over,' 331 moaned, his voice hoarse. 'All that's left for me is death. I guess all I can do is confess. I might as well tell you.'

'And why would you tell me, when you didn't open your mouth while you were being beaten to a pulp?'

'You figured it out. You read the solitary-wing log and found out that I'm a regular in solitary. Nobody even imagined what was going on, but you deduced what I was doing in there. I think you'll accept my terms.'

'What terms? I'm only a guard. If you want to negotiate, do it with the head guard or the warden.'

'No. They just want to kill me. You – you're interested in the stories. About me. About the prison.'

'I don't have the power to let you live.'

'I don't expect that. Just write down what I tell you. Don't remove a single word and don't add anything. Of course, you may not believe me. You might think I'm pulling your leg. But you can't edit it. You have to record what I say, word for word.'

'And why would I do that?'

'Somebody needs to record what is going on in here. So people will know what happened, when the war ends.'

'The regulations are to destroy documents after a certain time. No record exists forever.'

Prisoner 331 threw me a confident smile and pointed at my head. 'At least what's recorded in there won't disappear. The walls of this terrible place will crumble and documents will burn, but the memories in your head will remain. So don't you die until the war's over!' His eyes flashed.

I didn't know what to think. I didn't know what he wanted out of this. I doubted he'd tell me the truth. Even if he did, I was sure it would be bait for some scheme.

'Seven years,' he blurted out, disregarding my confusion. 'It's been almost seven years since I came to this hellhole.'

I picked up my pencil. The recycled paper waited hungrily to record his story.

'From the day I got here I dreamed of escaping,' he said. 'I dug the tunnel to escape from death, but it turns out what I dug was the road to death.'

Choi arrived at Fukuoka Prison in July 1938 for the attempted assassination of a prominent figure and the instigation of rebellion. He had spent half his life being hounded and the other half in prison. As a teenager he was pursued by the police for setting fire to several public buildings. The year he turned twenty he crossed the Tumen River. Manchuria was an ideal place for Koreans; they weren't oppressed by the Japanese Government-General of Korea or the vicious Special Higher Police, and they weren't subject to the violence of Japanese merchants. He settled in a Korean neighbourhood in Mukden. He frequented gambling dens and bars, shouting and cursing. He honed his fighting skills. Soon he was earning bundles of cash from the barwoman who pleaded with him to collect overdue bar tabs on her behalf, from the rice dealer who asked him to find the employee who'd stolen from him, and from the business magnate who tasked him with killing his cheating wife's lover.

One day he was hanging around a gambling den when a man with small rat-like eyes approached him. Choi drank with the man for a couple of hours, then packed his bags and followed him out of town. They walked for two days until they arrived at a cave in the mountains, where twenty bearded men in animal pelts were hiding, exhausted from anxiety and hunger. These men had lost everything to the Japanese. Their rice paddies and houses had been expropriated; their food, belongings and wives had been taken through allocated collection; their home towns and language obliterated. They were willing to do anything just to kill some Japs. The problem was that nobody had ever killed a single one. A man with a thick beard introduced himself as the commander of an autonomous anti-Japanese guerrilla unit; in reality, they were merely a gang of thieves who swung their fists at Korean merchants under the guise of building a war chest. The commander was a drunk and welcomed Choi's fists and big ideas, thinking that they would help the unit grow into the most feared in Mukden, but he soon kicked himself for his stupidity – Choi was not an obedient dog, he was a wolf. Choi became the leader of a subset gang that threatened the commander's position. The commander, unable to wrest control, leaked false information to a Japanese spy: that a man named Choi Chi-su was planning to lead an attack on the Kwantung Army's Mukden headquarters.

The Kwantung Army marched through the hills at battalion strength. Instead of mobilizing the troops, the Japanese commander waited for the guerrillas to emerge on their own. A long confrontation ensued. The rugged geography was on the rebels' side. The gang climbed over the cliffs and left the valley before the Kwantung Army reached the cave. Choi headed towards the Siberian Maritime Province with more than twenty men. They lived like wild creatures of the night, scaling mountains after dark and sleeping under leaves during the day. When they arrived at their destination, the gang had shrunken to fourteen; cold, hunger and beasts had reduced their ranks. Rumours about the fearsome band of thieves from Mukden preceded them to the Siberian Maritime Province, where they were organized under the command of the Russian Communists. That was where Choi encountered Marx's ideas; Choi's talent for fighting and dreams of destroying the Japs grew even fiercer. Six months later he'd turned into a loyal Communist. His unit attacked a Japanese ordnance corps and seized its train and assassinated a Kwantung Army general and commander; the Siberian Maritime Province soon became their territory. But it wasn't enough for Choi; he knew he was fated for greatness. Wanting more intense battles with more enemies, he headed to Vladivostok. He sneaked into the belly of a ship, covered in the stench of disintegrating produce and fish, and disembarked in brightly lit Tokyo Bay three days later.

The Communist organization extended like a vine everywhere; in Tokyo it was centred on Korean students studying abroad, who had learned about Communism from books and didn't know how to act on their rage. They stayed up all night memorizing manuals on fighting, but didn't know how to apply their learning to the Japs. They agonized over their sterile ideology, debating useless theory hundreds of times. Choi blamed books for delaying revolution; in his mind, writing was a tool that allowed the powerful to oppress the weak for thousands of years. The rich incarcerated the poor using law books, loan sharks oppressed the poor with their ledgers, and officials had used the king's directives to suck the people dry. He couldn't wait for a book-free world. He attended a Korean student meeting in Tokyo and mocked them: 'You so-called intellectuals have imprisoned yourselves behind letters,' he announced. 'You're weak. You're unable to take any action. That's what the Japs want – to create bookworms who can't act. You want to overthrow the Japs, but all you do is wriggle in the mud.'

Disgusted, Choi established his own Communist cell in the Tokyo area. Soon there was a spike in arson and attacks on officials, bankers and the heads of defence contractors. The Special Higher Police didn't realize that they were the acts of a foreign Communist; they thought they were isolated instances of increased violence as society became unsettled. Three years after he arrived in Japan, Choi planned the best plot of his life, the one attack that would return the whole warped situation to normal. It was 29 April, the Emperor's birthday. He would bomb the Emperor's celebration at Ueno Park, attended by high-level army generals, the Interior Minister and others. His assistant was a Korean student named Kim Gwing-pil, who had been studying chemistry at Rikkyo University when he received his conscription notice. He'd been on the run since then. Kim, who wore round eye-glasses, looked every bit the intellectual. Choi asked if he could make a bomb. Kim assented, requesting a hideout in return. He stayed up all night, reading books about gunpowder and explosives that Choi procured for him. No matter what happened, he had to make a bomb by 28 April.

Two days before the big event Kim handed over two bombs he'd made over several sleepless nights. Choi promised to send him money and buy a passage to Manchuria after the bombing. But the bomb Choi lobbed into the crowd didn't go off; he was arrested on the scene. The Special Higher Police caught up with Kim, who was wandering the Japanese islands without any escape funds. The prosecutor sought execution for Choi, but the Tokyo court sentenced him to life imprisonment. What they didn't know was how tenacious Choi was in biding his time. Choi wasn't angry at Kim. It wasn't the man's fault; it was the damn books he'd read. Inaccurate knowledge acted like a noose. If Kim was wrong, it was for the audacity of thinking he could change the world with a couple of books.

Choi's glares intimidated even the guards. He reeked of the wild. He was poised to attack on a moment's notice. Nobody knew what he would do next. When Sugiyama Dozan came to the prison fresh from Manchuria, Choi instinctively recognized his own untamed nature in the guard, and Sugiyama detected the Manchurian dust on Choi. The prison was a small, enclosed world and the two had to fight over this limited territory. Sugiyama called Choi into the interrogation room every few days. He had plenty of reasons – Choi had mumbled his answer to a question, he was late for assembly, he stared straight into the guard's eyes. Sugiyama's club would ram into Choi's eyelid, crack open his forehead, break his teeth. With eyes swollen shut, Choi stared down the pain. He had only one weapon at his disposal – his endurance.

'How would you like to die?' Sugiyama would ask as he pressed his boot down on Choi's neck.

Choi would grin, flashing his broken teeth. 'I don't want to die. If I die, I lose.'

Solitary confinement awaited him after each interrogation. It was as dark and quiet there as the inside of a coffin. Three days would pass. The cut near his eye would heal and the bruises would fade. Choi would go to the window, thinking he would suffocate from the stench. A weak wind blew through the ventilation window under the toilet. He would grip the bars as a wonderful scent wafted in – of life and hope, tender new shoots, overgrown spring grass, the scent of a young mountain bird's feathers.

One day something occurred to him as he walked out of solitary into the blinding sun. It wasn't enough simply to survive. He had to do something. First, he bulked up his weakened body. He began to do chin-ups on the bars of his cell and toned his muscles by doing squats and push-ups. When he was outside he walked around the yard to strengthen his shrunken heart. But his newfound focus only lasted a fortnight. He punched another prisoner and attacked a guard. What waited for him again was the smelly solitary cell. One week later he spat through his blood-crusted lips as he walked out of the cell. It was after this trip to solitary that he determined on new attempts at escape.

The first time he shoved the guard on duty and hurtled towards the wall. As he struggled to clamber up the high wall, a guard reached him and beat him. It was clumsy, an afterthought. It was too ridiculous even to call it an escape attempt, but the punishment was severe: ten days in solitary. The second time he volunteered for the night-shift work team and sneaked out of the workroom. He was caught climbing over the back wall of the prison. The warden was woken at home and rushed back to the prison. He viewed the entire incident as a challenge to his authority and personally interrogated Choi. Even a failed attempt deserved a summary conviction. But Choi wasn't executed; his stay in solitary lengthened to a fortnight, then a month. The curious part was that while most people couldn't make it out of their first solitary confinement alive, Choi walked out on his own two feet every time. Oddly, he tried to escape a third, fourth and fifth time, even though he hadn't fully recovered his strength. His attempts kept evolving and were as entertaining as a well-choreographed play or an acrobatics show. The time he sneaked into a military truck loaded with bricks made by the prisoners, it seemed he'd made it, until the truck was stopped just before it drove out of the gates. He almost succeeded the time he crawled through a narrow, 300-metre-long sewer pipe, until he lost consciousness from poisonous gas with thirty metres to go. Soon he and the guards came to a silent agreement. When a fortnight passed after his last stint in solitary, the guards moved first. They sent him back under the guise that he'd violated some trivial rule, before he could do something more serious again. The guards could stop Choi's violent behaviour and he could avoid the beatings. The solitary cell was occupied more often than not. So it was like clockwork; he and his gang went to and fro between Ward Three and the solitary cells like honeybees to a hive. Nobody thought twice about their trips, even though it happened at regular intervals. Until Sugiyama sniffed out the plot.

One day Choi was called into the interrogation room. Sugiyama held out a cigarette. Choi sucked on it deeply before hacking.

'I see you've forgotten how to smoke. Don't worry. If your plans go off without a hitch you'll be able to smoke as much as you want.' Sugiyama's sunken eyes glinted.

An artery throbbed in Choi's neck. This guard had a dog's nose, he thought. 'Whatever do you mean?'

'I ask the questions!' Sugiyama slammed his club down on the desk. 'I won't ask how long you've been at it. I don't want to know why you're digging the tunnel, either.'

Choi felt as though he had been dunked in cold water. But at least it was Sugiyama. If another guard had discovered the tunnel, he would immediately have pressed the emergency alarm. But Sugiyama thought the world revolved around him. Choi took a breath. 'Wouldn't it be easier to press the emergency alarm or report the tunnel to your boss? Why make things more complicated?'

Sugiyama let out a long trail of cigarette smoke. 'As soon as I do that, this incident leaves my hands. All the guards would get in on it. The machine gun on the watchtower would be aimed at the solitary cells and the searchlight would shine all around the prison. The guard dogs would chase after your scent. You'd be shot or mauled by the dogs and dragged back for your execution.'

'Are you letting me live?'

'No. I just don't want you to die at another's hands. We're not done here,' Sugiyama smirked.

Choi's heart sank, as though he were watching a heavy metal bar being lowered over the door to freedom.

Sugiyama continued slowly, 'You might think everything is over, but the battle has just begun. Fill up that rat hole with your own hands. You can't leave even a tiny gap. If you do that for me, I'll take your secret to my grave.'

'It's too late,' Choi said. 'The dirt from the tunnel blew away in the wind, so I can't replace it.'

'I'm sure you can figure it out. I don't care if you vomit dirt or if you dig another hole. Otherwise I'll have to send you and your idiot mole comrades to the cemetery.'

The hairs on Choi's forearm stood on end. He thought of each Korean who'd gone into solitary to dig that tunnel.

Sugiyama continued, 'If you don't like my terms, keep digging that tunnel and get out of prison. If you win, you're free. If I win, you're right back here. Wouldn't you say it's a fair fight?' Sugiyama looked at Choi with dark, brooding eyes.

Sugiyama continued to watch him over the next three months; the tunnel wasn't complete and escape seemed impossible. Killing Sugiyama was the only way. If he disappeared, the only person who knew about the tunnel would be gone. It wasn't an easy choice for a cornered mouse to bite the cat, but it wasn't impossible, either. Choi started to dig a new tunnel towards the cemetery, branching off the original tunnel to make it look as though he were simply digging to get enough dirt to fill up the first tunnel. Choi carefully observed Sugiyama's rounds. Finally the tunnel to the cemetery was complete. The night Sugiyama was assigned to make the overnight rounds, Choi crawled to the cemetery. He came up to ground level, uprooted a stake that marked a grave and waited, hiding around the corner from the solitary wing. Sugiyama's route was precise. Choi smashed the stake into the guard's shoulder as he rounded the corner. He heard bone breaking. Choi then held a spoon that he had filed down to Sugiyama's neck, prodding him towards the administrative wing. It was completely dark that night, without even a strand of moonlight. Sugiyama must have thought the heavens were on Choi's side. They went through the doors of the administrative wing and through to the inspection office. Sugiyama took out his bundle of keys and opened the small door; he was pushed along the corridor, past the inspection office, towards the central facilities. The block was deserted and silent. In the central building Choi led Sugiyama up the stairs to the banister. Sticky blood trickled down Sugiyama's neck.

'I'm sorry. But there wasn't any other way, was there?' Choi whispered.

Suigyama nodded. He knew there weren't any rules in war, just that you'd be killed if you didn't strike first. Choi snapped Sugiyama's neck, then tied him to the banister with the rope that he undid from Sugiyama's belt and stabbed him with his weapon. He was as skilled as a butcher handling a side of beef. He retraced his steps back to the cemetery, avoiding the blue searchlight that intermittently lit the darkness. Choi then calmly disappeared back into the tunnel.

Choi seemed spent. I put the pen down and blew on my hands. I was chilled, and not because of the sub-zero temperature in the interrogation room. 'It would have been easier to kill him in the cemetery or near the solitary wing. Why did you take him to the central facilities?'

One side of his mouth turned up in a cold smile. He spoke slowly, as if enjoying my terror. 'My purpose wasn't to kill him, but to escape. If I killed him near the cemetery or the solitary wing, the whole area would have been torn apart. The farthest place from the tunnel was the lobby between the administrative wing and the wards, the centre of the prison.'

'Where did you get the surgical needle and thread that you used to sew up his mouth?'

'I can get my hands on anything in this prison. I have skilled men: the craftiest, deftest pickpocket, an irresistible charmer, a con man who can seduce a nurse. And how convenient is it that the fancy infirmary is right here in the prison? It's child's play to steal a suture set.'

'So the intricate suturing is your work, too?'

'Remember, I grew up on the battlefield. I had to learn how to do many things. That was the only way I could survive.'

I put my pen down. What he was confessing would lead to his hanging. Why was he telling me this? What was he plotting? I summarized Choi's statement into a four-page report. I included everything he had confessed to me, but my report wasn't the entire truth. Even if everything I wrote down was accurate, it couldn't be truthful if anything was missing. I didn't record Choi's life as a fugitive or the emotional stand-off he'd had with the man he killed. I didn't write down the exact point in time when Sugiyama discovered the tunnel, or the fight over it. My report concluded with a simple cause and effect: Sugiyama Dozan found the tunnel and Prisoner 331 killed him to keep it a secret.

Things happened quickly after I submitted my report. Choi was thrown into a cell on death-row and a group of selected prisoners was ordered to fill up the tunnel. But unanswered questions continued to run through my head. Why, when he knew he would fail, when he knew what awaited him, did he put his life on the line, trying to escape in the most hopeless ways? And why did the warden let him live?

Three days later, I was called into the warden's office. I was given a promotion for my role in the discovery of the tunnel and the investigation of the murder. All the prison executives were there, including Maeda, the head of security, the head investigator, the head administrator and the head surgeon. The warden personally pinned a corporal badge on my cap. One man had been murdered, another was sentenced to death, while I was rewarded with a promotion. I felt hopelessly confused.

# A PIANO'S ENEMIES

The auditorium, bathed in light from the setting sun, looked like a painting. Midori was a priestess in prayer behind the piano. The piano laughed and wept beneath her touch. I realized I'd heard the beautiful notes she was now playing the first time I went to the warden's office. She turned to look at me. I averted my eyes and lowered my head; I'd been humming along.

'Schubert's "Der Lindenbaum",' she said. 'It's a movement in *Die Winterreise* and part of Professor Marui's repertoire.' She played on.

I wondered what the bleak title, the subtle, sorrowful allusion to melody and all the terse German words meant. 'I've heard it before, but I couldn't understand the lyrics.'

'Schubert devotees usually prefer the original lyrics. German is rough and turbid, so it goes well with the masculine tone and heavy atmosphere. *Die Winterreise* is a song cycle based on a serial poem by the German poet Wilhelm Müller. You can really understand the piece if you pay attention to the sound of the original language.'

She played another tune, low and sorrowful. I stole a glance at the neat parting in her hair. The sunset caressed her rhythmically moving shoulders.

'This is "Gute Nacht", the first lied in *Die Winterreise*.' She spoke without turning around.

That was when it came to me. 'Good Night.' It was the mysterious poem I had found in Sugiyama's pocket. I recited it aloud. 'As a stranger I arrived, as a stranger again I leave . . . Now the world is bleak, the path covered by snow.'

She froze like a salt pillar. Fear pooled in her eyes. Why was she so frightened? She must know something.

My face betrayed no emotions. I told her, 'I found that poem in the dead guard's pocket. He was a violent guard they called the "Angel of Death".'

She curled her white fingers into a fist. 'Don't talk about him like that,' she said warily, shooting me a hostile glance. 'You don't know anything about him.'

My mouth went dry. 'What do *you* know about him?' I asked, and turned around to hide my upset expression.

I heard the piano then, as mournful and majestic as a large collapsing building. I looked back. She had stood up, slamming both hands on the keyboard. Through her tangled hair that cascaded in front of her face I could see her wet eyelashes and the tip of her reddening nose.

'He wasn't violent!'

The heavy notes reverberated in my head. I thought about my promise to Choi that I would record the truth about Sugiyama's death. He had confessed everything, but I still didn't feel that I knew the truth. Really, I didn't know a thing.

'What was Sugiyama like then?' I asked, trying to appease her. Truly, I did want to know about Sugiyama Dozan's life. I knew she wouldn't know the whole story, either. But I wanted to know about the aspects of his life that Choi didn't tell me. The sunset was dissolving now, giving way to crisp darkness that settled beyond the windows.

She looked out. 'Sugiyama Dozan was a sensitive man. He knew music, appreciated poetry and loved life.'

What killed the gentle Sugiyama was this insane era, these times that demanded ever more blood, ever more hate, ever more death. Incarcerated in his uniform, he died in his own solitary hell.

One snowy winter morning two years ago, as a nurse in the newly established Kyushu Imperial University Medical School infirmary at Fukuoka Prison, Midori stepped onto the prison grounds. Specialists spent all day in the laboratories studying English medical texts, their eyes glued to microscopes, concentrating on significant research. If, thanks to these efforts, they could advance medical knowledge and develop groundbreaking new medications, they would be able to save thousands – even tens of thousands – of lives. Midori was proud to be a member of a team responsible for safeguarding life during this era of slaughter. Nursing was difficult work; she was assigned to double shifts every day.

She heard the name Sugiyama about a fortnight after she began working there.

'Sugiyama, that son-of-a-bitch. He's a butcher!' hollered a worked-up Japanese prisoner with a head injury. 'He clubs anything that moves. If he didn't have anyone else to beat up, he'd probably bust his own head open.'

A few days later, a guard came in clutching a swollen finger. Midori secured his finger with a splint and asked how he had injured it. He looked down at his bandaged finger and snapped, 'The Koreans got into a fight. Sugiyama clubbed one of them over the head and didn't stop. I ran over to pull him off, but he slapped me away, completely enraged. Eventually he did step back, but if it weren't for me, that Korean would be dead.'

Sugiyama again. What happened to the Korean who had been beaten like a dog? Was he in solitary, writhing in agony and cradling his broken bones? She realized she had never seen a Korean prisoner in the infirmary. She learned that the prison had a firm policy of disallowing unnecessary medical care for Korean prisoners. Unless there was a special circumstance, the guards sent injured Koreans to solitary confinement instead of the infirmary.

'I should actually thank him,' the guard was saying, grinning smarmily. 'I got to meet a pretty young thing like you.'

Sugiyama's name continued to come up frequently after that. A prisoner whose shoulder was shattered and a guard who got a fat lip both referred to him resentfully. The gashes and broken bones were enough to paint in her mind's eye a portrait of a cruel, merciless man who didn't care a whit about anyone else and forced his rage onto the world. Like a virus, rage spread its roots even into the hearts of good people; it eventually infected her, too. Tending to the cuts and broken bones, she grew hostile towards him. Sugiyama was evil. People like that should be behind bars.

Then, finally, she met Sugiyama in person. Every Monday morning at assembly 200 or so guards and sixty-odd doctors and nurses stood in rows in the auditorium; they acted as one, praising the Empire and the Emperor. The assembly began with a chorus of the 'Kimigayo', the national anthem, and ended with three rounds of 'Long Live the Emperor!' Midori chafed at its required reverence, but she stood in front and performed dutifully, to be near the piano.

One day, after assembly, she went up to the piano and opened the lid. She wiped the dust off each key with the tip of her finger, wondering whether it still played. She cautiously pressed a key. A low G grasped the ankles of those who had turned to leave. She pressed another key. A silvery F tapped their shoulders. Murmuring, the others waited for the next note. Midori set her hands on the keys and caressed and pounded them in turn. Music spooled out, like silk unravelling from a silkworm's cocoon.

A young nurse hesitantly sang along. "Mid pleasures and palaces though we may roam . . ."

The melody spread slowly. People's collective longing was expressed through song. They remembered each of their homes – the guard who'd left his wife behind in far-away Hokkaido, the conscripted guard who thought of his elderly mother in the mountains of Niigata and the intern who missed the meals around his family's dinner table in Tokyo.

'Home! Home! Sweet, sweet home! There's no place like home!'

Everyone lingered after the song was over. Only a long time later did the guards return to the cells, the doctors to the laboratories and the nurses to the infirmary.

Maeda came up behind Midori, furious. 'What are you doing? How could you play "Home! Sweet Home!" when you are to sing the "Kimigayo" with the resolve to sacrifice your own life for our country?'

It was only then that she realized what she'd done – she'd led the prison in singing an American song.

Warden Hasegawa approached with energetic, powerful

steps. 'Glorious! Good thing we didn't get rid of this piano. Otherwise we wouldn't have had the pleasure of listening to this wonderful performance.' He twisted his neat moustache and asked her who she was.

Director Morioka came up, his thick wavy hair neatly combed back, clad in a white coat and gold neck tie. 'This is Miss Iwanami Midori, a nurse in the infirmary. She studied the piano from before she entered primary school. She was a promising piano prodigy who won in the Kyushyu piano contest. When her father, a war-department executive, died in the Sino-Japanese War she was forced to give up playing, but – as you can see – she is still very talented.'

Hasegawa let out a delighted exclamation. Everything Morioka described contained all that he desired for himself, but had to satisfy through mimicry: the ability to purchase an expensive musical instrument, a sensibility to appreciate music, a sophisticated character.

The piano had come to the prison more than ten years earlier, before the start of the Second Sino-Japanese War, when Fukuoka was a peaceful city known for hosting a large contingent of foreign businessmen on leisure trips. Stevenson, an American importer and a music lover, wanted music to flow through the utilitarian prison. The day the piano arrived, Stevenson held a small performance by an amateur choir that he led. Since then, the piano had languished in a corner of the dark auditorium, covered in dust. Disinterest, humidity, dust, bugs and mice had all attacked it. The strings lost their innate sounds and the frame warped. Many suggested that the eyesore be tossed, or hacked apart to donate the steel strings to the war effort.

'Awful sound,' said a rough, creaky voice behind Hasegawa. Everyone turned to look at the guard with wide, sturdy shoulders and a long scar down his cheek. He was looking down at the keys disapprovingly.

Midori closed the lid and stood up. 'I'm sorry if you didn't like my playing.'

'No need to be sorry. Your playing isn't what's awful. I don't have the ability or the desire to judge how you play.'

Hasegawa tensed his small, hard body. 'Sugiyama!' he shouted. 'How can you say something like that? You don't know a thing about music!'

Midori shivered. It was that menacing butcher, the monster who broke countless bones and ripped flesh.

Sugiyama replied tersely, 'I don't know much about music, but I do know about sounds.'

'What? What could you possibly know about sounds?'

Instead of answering, he approached the piano and put a hand on the keys. Hasegawa watched him in surprise. Sugiyama pressed two keys at the same time. He pressed five keys down. A heavy, powerful noise filled the auditorium. He closed his eyes, gauging the resonance and power of each note. 'This piano has lost its sound.'

Hasegawa's eyebrows shot up. 'Nonsense! Nobody has even touched this piano in the last ten years!'

'Not playing a piano is worse than pounding on it. Because of the humidity in the wood, the notes can't stretch out. The strings lose their bounce, become warped and are unable to let out a precise note. A piano that can't make a proper sound is no better than a dead one.'

Hasegawa smirked. 'Sugiyama, don't you dare think about getting rid of a perfectly fine piano by treating it like a broken piece of rubbish. It was abandoned for ten years, but today it finally met a proper player.' He turned to look at Midori with a gentle expression.

Midori pressed one key with her right thumb and another with her little finger. The low and high G notes stretched out in parallel lines. 'These are exactly one octave apart, sir. But the G I pressed is a black key. It's G#, not G. G is a half-note lower. Its resonance is also shaky. The notes are slightly off and the vibrato is not quite right.'

Hasegawa turned to Sugiyama with displeasure. 'How did you know about the condition of this piano?'

'Before I enlisted I worked at a piano shop and learned a little, over the tuner's shoulder.'

'Then fix it!'

That evening Sugiyama crouched on the auditorium floor and opened a leather bag filled with a variety of metal tools, tongs, wrenches and pieces of leather. He caressed the piano as he would a beloved pet. He opened the lid; he was surrounded by the faint forest scent of antique wood. The piano-felt was ragged.

'G.' His monotonous voice was brittle.

Midori pressed the key confidently. The silence was broken by Sugiyama's voice, followed by the piano. He wound a piece of leather around the bolts and tightened the strings. His expression reminded Midori of a doctor listening to the patient's heart through a stethoscope, or a surgeon preparing to operate on a doomed patient. Sugiyama was holding tongs instead of a scalpel, but he was as powerful as a surgeon who made the lame walk, the blind see and the dying live.

'It's improving,' she offered. 'The note is precise and the vibrato sounds better, too.'

He didn't seem satisfied. 'I gave it a basic tune-up, but I need tuning instruments and other materials to do it correctly. A hammer and tuning driver, one spring-adjustable hooked needle, new steel strings, glue, wax for shining and a fine polishing cloth . . .'

He appeared worried that he wouldn't be able to find what he needed in these times of shortages and rations. Pianos, once objects of envy, had become the target of rage. No one would buy them, so they were hidden away in rooms or attics like clandestine children, covered with dust, forgotten.

'I'm going to try the piano shop in town. I may be able to find tuning instruments.' He started putting away his pliers, metal rods and leather ties.

Midori recognized those pliers; the patients she'd cared for had sported bloody bruises on their fingers made from those steel tips. She'd seen lash wounds on their backs the same thickness as those leather ties. This violent guard menaced powerless prisoners, but he was also the only person who could recover this piano's sound. Which was his true self?

'What do you use those tools for?' she asked cautiously.

Sugiyama's pupils flickered like candlelight in the wind. 'Why do you want to know? We each do our jobs. I rough people up, and you treat them. I tune the piano, and you make music with it.'

'What is it exactly that you do?'

'My job is to purify the warped brains of those who believe they're saving the world, but are really befouling society – Communists, nationalists, anarchists. So don't meddle.' He tossed her a cold smile and stalked out of the auditorium, leaving her behind in the murky darkness, the metal instruments in his bag clanging with each step he took.

Two days later, Sugiyama went into town. The piano shop there had closed a long time ago. He pounded on the door for a long time until it opened. The bald, moustachioed owner was as lethargic as a dust-covered piano. Sugiyama explained that he was seeking a tuning kit and repair tools. Resigned, the owner opened the door to the storage room. There wasn't much that was usable, but Sugiyama took a few tools and walked through the grey streets back to the prison.

Midori was waiting for him in the auditorium. Without a word, Sugiyama opened up the piano, revealing hundreds of nuts and dozens of strings, and the crossbeam that stretched across. He tightened hundreds of tuning pins and strings and bearings and nuts.

'Try any key.'

She played 'Carry Me Back to Old Virginny'. Her playing sparkled, recalling for him the image of a rainbow, summer rain, amber. Sugiyama glanced at her fingers, which flew across the keys like butterflies, at her thin ankles above the pedals. He softened, looking nostalgic.

'Tuning isn't something you can learn in a day or two,' Midori suddenly said. 'It's obvious you didn't just pick it up — you managed to tune this piano without any real tuning equipment.'

Sugiyama flinched.

Midori could tell that he was recoiling from a memory.

He fixed his gaze on the rusted strings. 'It was just to survive,' he muttered. 'It was a decent way to rip off the rich. I didn't dare play, so I learned how to tune.'

She knew that couldn't be the whole story. His tortured expression wasn't that of someone who remembered trying to make a few yen here and there. When he was tuning the piano, he was an artist searching for the best sound.

She shook her head. 'No, I can tell. Your voice is tender, almost loving, when you call out a note from the other side of the piano. All of your senses are focused on the sound. You're reading the player's heart.'

But the man in front of her had turned back into a stern prison guard. He looked tired, like an exile pursued by his golden-hued past. He didn't reply, instead tending to the piano carefully, separating strings and actions, wiping away the rust with soft leather and recovering standard pitches. He reversed the damage to the hammer and damper. He adjusted the resistance and working range of the keys and found a uniform touch. The piano slowly regained its elegance; the sounds gradually recaptured their colours. His voice became stronger as well. 'G!'

A few weeks later, Warden Hasegawa and Director Morioka walked into the auditorium together. They were all smiles, thrilled that the piano was returning to its former glory. Hasegawa was positively vibrating; he was honoured to be in the presence of a respected Fukuoka luminary. He looked at the piano with reverence as though he wanted to bow to it in gratitude, then shot a doubtful look at Sugiyama, who was still busy working on the instrument. He didn't know what the guard was doing, but he was forced to trust him.

'Thanks to Miss Iwanami's wonderful playing, we'll be able to have piano accompaniment at all official events, including, of course, our weekly assemblies,' Hasegawa announced.

Morioka didn't answer right away. Hasegawa stared at him impatiently.

'It would be a waste for this instrument and player to accompany the assemblies,' Morioka said finally. 'We need a bigger stage. What do you think about organizing a larger concert?'

Though slightly taken aback, Hasegawa nodded eagerly. 'You are entirely correct, of course, but this is a prison and we don't have the time for practices—'

Morioka gently cut him off. 'Actually, the fact that this is a prison makes this the ideal venue. What if we had a concert for peace, direct from a criminals' den? We will be coaxing beautiful music out of a desolate place. We could invite a famous singer from Tokyo as well as high-level officials, both Japanese and international. What do you think?'

Hasegawa's eyes glimmered at the thought of being part of this ambitious project. 'You have an outstanding artistic vision, Director!' he cried. 'But would a famous singer come here?'

Morioka walked over to the piano. Hasegawa followed him awkwardly. 'You know the singer Professor Marui, right? He is a supporter of Miss Iwanami and offered to help her study in Tokyo.' He turned to look at Midori. 'Miss Iwanami! Brief the warden about the plans for Fukuoka Prison's peace concert. It's ultimately his decision.'

Midori stood up. 'Sugiyama-*san* did his best, but he couldn't find all the tuning tools and parts in town. That's when I thought of Professor Marui. I thought he might be able to help us. I know I may have overstepped my place, but I sent a letter asking him for tools and new parts to revitalize the prison's old piano.'

'And?' Hasegawa cut in impatiently. 'What happened? Did Professor Marui reply?'

She nodded. 'Yes. From Tokyo we received a tool set, parts and new strings. I wrote back that once the piano was tuned, I would be honoured to accompany his rendition of *Die Winterreise*. He thought it was a wonderful idea.'

Hasegawa couldn't believe his ears. The foremost singer

in Japan would perform in his prison! A smile began to form on his face. An International Peace Concert at Fukuoka Prison – the benefits of a good press would be incalculable. The music would float out from behind bars and reach a nation exhausted from war and austerity. Hosting such a meaningful event meant that he could invite high-level officials of the central government, including the commanders of the army, navy and air force, and military Diet members. This might help him get a job at the Interior Ministry. Soldiers ruled during wartime, but afterwards it would be the bureaucrats' era. This concert could deliver him to the core of power. Hasegawa clenched his teeth with determination. 'We must begin to practise immediately.'

Midori finished her story and started to play. As her fingers sprang across the keys, the keys pushed up the hammers, the hammers pounded the strings, and the strings trembled and vibrated. One note led to another and seeped into the dark, dry air. I felt my despair lifting; from within me bubbled hope for life, making me want to hold someone's hand and fall in love.

I started to sing along: 'Carry me back to old Virginny . . .' My heart hammered, a clamour in the calm. It was enough to make me want to hope, even in these turbulent times.

After she finished playing I asked, 'Why would Sugiyama have the lyrics of *Die Winterreise*?' I was afraid to hear the reason, but I had to know.

She swept up a strand of hair. 'He always kept poems in his shirt pocket. He loved poetry and gave everything to it.'

Untuned strings roared dissonantly in my heart. He loved poetry? He, who callously destroyed books? The face of the young poet hovered in front of my eyes. Hiranuma. He must know something. Maybe he knew everything.

# LET ME LOOK UP TO THE HEAVENS WITHOUT A SPECK OF SHAME UNTIL THE DAY I DIE

According to the incineration log, Hiranuma Tochu's documents were burned on 2 April 1944, immediately after he arrived at Fukuoka Prison. On the log were the names of unfamiliar Korean authors written in Chinese characters – Kim Yeong-rang, Baek Seok, Yi Sang, Jeong Ji-yong. Next to them were titles of books, a mixture of Chinese characters and *katakana*. *Poetry of Yeong-rang, Poetry of Jeong Ji-yong* . . . Most were volumes of poetry, but there were also copies of a Korean magazine called *Sentences* and books in English. The next incineration date was 3 April 1944. Sugiyama had written down all the names of the burned poems in his cramped hand.

1. *Prologue*
2. *Until Dawn Comes*
3. *Cross*
4. *Another Home*
5. *Night Counting Stars*

The numbers went up to nineteen. In the notes column he had written: '19 poems, to be included in the unpublished

*The Sky, the Wind, the Stars and Poetry'*. Under that were the numbers twenty to twenty-nine. In the notes column was the following: 'According to Detective Koroki, the prisoner translated the poems into Japanese at Shimogamo Police Station in Kyoto.' So Hiranuma had been arrested and brought to Shimogamo Police Station in Kyoto. The arresting officers confiscated dozens of seditious books and poems, and made Hiranuma translate his poems into Japanese. And of fifty or so poems, nineteen had been intended for inclusion in an unpublished book of poetry. The remaining poems seemed to have been written in Tokyo and Kyoto.

Sugiyama Dozan and Hiranuma Tochu. Sugiyama the censor ruined Hiranuma the poet, and Hiranuma hated Sugiyama for it. They were in stark contrast to each other – one was the shadow and the other the light. But they were linked by poetry. So why did Sugiyama have poems in his pocket and desk drawer? What role did poetry have in their relationship? To find out I had to interrogate Hiranuma.

Prisoner 645 sat straight-backed on the old wooden chair in the interrogation room. The humidity-spotted walls accentuated his gaunt, pale face. He was slight in his too-large prisoner uniform. I assumed an impassive demeanour as I flipped through the file, but I was feeling anxious. I told myself to calm down; Hiranuma was the one who should be worried.

'Did you catch the murderer?' he asked.

His question knocked the breath out of me. I'd already lost my authority. I took off my sweat-soaked military cap and decided to confide in him. There was no way he would tell me the truth if I didn't. 'It was a prisoner named Choi Chi-su. He killed the guard when his escape plot was discovered.'

Hiranuma nodded. Dark shadows were cast under his nose and on his stubbly chin. The bruise on his eye was turning yellow. 'So you got the murderer. What do you want from me?'

'I have the facts, but not the truth.'

He scanned my face. 'Facts and truth . . .'

I recalled Rilke's book of poems in his box of confiscated books. 'It was a fact that Rilke died from being stuck by a rose, but that wasn't the truth. The thorn caused blood poisoning that spread bacteria throughout his body, but that wasn't the cause of death. It was leukaemia. On the other side of a fact lurks another truth.'

'You don't say?'

'Yes. He wrote his own headstone to say: "rose, o pure contradiction, desire to be no one's sleep beneath so many lids". That is suggestive of the secretive essence hidden on the other side of a beautiful rose.'

He searched my face. My argument was, in essence, revealing to him the kind of person I was; he was reading me as I sat in front of him.

I made an effort to regain the terse tone of an interrogator. 'Why did Sugiyama Dozan copy out your poems?'

He shook his head. He looked firm – he couldn't, or wouldn't, tell. Noting my disheartened expression, he spoke, with the finality of scattering wet dirt into an open grave. 'Accept the facts that have been revealed. The truth only makes everyone suffer.'

I shook my head violently as if to fling off the wet dirt. The wall in front of me swayed like a thin, undulating piece of paper. 'Even if it's presented as the truth, a lie is a lie. A little knowledge is a dangerous thing.'

He hesitated. 'What is it that you want to know about Sugiyama Dozan?'

'His life.'

'Not about his death?'

'I need to know about his life to understand his death. Only when I know how he lived will I be able to know why he died.'

'It would be easier to ask your fellow guards about his life. Why are you asking me, of all people?' Hiranuma seemed anxious to leave as soon as possible.

'Because you're the one person who really knew him.'

He studied me carefully. After a long time he replied in a calm voice, 'He was a poet. He was the most wonderful poet I've ever met.'

Sugiyama Dozan was a poet. But not at first. At the beginning he was quite different. He despised literature and looked down on those, like Hiranuma, who believed they could make something out of words.

Hiranuma came to Fukuoka Prison in the spring of 1944. With fourteen other men he stepped behind walls that aged him instantly. Exhaustion and fear grew like liver spots on his face, his bones protruded, the heels of his sockless feet cracked and the back of his frost-bitten hands chapped. With dim eyes he gazed at his reality – the barbed wire, the bars and the thick steel doors that blocked his vision. He was puzzled as to why he was here, dragged in by a few lines and a couple of documents – his banned Korean poems, police reports, the prosecutor's indictment and the judge's ruling. At Fukuoka he moved slowly, passing through the shadows of the tall watchtower and the cold brick walls. He went into the disinfection room and was doused in white powder. He was given an old prisoner uniform. He wondered whether the person who'd worn it before him had left this place alive. He walked along the long corridor into the musty unknown, his own feet crushing his consciousness. Cell 28, Ward Three. That first night he hunched in a corner like a crumpled piece of paper as despair soaked into his marrow.

The Korean prisoners were clustered together at the sunny spot below the wall, when they heard a thin, smooth, wind-like whistling. Sugiyama slid the club out of his belt and looked for the source. It was Prisoner 645, standing at the foot of the bare hill. Sugiyama's steps instinctively quick-ened into a run.

'645! What are you doing here, all alone?' Sugiyama's voice, out of breath, was on edge. He aimed his club at the young man's neck, ready to break his shoulder.

645 stopped whistling. 'Is it a crime to whistle?' he asked gravely, his voice sinking like sediment.

This young man was everything Sugiyama derided: a recalcitrant Korean political prisoner who violated the Maintenance of Public Order Act, and an intellectual on top of that. With the tip of his blood-crusted club, Sugiyama pushed the young man's chin up. 'Listen carefully. This is Fukuoka Prison and I'm Sugiyama Dozan. You're behind bars. You can't whistle. And you certainly can't write.'

'So what can I do?'

'It would be easier to ask what you can't do.'

'Then what can't I do?'

'You can't do whatever it is you're trying to do right now!' Sugiyama's teeth were set on edge. A flock of black crows flew up noisily into the ashy sky.

'One's heart can't be incarcerated or taken away.' 645's voice rustled like a leaf in the wind, lustreless, tired and trembling.

Sugiyama despised the educated. They were arrogant, and clueless. With their puny words they sucked off someone else's sweat and tears, mumbling nonsensical poems and reciting unintelligible phrases. 'No lies and exaggerations and sweet talk allowed here. This is Fukuoka Prison, and I'm watching your every move.' Sugiyama swung, and his club landed heavily on 645's shoulder; the young man fell to the ground, his shoulder dislocated.

He looked up at Sugiyama, his face contorted in pain. Sugiyama was struck by the look in the prisoner's eyes – they were filled with pity, not resentment.

Back in his office, Sugiyama flipped through the log of confiscated items. 645. Hiranuma Tochu. The log showed that he had an unpublished poetry collection, *The Sky, the Wind, the Stars and Poetry*, thirty additional poems and a total of twenty-eight books. Sugiyama headed to the library. Boxes were lined up on the shelves. Sugiyama opened Hiranuma's box. He saw faded titles on dirty, well-worn covers; books by Fyodor Dostoyevsky, André Gide, Francis Jammes, Rainer Maria Rilke and some Korean writers. He spotted a bundle of paper shoved into one corner.

*The Sky, the Wind, the Stars and Poetry.*

Cautiously, as if he were searching an enemy camp, Sugiyama turned the first page. And with stern eyes he glared at the neat strokes:

PROLOGUE

– The Sky, the Wind, the Stars and Poetry

*Let me look up to the heavens*
*Without a speck of shame*
*Until the day I die.*
*I was in agony*
*Even from the wind rustling among leaves*
*I shall love every dying being*
*Singing of the stars*
*And I shall walk*
*On the path given to me.*

*Tonight too the stars brush against the wind.*

These average, nondescript sentences pummelled Sugiyama's temples. How could ten lines make him breathless and dazed? He didn't realize that reading a single poem was equivalent to getting to know the world inhabited by the writer, expanding his senses beyond the usual five. He stuffed the manuscript back in the box. He wanted to flee – from this man, his writings, this poem. Sugiyama was firm in his belief that writing was a contaminant; it ruined people, concealed weak spirits and unmoored pity, ridiculous optimism and foolish dreams. Writers led an idle life in the name of romance, dazzled by clever lines, infected by anarchism. Poets believed they could change people and the world. Sugiyama straightened his guard cap. He would banish this absurd poem that flickered its evil tongue. He banged the square, long-handled stamp onto the manuscript:

To Be Incinerated.

He dipped his dry pen into the inkwell and filled out the incineration log:

Prologue (*The Sky, the Wind, the Stars and Poetry*) — Author: Hiranuma Tochu

His hand, holding the pen, trembled. His office felt unusually cold. He put his pen down; the young man's pale face loomed in his memory. Sugiyama hesitated for a moment. There was no need for this to be incinerated right away. He should first interrogate and punish the prisoner who wrote this seditious poem.

War dragged on. Prisoner 645 was curled up on the floor of his cell. Last summer his life had ended in a single instant, and nightmares had slammed him against the cold floor. He was no longer a university student, a young man agonizing about the times; he wasn't spending every waking moment reading or taking long walks. Now he was 'an element of the Korean Independence Movement' implicated in the 'Kyoto Korean Student Nationalist Group Incident'.

On the morning of 14 July 1943 a handful of burly men rushed into Takeda Boarding House. They were Special Higher Police detectives from Shimogamo Police Station in Kyoto. They grabbed Hiranuma's arms as he was about to step out of the house. The detectives threw him into a holding cell at the station, but did nothing more for two days, as though they enjoyed watching someone go mad behind bars. On the third day Hiranuma was called into the narrow box of an interrogation room. Across from him sat Detective Koroki, who opened the thick file on the desk containing a police surveillance log detailing Hiranuma's every movement during the preceding year: how many people drank how many bottles of what kind of liquor in which bar on which day, what they discussed and what time he returned home and switched off the lights.

According to Koroki, Hiranuma's cousin, Song Mong-gyu, had been arrested with other conspirators four days earlier. Song was the alleged leader of a seditious organization, and Korean students who didn't even know each other were linked through him. Song had made the police blacklist for his past enrolment in a Chinese officer school. The exact account of the incident, accomplices, the charge and prison term were arranged in a perfect script. The incident, later known as the Kyoto Korean Student Nationalist Group Incident, occurred when Song and Hiranuma allegedly gathered Korean students in Kyoto and plotted to fight for Korean independence and support Korean culture. The Special Higher Police detectives simply took issue with anything to do with Korea, and Hiranuma happened to be Korean. Koroki tossed a bundle of papers on the desk. Hiranuma recognized the scent wafting from his manuscript of poems – that of a warm *tatami* room, accidentally spilled ink, dreams that vanished into the ether – and looked down at the bundle before him.

*The Sky, the Wind, the Stars and Poetry.*

Scenes from his former life flashed past his eyes: the blue sky outside the windows of a lecture hall, the wind brushing tree branches on a hill, the stars filling the night sky, and the poetry he read, copied down and created.

'Nice lifestyle you've got there,' Koroki spat out. 'Patriotic young men are dying on battlefields while you scribble poems like a little girl. Translate these into Japanese! Your poems will prove your ideology. The original manuscript will be destroyed.' He smiled, his face crinkling like Mephistopheles.

Hiranuma gazed at the dry pen, black ink and his mother tongue. The poor-quality government-issue paper was waiting for something to be written on it. But writing his poems in Japanese was to trample on his own soul. At the same time, he was starving to write something, anything. Like a famished young man grabbing a spoon, he snatched the pen and dipped it in ink:

## EASILY COMPOSED POEM

*Night rain whispers outside the window*
*Of a six-mat tatami room in a foreign country,*

*Though I know a poet follows a sad calling*
*I write down a line of poetry,*

*With the tuition envelope sent*
*Imparting the warm scent of sweat and love*

*I hold a notebook under my arm*
*And go to a lecture by an old professor.*

*When I think about it*
*I lost*
*One, two, all my childhood friends.*

*What do I wish for?*
*That I alone sink?*
*They say life is difficult*

*But it is embarrassing*
*That this poem is so easily composed.*

*A six-mat tatami room in a foreign country.*
*Night rain whispers outside the window,*

*Turning on the light to drive away a sliver of darkness*
*My final self waits for morning, a new epoch.*

*I offer a small hand to myself*
*The first handshake of tears and solace.*

After they were translated, Hiranuma's poems were burned. He was sent to a solitary cell in the prosecutor's office. On 22 February 1944 the prosecutor indicted him and his cousin as leaders of the incident. The trial began on 31 March, with Judge Ishii Heiyo of the Second Criminal Investigation Department at the Kyoto Regional Court presiding. Judge Ishii found the prisoners guilty of violating Clause V of the Maintenance of Public Order Act, which stated: 'Individuals who organize an association with the purpose of changing the forms of state, support such an association, or consult, instigate or propagandize to implement such a purpose, or act in order to carry out said purpose, will be subject to a sentence of no less than one year, but no greater than ten years.' Hiranuma received a sentence of two years. His release date was 30 November 1945, taking into account the 261 days he spent in detention prior to his conviction. He was no longer free, but he hadn't ever known how it felt to be free; no Korean was free. Hiranuma stepped into Fukuoka Prison, counting the remaining days of his sentence.

*

Sugiyama opened the door to the interrogation room. He approached Prisoner 645 stiffly, wanting to appear rock-solid, and sat down across from him. 645's lips were dry and cracked, as though they'd been salted. His thin, wrinkled red prisoner uniform, its collar threadbare, looked like a piece of dirty, cast-away cloth.

'645! You brought this in with you.' Sugiyama tossed a leather-bound book onto the desk. Its title, *The Complete New Testament and Psalms*, was embossed in gold on the black leather cover.

With trembling hands, Prisoner 645 grabbed the book and inhaled its scent of leather.

Sugiyama snapped, 'This was allowed in only because it's in Japanese!'

645 flipped through the book like a starving child. The thin pages of the Bible fluttered. He found the page he was looking for and read feverishly:

Blessed are the poor in spirit: for theirs is the kingdom
   of heaven.
Blessed are they that mourn: for they shall be comforted.
Blessed are the meek: for they shall inherit the earth.
Blessed are they which do hunger and thirst after right-
   eousness: for they shall be filled.
Blessed are the merciful: for they shall obtain mercy.
Blessed are the pure in heart: for they shall see God.
Blessed are the peacemakers: for they shall be called the
   children of God.
Blessed are they which are persecuted for righteousness'
   sake: for theirs is the kingdom of heaven.
                                  — MATTHEW 5:3–10

He was a different person when he lifted his head; he was no longer haggard or nervous. His gaze was peaceful. Who had consoled him? What had brought him peace?

Sugiyama took his hand off the club by his waist. 'Unbelievably foolish. Believing in God in times like these . . .'

'It's better than not believing in anything.'

Sugiyama shook his head. In his mind, God was merely an excuse. The powerful killed and launched wars in His name and the weak closed their eyes to injustice, telling themselves it was God's way. 'I would think it's better to believe in yourself before God.'

'I believe in God in order to believe in myself.'

'So you're not seditious. You're just stupid.'

'If believing in God is stupid, then you are, too. You believe in God, just like me.'

Sugiyama was suddenly afraid that he might tumble into the darkness of 645's eyes. 'I've never believed in God. Not for one second!' He slammed his club onto the table, shattering the dry air.

645 flinched, but forged on. 'You hate God as much as I love Him. Or maybe you actually hate Him more than that. We each love or hate God in our own ways. If He didn't exist there would be no reason for you to hate Him.'

Sugiyama didn't want to get tangled in showy sophistry. 'Maybe that's true. God may exist. But not here. Because this is Fukuoka Prison. If God existed here, then He's not loving. He's cold and cruel. Because He let you live. Here, staying alive is a curse.'

'No matter where you are, no matter which side you're on, being alive is a blessing.'

Sugiyama gave him a sharp look. 'Don't yammer about

death to me. Even I don't know about death, and I spent my life with an arm around it.'

'I'm not talking about death, I'm talking about life.'

Sugiyama's eyes burned red. The young man's calm stare and the guard's heated gaze met in the air, tussling silently. 'I read a poem of yours. Since you said the poem was the road to understanding your truth, I figured the quickest route would be to read it. But you lied. There was nothing to be found in your poem. It was the weak, emotional drivel of an immature girl.'

The young man's brow furrowed.

Sugiyama felt triumphant, believing that he'd hurt Prisoner 645's pride. But the lump of emotion he'd sensed when he read 'Prologue' remained steadfast. Feigning calm, he said, 'I did think of one thing when I read your poem.'

Prisoner 645 looked up at him.

Sugiyama hesitated a moment. 'You don't need to believe in something like God.'

'Why's that?'

*Because He's already in your heart.* But Sugiyama swallowed the words. He didn't want the prisoner to know that he'd been moved by a silly poem.

His cap pressed low over his eyes, Sugiyama walked down among the narrow bookshelves. The dark quiet seeped into his body. He heard a low whisper. He stopped and listened, but the sound disappeared. Was he hearing things? As he aged, his own body was attacking itself. His eyes dimmed, his ears heard phantom sounds, his joints creaked, his skin sagged and his bones were unable to hold up his weight. That was Sugiyama's current stage of life. He'd lived so roughly that his body was deteriorating quickly.

He found himself standing in front of the shelf holding box 645. He looked down and was startled to find his hands already holding the box. This is what happens when you get older, he thought to himself. Your body doesn't listen to you any more. The manuscript he'd stuffed back in the box was still there. Sugiyama drew in a sharp breath, promising himself that he wouldn't be shaken by sentimental feelings, no matter what. He collapsed into his chair and turned the thin page with his stubby fingers:

### Night Seen On My Return

*I return to my small room as though returning from the world and turn out the light. Leaving the light on is ever so exhausting as it is the extension of day –*

*Now I should open the window to air out my room, but when I look outside it is dark like the inside of the room, like the world, and the path I took through the rain is still wet.*

*Without any way to wash myself of the day's pent-up anger I quietly close my eyes and a sound flows through my heart; ideology ripens on its own like a crab apple.*

Sugiyama's voice, hoarse from yelling and swearing, was reading the poem out loud reverently as though in prayer. He was afraid he would be weakened by the beauty of the words and their warm consolation, but he couldn't take his eyes off the poem. His life had been one long wearisome struggle; he deserved some relief, even briefly. Some men went around with their pasts pinned to their chests like medals, gloating about the number of men they killed or maimed in battle; to him, the past wasn't something to be proud of. His life had been wind-swept and precarious, like a winter river topped with thin ice. He'd been born into stench, into the dust. Soon after birth he was abandoned at a fish market on the Kobe coast. A few merchants at the market looked after him. By the time he was seven, he was cleaning fish; by the time he was twelve he was out on a boat. His hard work helped him mature physically faster than his peers and his strength soon became his sole asset. When he was fifteen a group of Kobe riff-raffs picked a fight with him. He shattered noses and cheekbones and arms. When five more thugs came after him, he sent them packing with broken teeth and shattered wrists. The merchants began to avoid him and the captains didn't want him on their boats; the fish market spat him out. The gang had threatened the merchants and captains, forcing them to cut their ties with him out of revenge. Sugiyama had nowhere to go. He ended up joining the very gang that had been the cause of his problems. Life in the back alleys wasn't always bad. The rules made sense to him. If you didn't eat, you would be eaten; whatever you didn't steal, you would lose. His fists were precise and efficient. Soon a modifier followed his name: he was Sugiyama the Dog, Sugiyama the Butcher.

One day he was pacing the garden of a high-level official's house that he'd been assigned to guard. He heard something – a piano. Sugiyama looked up at the second-storey window, searching for the source, and saw the undulating, round shoulders of a young woman. That brief moment altered him forever. He was twenty years old. The notes of the piano coasting on the fine flow of air tugged at a heart that knew nothing of music. He knew he would worship that sound for the rest of his life. Something began to form inside him, feelings that had atrophied in the years ruled by punches. Little did he know that an eye for beauty was tucked away in his nature. The notes created a web and hung in the air. He felt at peace; the music flowed through his veins and rattled his dead heart.

A few days later he decided to learn how to tune a piano. He began working as an errand boy at a piano shop in Kobe. His touch with the piano was inborn; in a mere instant he learned skills that took most people three years. He didn't know whether it was because of a natural artistic sense and excellent hearing or because of the young woman. Within a year he'd become a tuner, handling delicate strings with the same hands he'd used to beat people with. He caressed the piano, imagining he was touching her, and she played for him. But their happiness was as fleeting as a drop of water on the surface of glass. The year he turned twenty-four a red notice struck him across the face and he was conscripted. As a soldier, he suffered through snowstorms, sandstorms and mud, dust, exhaustion and death. Somehow, he survived. He thought of her all along. Surviving was the only way to preserve the sound of her piano; surviving was the sole blessing in his life.

Or maybe it was a curse.

# HOW DO SENTENCES SAVE THE SOUL?

The warm April breeze wafted over the towering walls and scattered a subtle scent around the desolate prison; flowers opened and dusted pollen into the air, luring honeybees. Blood circulated anew in the prisoners' faces, festering toes healed and new flesh grew on cracked hands. All Hiranuma wanted was to survive this place. If he lived, he could write poetry again. Every morning, before he got up, he erased the numbers he'd etched on the wall next to his head, bitterly resolute, counting down the days to 30 November 1945.

The prison was a melting pot of the human condition. Housed here were ideological prisoners and assassins, con men and fugitives. They shared only one trait: they all insisted on their innocence. But they were all lying. Their wrongdoings weren't serious, sometimes not even crimes: they didn't deserve to be thrown behind bars. A docker had chased after a woman he loved and was accused of raping her; a guard overseeing a conscript's forced-labour unit got him in prison out of hatred; a man knocked on his boss's door to ask for back-pay and was charged with attempted murder. Everyone talked about their heroic exploits, and each time someone spat out indifferently, 'Hell, there's nobody here who isn't falsely charged!' The prisoners launched violent attacks on one another. Hiranuma felt only pity. He thought violence was the only way for prisoners to stand up against their fate.

One day, during their daily outdoor break, an old man with short greying hair and a wily look came up to Hiranuma. 'You're so gentle,' he remarked, air whistling out of the gaps in his teeth. 'You don't belong in here. What crime did you commit that brought you to this place?'

'Violation of the Maintenance of Public Order Act,' Hiranuma answered curtly, digging the dead grass. He could see green sprouts under the dried roots.

'Maintenance of public order, my arse,' the old man grumbled. 'They're trying to do away with Koreans. I had a high-interest loan, but the Jap financier brought a charge against me, saying I wasn't paying back the interest. I've been here two years. Is that what happened to you?'

'No. I wrote some poems in Korean.'

The old man clucked his tongue. This boy wasn't just naive, he was foolish. Their world was one in which Japanese was taught in primary school and no one was allowed to utter a word in Korean. He squinted at Hiranuma. In his mind, educated people like this boy who did useless things were what caused Korea's demise.

A small man with beady eyes came up to them. He brushed his hand over his shaved head and blinked, looking all around him. 'Old man, are you crazy? What are you doing? What if the Choi gang sees you?'

Everyone knew that Choi monitored the prisoners and hand-picked those he wanted for his gang. Since Hiranuma's arrival, this university student had been Choi's main focus.

The old man grinned. 'Don't get so worked up, Man-gyo! Do you even know why Choi is anxious to get this boy in his gang?'

'I don't. Do you? Is he made of gold or something?' Man-gyo snapped impatiently.

The old man turned serious. 'I don't know whether he's a mound of gold or a mound of shit. But since Choi is interested, it's clear he's not just anyone. If we get him first, Choi won't be able to boss us around.' The old man rubbed his dry palm against his beard, speaking about Hiranuma as though he weren't standing beside him.

'Shit! And if he's not worth it?'

'You don't know the first thing about selling something, do you?' the old man said dismissively. 'You need a good eye to notice whether something will make you money. And you need gumption. The more money you can possibly make, the more danger you have to risk. But you don't know any of that. Your fate is to sell cigarettes and crackers and stick your nose up the guards' behinds.'

Man-gyo settled down. The old man gave him a look, prompting him to take out a dirty cigarette from a seam in his uniform and offer it to Hiranuma, who waved his hands, refusing this small luxury.

Man-gyo shoved the cigarette back into his uniform. 'I'm investing, so if it's a good deal you have to split it with me!' He moved away, looking around furtively.

The old man stroked his jagged beard. 'You might be wondering how cigarettes are circulated in the prison. Well, you see, wherever people live there is trade. A proper merchant can buy and sell even death. That Man-gyo, he may never be a big fish, but he's an innate peddler. He began to bring things in from the outside six months after he got here. The guards are hungry, too. Bribes got them to look the other way.'

Hiranuma didn't know whether to feel hopeful that his fellow man had a persistent will to live or to despair at the tenacity of human greed.

The old man read his hesitation. 'If you have to bet on something, I suggest you choose hope. If you go with despair, what's left over is even greater despair. In my experience, believing that the sale will be a success leaves more profit.' He blinked his crusty eyes and asked, 'What will you sell?'

Hiranuma shook his head. He had nothing. If he had books he could sell a few to a used bookshop, but they were useless now. *Sentences*, *Criticism of the Humanities*, *Poetry and Opinion* – they'd been confiscated and were either mouldering in the inspection office or had been burned.

'Everyone has something to sell. If you don't, you can sell your body. If your body's damaged, you can sell your life. Son, you studied at a university! You were fortunate enough to study abroad in Japan! If you can read and write in Japanese, you have something to sell.'

'How could I possibly sell that?'

'We're allowed to send out a postcard written in Japanese once a month. But most prisoners are illiterate. Forget Japanese – they haven't even learned Korean properly. You can write postcards for the prisoners who can't write. Since Korean is banned, you can translate what they tell you and write it in Japanese.'

'There must be other Koreans who know Japanese.'

'The censor here is incredibly strict. He'll destroy your postcard if there's a sentence that is even a little bit problematic. You'll also get a beating. A couple of prisoners wrote postcards for others, but when they almost died from the beatings, nobody wanted to do it any more. Lots of people are itching to send out postcards. Can't you see the money piling up?'

'But you just said you can die from a single wrong word.'

'That's why you're the right man to do it. You're a literary man who knows about writing, so you can avoid expressions that will get censored. And you can make money.'

Hiranuma frowned. 'How could I make money off penniless Koreans?'

'The Japs in Wards One and Four are always looking for people to do their work for them. So the Koreans sell their labour. In exchange for writing a postcard in Japanese, you can get them to work for a Jap for a day and take their wages. Then everyone wins.'

'You're saying I'm to sell Korean manpower to the Japs?'

'That's the deal. If they register as patients with the guards that wcrc bought off, they can avoid physical labour here, and that's how they can fill in for the Japanese.'

Hiranuma was disgusted. 'I can't make my countrymen suffer.'

The old man shook his head. 'And here I was, thinking you were smart. With your talents you can help the illiterate send news home. But you're going to decline. Are you stupid? Or cruel? Most prisoners can't send word to their families. If you aren't going to help them, what's the point of your education?'

Hiranuma pondered the questions for a long while. 'How much do you get for a day's work from the Japs?'

'Four *sen*. That's the official price.'

'So how much do I get?'

The old man's eyes glinted. 'We'll split fifty-fifty. Two

*sen* each. But considering that I'll take out Man-gyo's cut and the bribe for the guards from my share, it's actually a better deal for you. Take it or leave it.' The old man waited expectantly.

Hiranuma gave him a short nod. The old man grinned, and scurried around to publicize his new service. The news about the ghostwriter quickly and quietly spread throughout the cells. But people didn't approach Hiranuma as he stood under the prison walls. Everyone knew that evading censorship was as precarious as balancing on a straw cutter. Emotional expression, descriptions of the reality of prison life, questions about the war were all immediately blacked out, and both the sender and the writer of the problematic postcard would be called into the interrogation room for a beating. The old man decided that the only way to convince the fearful prisoners was to be the first. He stood in front of Hiranuma and called out his letter in a loud voice so that all the Koreans could hear.

'Dear Suna, the spring I've been waiting for isn't coming to this prison, which I so want to leave. They say spring has come, but damn it, the cell floor is like ice and the guards run wild. People are dying all around me and it doesn't even make me flinch.' The old man shouted out expressions that went well beyond the danger zone, as though determined to be caught.

Hiranuma's pencil raced across the postcard transcribing the old man's sardonic voice. The prisoners crowded around, curious as to whether the pale writer could repackage the old man's complaints. When he finished writing, Hiranuma read out in Korean what he'd written. The old man's intent and feelings were intact, but his overt complaints had been restrained. The courier collected the postcard. The prisoners were tense. Each cell whispered and bet about the fate of the missive. Two days later the postcard was sent off, but the old man wasn't called to the interrogation room. Silent cheers spread through the cells. The prisoners finally understood who 645 was: someone who would help spirit their souls to the outside.

One by one, prisoners came looking for him. Before Hiranuma wrote their postcard, he asked them who they were sending it to, what their relationship was, what memories they shared. He carefully observed the way they talked and the words they liked to use. He wasn't simply writing down what was dictated. He constructed a cover that would camouflage the true meaning of what they wanted to convey. When he read back what he had written, the men shed tears, as they heard their true feelings put into words. Hiranuma shaped the desperate sentiments of the prisoners while avoiding the blade of censorship, a perilous high-wire act. A fortnight after the postcards were sent out, answers began arriving, slashed intermittently with black ink, only traces left of undesirable words that didn't pass Sugiyama's censorship. The letters sparkled with hope and love. Hiranuma read them out; even if Sugiyama blacked out all of the lines he could resurrect the words, read what was hidden and what couldn't be said, revealing unshed tears and undreamt dreams. Hiranuma felt alive again. More and more prisoners rushed to secure his services; the old man fashioned ledgers out of scraps of wood and kept records written with a lump of coal. Hiranuma grew busier, the old man's books grew fatter and Man-gyo busily scurried off to the Japanese wards to supply labour.

'It's a hit, Dong-ju,' the old man said, grinning. 'People are lining up. If they've done it once, they'll naturally come again. If you reduce the silly interview time, then the poor saps won't have to wait so long.'

Hiranuma was editing a postcard he'd just written. 'But if we get caught it'll all be over,' he murmured. 'Don't you want to keep doing business?'

'You're right! Just keep doing what you're doing. We're doing pretty good.' The old man shook his head and looked at his log. 'Forty-five prisoners wrote postcards in a fortnight. So that's 180 *sen*, and your share is ninety *sen*.'

Man-gyo came up to them. 'You need anything? Cigarettes? Rice? Sugar cubes or red-bean jelly? I can get you anything.'

'I could use some labour. How much for a day?'

'We get four *sen* from the Japs, but I can't charge the full price for a business partner, can I? How about half? Two *sen* a day!'

Hiranuma smiled. 'Okay. I'll use the people I write postcards for.'

The old man's face fell. 'Look at this boy! A real wolf. You're trying to take the meat meant for someone else's belly.'

Man-gyo looked from one man to the other in confusion.

Pitying him, the old man explained what Hiranuma was proposing to do. 'If Dong-ju writes a postcard, we get four *sen*. That's the cost of the labour of the man who sends the postcard. We get four *sen* from the Japs and send the postcard-writers to them. We take half and this boy gets the other half. But now he's going to repurchase the manpower of the man who asked for the postcard. And for two *sen* a day!'

Man-gyo grew concerned. 'Then we don't have a worker to send to the Japs, and our business . . .'

'Is over.'

Man-gyo looked alarmed.

Hiranuma jumped in to reassure him. 'Don't worry. I'll

have the man work for the Jap, and then you can give him the two *sen* you would have given me. Then everyone wins. You and the old man can keep earning your cut, the Koreans will make money for their labour, and the Japs can find a Korean to do their work for them. Of course, the guards will keep getting a nice bribe, too.'

'Then you don't get anything,' Man-gyo said. 'Shouldn't you get something out of it? You're doing the writing, after all.'

'I do get something out of it.'

'What?'

'I can use a pencil and paper every day. As long as I can write something, I don't care what it is.'

It was an ideal arrangement, but the old man and Man-gyo didn't realize how good they had it.

Sugiyama opened the outgoing post box after his afternoon rounds and found four postcards inside. He settled into his chair. One was by a Korean prisoner sending a postcard to his wife. The neat handwriting succinctly relayed what he wanted to say. He spoke of the prison, but he didn't complain, and while he wrote about pain, he seemed relieved. Sugiyama was a little suspicious, but he couldn't pick out exactly what was unsanctioned. The second postcard was to a prisoner's mother. It was in the same hand as the first one, but its writing style and expression were different, as though a completely different person had written it. He couldn't find anything problematic about this one, either. This phenomenon repeated itself again and again. The writer knew which words to avoid. Sugiyama suppressed his scepticism and stamped the blue *Censorship Completed* mark in the middle of the postcards. He leaned back and rubbed his dry eyes. He suddenly sat up as he picked up the last postcard:

More than anything, you should know about the censor officer's generosity. If I had known that he was this gracious, I would have sent a postcard earlier on. I didn't send word because I was afraid it would be censored. But thanks to his magnanimity I could read your postcard without a single word being deleted.

A thought struck him: the author of the postcards was writing all of this with Sugiyama in mind. He could tell there was something fishy going on. He would show this brash prisoner what would happen to someone who played pranks on him.

Prisoner 645 sat ramrod-straight on the hard chair, much like his neat handwriting. Sugiyama lowered his voice. 'The postcards you wrote were for me. You knew I would read them.'

Hiranuma's brain whirred. One wrong step would cripple him and the prisoners who had asked him to write the postcards.

'I know you're crafty. But it doesn't work with me. I know you're the one who's behind all this!' Sugiyama shouted. He avoided meeting Hiranuma's eyes, afraid that doing so would change his mind.

'Yes, you caught me. But it was worth it. I learned a lot about you.'

Sugiyama's heart sank – had 645 been conducting a secret investigation of his life? He could guess how it happened: 645 would have written his first postcard very carefully, suppressing any emotion and avoiding any expression that might become a problem. After that first postcard passed review, he would have gradually got bolder. One day he would have slipped in a suspicious word, and on another he would have cleverly inserted a phrase with dual meanings. He would have figured out how Sugiyama took the meanings of the words, inferring from the blacked-out letters the prisoners received which expressions Sugiyama disliked. Sugiyama had been fooled into thinking that he was in complete control. He hadn't been watching Hiranuma; in fact, Hiranuma had been looking straight into Sugiyama's heart.

The thick veins in Sugiyama's neck thrummed. 'You've gone too far. I'm no writer, but I'm not so stupid that I don't realize what's going on.' He was incensed; he gritted his teeth and rubbed his hand over his prickly hair. 'You knew you'd get killed, but you still tried to fight me!'

'You can't kill me.'

'You knew full well that you'd be beaten if your plot was revealed!' It dawned on Sugiyama that the prisoner was right. If he were the type of censor who would kill a man for writing postcards, he would have been stricter with several of Hiranuma's postcards. Hiranuma must have sensed that Sugiyama didn't catch the seditious undertone of the postcards or had looked the other way. That quiet passage of the postcards informed Hiranuma that this guard, no matter how violent, wouldn't be able to beat him, let alone kill him. Sugiyama shook his head. 'Don't you know they call me The Butcher?'

'I know more about you than your nickname.'

'Oh, really. And what do you know about me?'

'That you understand and love the secrets harboured by words.'

Sugiyama smirked. But it was true that he'd seen the

world; the roots of the sentences created a gigantic forest of meaning. His voice hardened. 'What makes you say such foolish things?'

'Because I know the real you. You yourself aren't even aware of who you are.'

Sugiyama recognized that the young man was taunting him. He had to fend him off. He had to fight with vocabulary sharper than knives and with sentences more fatal than spearheads. The odds were against him: Hiranuma was an intellectual, while Sugiyama had barely thrown off the cloak of illiteracy. Sugiyama sensed that he was being dragged into a black, unfathomable swamp. But there was nothing he could do. The battle had begun; all he could do was fight.

Under the shadow of the wall, Hiranuma continued to listen as the men in front of him sobbed and yelled and shook their fists. He soon became familiar with their stories; what their childhoods were like, what crimes they'd committed, how wronged they felt. He wrote postcard after postcard, recalling their voices, expressions, intonation. He had to accurately convey what they wanted to say, but delicately plant two or three other meanings in one phrase to avoid censorship. Each morning Hiranuma woke up from the same dream, drenched in ink-black sweat – the red censor stamp was branded on his forehead. He didn't know when Sugiyama would tire of this game. But on the other hand, if the censor was firm, the rules Hiranuma had to toe became simpler. He was persuading the censor, one postcard at a time, in a slow and insistent seduction.

Sugiyama felt himself changing. He was getting pulled into the prisoners' writing, so much so that he subconsciously looked forward to the postcards. The faint letters written on the brownish paper contained longing and hope, tears and sighs between each line. Reading them made him feel relaxed, as though submerged in a warm bath. All day long Sugiyama felt overcome. He struggled to get away from the tug of those postcards. He handled the prisoners with even more cruelty.

Hiranuma observed Sugiyama from far away. The guard was becoming more and more violent. He swung his club and swore and hollered. Hiranuma smiled to himself. It was working. Violence was the final line of defence. He could tell that Sugiyama was in flux. A letter had arrived a few days ago from a prisoner's wife. Sugiyama had censored the letter, which was streaked with red lines. But Hiranuma could still read the words underneath; before, Sugiyama would have completely obliterated the sentences with black ink. Now, Hiranuma thought, he could begin using bolder, more overt expressions.

# O MY SORROW, YOU ARE BETTER
## THAN A WELL-BELOVED

Sugiyama glanced at a postcard written by a prisoner to his thirteen-year-old son; it started off with praises for the beauty of the season and went on to describe the burdens of war. Imprisonment, destitution, death . . . These were bold words, the first overt descriptions of the war in a postcard. Sugiyama rubbed his stamp on the red ink pad.

Don't despair that Father isn't there with you. No matter how sad you are, no matter how difficult it is, you can always learn from pain. Pain can destroy us, but it can also help us grow. Francis Jammes, a wonderful French poet, wrote in a poem entitled 'Prayer for Loving Sorrow': 'O my sorrow, you are better than a well-beloved.' In another he wrote, 'These are the labours of man that are great.' Read his poetry collection when you have a chance, you'll learn about retaining hope and gain the courage to stand up to any hardship.

It was a daring message, but there wasn't really a reason to censor any of it. After all, the postcard was encouraging the child to embrace pain. Sugiyama thought for a moment. Was he expressing criticism and scorn for the challenges of the times? Or was he merely offering his son a burst of hope to help him come to terms with his sadness? Sugiyama realized that he would have to read the poems mentioned in the postcard to determine that. His impatient feet led him to the library of confiscated documents. He dug through Prisoner 645's box and found a yellowed old book, *The Poetry of Francis Jammes*. He opened the book and scanned the table of contents: 'Prayer to Go to Paradise with the Donkeys', 'Prayer to Have a Simple Wife', 'The House Would Be Full of Roses', 'Orchard with Raspberries in the Sun', 'These Are the Labours'. The pages created a breeze at his fingertips. He took in a deep breath and started to read 'Prayer for Loving Sorrow':

> *I have nothing but my sorrow and I want nothing more.*
> *It has been, it still is, faithful to me.*
> *Why should I begrudge it, since during the hours*
> *when my soul crushed the depths of my heart,*
> *it was seated there beside me?*
> *O sorrow, I have ended, you see, by respecting you,*
> *because I am certain you will never leave me.*
> *Ah! I realize it: your beauty lies in the force of your being.*
> *You are like those who never left*
> *the sad fireside corner of my poor black heart.*
> *O my sorrow, you are better than a well-beloved:*
> *because I know that on the day of my final agony,*
> *you will be there, lying in my sheets, O sorrow,*
> *so that you might once again attempt to enter my heart.*

Sorrow was something better than a well-beloved. Sugiyama understood that instinctively. A man's will for life could be broken, but he would stand firm again; his desires could extinguish, but burn bright once more. A man's acceptance of a lacklustre reality would make him even stronger. He leaned against the hard back of his chair.

Another page caught his eye: 'These Are the Labours'. He looked back at the postcard he had finished censoring. This was the right one. 'These are the labours of man that are great.' Sugiyama felt triumphant. He'd caught Hiranuma red-handed; the fool had put in a secret code, probably a seditious one. The child would read Jammes's poems and discover the hidden meaning. Could it be that this postcard wasn't meant for his son at all, but for some nefarious element? Sugiyama could guess at the rebellious meaning of this poem — something to the effect of giving your life to liberate your country, or inciting others to disregard their comfortable lives and resist the Japanese:

## THESE ARE THE LABOURS

*These are the labours of man that are great:*
*he who puts milk in the wooden vessels,*
*he who gathers wheat-ears sharp and straight,*
*he who herds cattle near fresh alders*
*he who bleeds birches in the forests,*
*he who twists willows near rushing brooks,*
*he who mends old shoes*
*near a dark hearth, an old mangy cat,*
*a sleeping blackbird and happy children;*
*he whose weaving makes a steady sound,*
*when at midnight the crickets sing shrilly;*
*he who bakes bread, he who makes wine,*
*he who sows garlic and cabbages in the garden,*
*he who gathers warm eggs.*

He was stunned. No matter how carefully he read the poem, there was nothing seditious about it. There was no hidden code or concealed plot. The poem merely praised leading a peaceful life, at one with nature, a humble existence in the countryside. It celebrated waking to the crow of the rooster and working hard, before falling asleep to the sound of crickets. Sugiyama's gaze dulled. He didn't believe in happiness – it existed only in the chatter of weak romantics. He worked hard to dismiss the small peace inherent in the everyday, because he'd never been happy. Could it be that he'd ignored contentment, thinking it a desperate dream?

After a very long time he stamped the postcard with a bang, marking it with the blue *Censorship Completed* stamp. He was a failure; he hadn't discovered any banned communications. The postcard would fly to a young boy waiting for his father in a shabby shack in the alleys near Kobe harbour. The boy would read Francis Jammes. The postcard would deliver him the grit to deal with the weight and pain of life during wartime.

After that, unfamiliar names and phrases began appearing in outgoing post, including stanzas cited in ways appropriate for each recipient's age and situation. Hiranuma seemed to have in his head a huge catalogue of poems perfect for any situation. One prisoner sent a postcard to his wife containing the entirety of 'Prayer to Have a Simple Wife'. A man sending a postcard to his girlfriend included a love-poem by Goethe. Sugiyama scoured the library to look for the writers and works cited in each of the postcards. He didn't miss a single name or book. When he spotted Tolstoy's name, he read all of Tolstoy's books. Night after night he wandered amid the suspicious phrases. He couldn't find anything to censor, but that didn't lower his wariness.

The prisoners changed, too. Smiles replaced their curses. A single phrase pushed men who didn't think past that evening to start counting the days until their release. Men who fought incessantly became calm; the brawls that occurred on a daily basis decreased. Sugiyama watched the men hold replies from their loved ones, wiping away tears with their sleeves. Every change seemed to stem from the postcards. He began to wonder; one sentence seemed to change a man, and the world seemed to change, one man at a time.

As summer deepened, Sugiyama spent one entire night reviewing a postcard from a prisoner to his son. It was a reply to the son's complaints of being teased because of the family name they had chosen to acquire. Kaneyama was painfully obviously Korean — it was simply the Japanese pronunciation of the Korean surname Kim, plus the Japanese suffix 'yama'. The postcard consoled the son, telling him that dealing with insults was the stepping stone to living a proud life:

Don't be sad about your name. In *Romeo and Juliet* Shakespeare wrote, 'What's in a name? That which we call a rose / By any other name would smell as sweet.' A name isn't important. What's important is having your own scent.

Sugiyama found a reference to the play in the log of confiscated documents and rushed to the library. He found it in box 486. Discovering that Shakespeare was British, Sugiyama let out a yelp of joy. It would be easy to find this undesirable; after all, this writer was from an enemy country. He cautiously opened the dangerous book. It turned out to be a love-story. Romeo, a son of the Montagues; Juliet, a daughter of the Capulets; a ball; a romance that couldn't be consummated because of the feuding families. He flipped faster through the pages. A duel between Mercutio and Tybalt, death, exile, Juliet asleep after taking the potion from Friar Lawrence. Romeo drinking poison. Juliet stabbing herself in the heart.

He sat back, haunted by the beautiful scenes in Verona, the conversations between Romeo and Juliet and the afterglow of doomed love. Sugiyama shook his head to clear his thoughts. *Romeo and Juliet* was clearly problematic. Not only was it by a writer of an enemy country, but it was also all about a decadent love, and the death-filled conclusion stank of pessimism. But he couldn't pick up his red stamp. Had his censorship criteria turned too compassionate? He didn't want to be rash and stop the postcard's transit. Otherwise, who would console the child? He finally thought of a compromise. If he questioned Hiranuma, he could obtain a more accurate interpretation.

The sunlight seared the prison yard. The thick brick walls radiated heat and the workroom boiled as if they were the inside of a pot. During their free time prisoners rushed to the shade provided by the walls as though they were escaping hell. They sat around and talked urgently, hungrily. One man would speak passionately for a while, then another man would start. They took turns, like actors onstage.

Sugiyama shook his head. As he crossed the yard, hot air snaked around his calves under his gaiters. He walked the way he typically did, his upper body swaying from side to side and his legs spread apart, taking big steps. Prisoners shrank away from his arrogant, militaristic gait. They didn't know it was the only way he could stand the pain from a gunshot wound in his thigh. He headed to the hill, the site of the execution range and the cemetery. Three tall poplar trees stood side-by-side, but their sparse branches didn't create any shade. The prisoners murmured about ghosts wandering here, nooses still hanging around their necks; the guards, too, disliked patrolling the area at night.

Hiranuma was sitting against a tree. Sugiyama could hear him whistling.

'645! Whistling, are we? Feeling good then?'

Hiranuma didn't answer. His eyes were cool and empty.

'Hiranuma Tochu!' Sugiyama shouted. 'Answer me! Will you bark only if I beat you like a dog?' He used his club to push the prisoner's chin up.

Hiranuma looked down. 'My name isn't 645 or Hiranuma Tochu. My name is Yun. Dong. Ju.'

Sugiyama tensed. Was this a trap? Did he toss in that bit about Shakespeare, about names and existence, to pull Sugiyama into this long-standing controversy over Koreans being forced to take Japanese names? Even better. Then they wouldn't need to talk around the subject.

Sugiyama smiled and plucked a blade of grass to chew on; its bitterness filled his mouth.

'Yun Dong-ju or Hiranuma, who cares? You're you, whatever you may be called.' Sugiyama recalled Juliet's words, which he'd read the previous night:

> O Romeo, Romeo! wherefore art thou Romeo?
> Deny thy father and refuse thy name;
> Or, if thou wilt not, be but sworn my love

*And I'll no longer be a Capulet.*
*'Tis but thy name that is my enemy:*
*Thou art thyself, though not a Montague.*
*What's Montague? It is nor hand, nor foot,*
*Nor arm, nor face, nor any other part*
*Belonging to a man. O, be some other name!*
*What's in a name? That which we call a rose*
*By any other name would smell as sweet;*
*So Romeo would, were he not Romeo call'd,*
*Retain that dear perfection which he owes*
*Without that title. Romeo, doff thy name,*
*And for thy name, which is no part of thee,*
*Take all myself.*

'A rose by any other name still smells the same,' Sugiyama continued stiffly. 'A name means nothing. What's important is your essence. Whether you're Yun Dong-ju or Hiranuma Tochu, you're a cheeky, stubborn Korean.'

'A name is the symbol of one's very being,' Hiranuma protested in a low voice. 'It represents not only someone's face and body, but also his memories, dreams, past, present and future. Just as a single word can contain various feelings, one sentence can espouse a variety of meanings.'

One sentence can espouse a variety of meanings? Then it surely meant that the arsehole had used Shakespeare's words to convey multiple thoughts. A rose by any other name was still fragrant, but it was no longer a rose if it wasn't called a rose. Even the most fragrant rose will lose its scent and fade as time passes, but its name will live on, and the utterance of the word 'rose' will recall its beauty and scent. The rose may disappear, but the name never would.

Hiranuma pushed on, ignoring Sugiyama's mounting

confusion. 'Juliet's soliloquy is a paradoxical expression of the fact that a presence is defined by a name.'

'Paradoxical?'

Hiranuma explained that it was a way to emphasize how something was said by not saying it, and to assert that it was true by saying that it wasn't. Something clanged in Sugiyama's head. A sentence could be interpreted the opposite way, depending on who read it? Then was Juliet's request to discard the name really a clarification of the fact that names defined everything? Romeo and Juliet despaired because of their families, because of who they were. Their love became a tragedy. If they cast away their names, nothing would have stopped the consummation of their love. But in the end they couldn't discard them; their names defined their existence, and that made their love ever more star-crossed.

'My name is Yun Dong-ju,' Hiranuma said, his voice steely and dignified.

Sugiyama glared at him. 'That's not your name. Don't you know that Korean is banned?'

'Without the name Yun Dong-ju, I'm nothing. Hiranuma is a mask that the Japanese force me to wear.'

His words were pedantic and ridiculous. Or were they? Working in his small cell, this degenerate had slipped books into postcards to seduce and brainwash Sugiyama.

Sugiyama swatted his sweat-soaked hat on his thigh. 'Shut up! Nothing's changed.'

'No, you've changed.'

Hiranuma was right. If he hadn't read *Romeo and Juliet* he wouldn't be engaged in a silly argument about roses and names. He had to keep his guard up. Sugiyama balled his fists, but they trembled as it dawned on him that he couldn't return to who he'd been before. He was afraid of what he'd become; a person who could be transformed by a book.

As the summer wore on, Sugiyama wandered the maze of neatly lined bookcases every night. His censorship duties had exploded, but he wasn't resentful; he found himself looking forward to the postcards. Then, one day, he put down his red pen for good. He wasn't reading the postcards to censor them any longer. Instead he was heartened by the neat handwriting, warm exclamations, delicate adjectives and familiar nouns. He followed the trail of codes hidden in the postcards. He read his way through Dostoyevsky, Valéry, Baudelaire, Gide, Homer, Dante, Shakespeare and Cervantes. He was changing, willingly. He became addicted to the printed word. He grew anxious if he didn't read something — anything. Had he been brainwashed? He couldn't do anything about it, if it were so.

The rainy season arrived at the prison and falling water undulated like a sheet being drawn through the air; everything beyond it was hazy, undefined, unmoored. By the time the rain stopped, one season would have passed and another would be dawning. Sugiyama knew that the August sun would cool and the September wind would begin to blow. He stayed up late one night, looking at the long shadow cast by the tall watchtower in the yard. He'd read a postcard the previous night with a poem written on it — 'Day in Autumn' by Rainer Maria Rilke — and he couldn't stop thinking about it.

## DAY IN AUTUMN

*After the summer's yield, Lord, it is time*
*to let your shadow lengthen on the sundials*
*and in the pastures let the rough winds fly.*

*As for the final fruits, coax them to roundness.*
*Direct on them two days of warmer light*
*to hale them golden towards their term, and harry*
*the last few drops of sweetness through the wine.*

*Whoever's homeless now, will build no shelter;*
*who lives alone will live indefinitely so,*
*waking up to read a little, draft long letters,*
*and, along the city's avenues,*
*fitfully wander, when the wild leaves loosen.*

Dong-ju had sent him an autumn greeting hidden in a romantic, introspective prayer.

# FROM WHERE DOES THE WIND COME
# AND WHERE DOES IT GO?

Sugiyama walked into the new season, his eyes squinting. Autumn smelled of sunlight and pungent fallen leaves. The small, square sky above the prison looked like a piece of blue cloth, framed by solid walls sprouting sharp thorns. Caught in the barbed wire, the afternoon sunlight flashed like the scales of a fish in a net. Prisoners continued to arrive; many others left, some limping, others covered by a straw mat. The eyes of the surviving prisoners turned chilly, reflecting the season.

Sugiyama walked up to Hiranuma, who was leaning against a poplar tree. 'What is it about poems that brought an intellectual like you to prison?'

Hiranuma stared up at the sky without answering. After a long time he said, 'Poetry is a temple of words.'

A temple? That made no sense. A temple was for pure and holy souls, where sinners asked for forgiveness, the downtrodden were consoled and people prayed for eternal life. So poetry consoled the soul and allowed you to dream of eternity? It sounded romantic. *Who believes in romance these days?* Sugiyama hawked and spat out his disdain.

'Poetry is reflective of your soul,' Hiranuma went on quietly. 'It is casting a bucket into a dark well and drawing up the truth. We're reassured by poetry. We learn from it, and ultimately it saves us.'

'A temple is there to help people who are beaten down by life. How can a stupid poem do that?' Sugiyama raised his voice. 'You're the only one who can help yourself. A cruddy poem that conceals its true purpose behind shiny words can't do that. I'm just on this side of literacy, but I won't be fooled by the crazy talk you people spout.'

'You may have only recently become literate, but you're already a skilled writer. You understand metaphor and symbolism. You appreciate the significance of language. Even your curses are poetic, you know. Even when you insult someone, you freely employ symbolism and metaphor.'

'Symbolism and metaphors? You're making shit-waves! A lie's still a lie even when you use crafty wordplay. It's the same crap as waging war for peace, and parting ways because you love each other.' Sugiyama huffed like an enraged bull.

Hiranuma smiled faintly, fatigued. 'See, you just did what I was talking about. Making shit-waves. You used a metaphor to describe useless words. You blew life into that sentence. You helped me see an ordinary concept in a completely different way.'

'That's ridiculous. Cursing can't be poetic!'

'Sure it can. Your curses are rooted in truth. Sometimes illogical lies can become the truth. So that's when it would make sense to say a beautiful war or a sweet farewell.'

'A beautiful war? Someone like you doesn't know anything about war! You can't even imagine how a man gets destroyed on the battlefield, how he dies. Have you ever slept in a bloody puddle, covered by flies? Have you ever been caught by the enemy and, not knowing whether you were dreaming or awake, told them where your fellow soldiers were hiding? That's war. Filthy.' His voice broke and dropped. Sugiyama had always known he was damaged. But perhaps things could be different. Maybe he still had a soul somewhere, small and desiccated.

Hiranuma gave him a sympathetic look. 'You're right. I don't know much about war. But I'm the same as you. I hate it.'

Sugiyama grimaced. 'So if swear words from an illiterate man can be poetry, everything I write must be a poem.'

He looked up at the mass of white clouds surrounding the poplar trees.

'Of course. You've already written them.'

'I'm no poet.'

'A poet doesn't make poems. The writing of poetry makes the poet.'

Sugiyama looked down at his worn boots as birds flew up from the trees. They had tramped through bloody battle-fields and prison-yard dust; they had kicked and stomped on others. They were old and scratched, just like his life.

Sugiyama murmured penitently, 'I'm not a pure man, like you,' then froze. The words locked inside his body tore at his face. He wasn't a pure man, he wasn't even a man. He was a monster that had destroyed the innocent.

'Life is poetry,' Hiranuma said. 'You write poems the way you live your life.'

Sugiyama wished the young poet's words were true. If speaking the truth was calling beautiful something beautiful and throwing curses at dirty things, he might already be a poet. At least his curses were true in their rage. Sugiyama suddenly regretted learning how to read and write, as it had made him read Hiranuma's poems. He could sense his former self falling away; he was no longer a cold guard or a strict censor. He was now an excitable boy who couldn't wait to become a poet.

A few weeks later, Hiranuma stood leaning on a poplar tree, whistling a tune.

'Yun Dong-ju!'

As three unfamiliar clunky consonants – the name that had been taken away, destroyed and covered in dust, the name that didn't exist any more – hit his ears, Dong-ju stopped whistling. The answer, 'Yes', was stuck in his throat like a fish bone; his throat ached.

After a long time he spat out, 'Yes!' in a voice that wasn't Hiranuma Tochu's. It was Yun Dong-ju's.

'Don't you know any other song?' Sugiyama asked.

Dong-ju stared at the guard.

'Even I know that song now, since all you do is whistle that same tune. I don't even know what it's called.'

'It's a Negro spiritual called "Carry Me Back to Old Virginny",' Dong-ju finally replied. 'The American Negro slaves sang it, longing for home.' He smiled bitterly. The world was unkind and time was cruel; they each betrayed hopes and dashed dreams.

Sugiyama looked over at the prisoners who were mumbling among themselves and changed the subject. 'Why are Koreans so talkative, anyway? All they do is sit around and yak.'

'Everyone has stories,' Dong-ju murmured. 'From where does the wind come and where does it go—'

Without realizing what he was doing, Sugiyama uttered the rest of Dong-ju's poem. 'The wind blows / and my suffering has no reason. // Why does my suffering have no reason? // Never loved a woman. / Never sad about the times. // The wind keeps blowing / and my feet are planted on a flat rock // The river keeps flowing / and my feet are planted on a hill.' Dismayed that he'd recited the poem, Sugiyama snapped, 'Only a scientist would know where the wind comes from and where it goes. How would a stupid poet like you know that?'

Dong-ju bowed his head at this irrefutable truth. Poetry couldn't shed light on the origins of the universe or about life and death. A poem bound by logic became meaningless.

He said drily, 'You might not know how, but you can feel it. The sensation of the wind tickling your skin, the small grains of sand floating along with the breeze, and the scent of the seasons.'

'And what's the point of feeling all that?' Sugiyama asked, swallowing the rest of his sentence: *when the world is engulfed in flames and young men are dying like ants.*

Dong-ju wasn't sure. He had an inkling that language was the only tool with which to reveal the barbarism of war. Only the purest language could testify about the most brutal era. Dong-ju looked beyond the walls. Multicoloured kites were flying in the sky near the harbour far away. They glistened like a school of grey mullet swimming against the current. At that moment a blue kite soared up from the other side of the wall, bobbing in large, bold movements, like a shark chasing all the other kites. Dong-ju shaded his eyes to watch.

'What are you staring at?' Sugiyama huffed. 'They're just kids playing with kites.'

'Well, every detail is revealing. You can tell what kind of person is controlling any given kite. What their personality is, how old they are.' He pointed upwards. 'This one's a girl, about thirteen or fourteen. When you look at the speed of the kite when she runs, it's not an adult's gait. But she's not very young, either. When you consider the intricate movement of the kite, it's clear she's not a boy. She's fearless and curious and competitive. She's also lonely.'

'How can you tell all that?'

'The other kites fly up around the shore, so far away that we can barely see them. Everyone goes there because the sea breeze can carry the kites higher. This blue kite was over there a week ago, too. But then over the last week it kept drifting closer to us. When you consider that the girl's flying a kite where the other kids don't play, it's clear she doesn't get along with them. But she's really good at flying the kite.'

'Not bad,' Sugiyama said, smirking. 'All that from the position and movement of the kite, huh?'

Dong-ju's eyes sparkled. 'There are so many things you can understand, even if you don't see it yet. You could see the wind if you wanted to.'

'Nonsense! I'd believe you if you said you could show me a ghost. Some guards have seen dead prisoners haunting this hill. But the wind?'

Dong-ju smiled.

The next day a loud siren blared through the work area. Sugiyama stopped in the middle of the yard; he noticed that everyone was still. Nobody was cursing or fighting; the prisoners looked peaceful. Their eyes were glued to a dot in the sky, wriggling in the afternoon sunlight. A red, diamond-shaped kite wagged its long tail. The prisoners let out a shout. Sugiyama's blood froze. He reflexively turned to look up at the poplar hill – Dong-ju was standing there, busily handling the spool. Sugiyama whipped around to look up at the watchtower. The barrel of the machine gun, which should have been placed parallel to the wall, was arcing towards the hill. Sugiyama sprinted across the yard, panting, his blood now boiling. The wind was whipping the hill and Dong-ju's eyes were fixed on the kite, his hands busy with the lines. His expression was peaceful. Sugiyama's club rammed into the young man's shoulder. The resulting thud reverberated through Dong-ju's body as it crumpled like a poorly hammered nail. Dong-ju heard his bones snap.

'Are you trying to get yourself killed?' Sugiyama shouted. 'Are you trying to get shot?'

The kite, taut with the wind, snatched the spool out of Dong-ju's hands. The spool rolled along the barren ground. The kite wagged its tail dispiritedly before sinking.

'Did you see the wind?' Dong-ju moaned. 'Did you see how the wind lifted the kite?' He grinned, his white teeth stark against the blood trickling down his forehead.

Sugiyama let go of his club. He did see the wind. It blew in from the valley, pregnant with the scent of the forest and the eerie silence of the cemetery and the movements of the poplar branches, and tossed the kite high into the sky. He kneeled and glanced at the watchtower; the guard manning the machine gun, seeing that the prisoner was under control, returned to his original position. Sugiyama heaved a sigh and sprawled on the ground. The kite that had soared in the vast sky was nowhere to be seen. Instead it was on the ground, made not of paper, but undergarments. Scraps of fabric stitched together made up the tail; poplar branches, not bamboo, formed the shaft; unravelled threads from the seams of a prisoner uniform had been twisted together to make the lines. Sugiyama pulled at Dong-ju's uniform and saw that he wasn't wearing underwear. His sleeves and trousers were much shorter than before. He realized that Dong-ju had used the rice from his meal to glue together the kite. 'You almost got yourself killed for that damn wind!'

'Thanks for saving me.'

'No need to get a big head. I'm just doing my job, suppressing a problem prisoner.'

Dong-ju just looked down. Otherwise Sugiyama wouldn't have sprinted up the hill and pushed him behind the poplar tree, or clubbed him so viciously, forcing him into a ball. He wouldn't have stood over Dong-ju to block the gun-sight with his wide back.

Back in the censor's office, Sugiyama filled out a medical treatment form for Dong-ju. It was the first time he'd done such a thing.

Sugiyama was called into the warden's office. Hasegawa pushed up his round glasses and stared out of the window. Maeda sprang to his feet, brushing away Sugiyama's salute. 'Sugiyama! What the hell were you doing? Where were you when that prisoner was inciting the others?'

Instead of answering, Sugiyama looked down at his boots. Truncated images flashed through his head. Men gazing up at the blue sky; the red kite floating up with the wind; the young man winding up the lines on the hill; the gun barrel moving upwards; the splattering of blood; the interrogation room where he dragged the poet. None of that felt real now.

'Today, around 4 p.m., Prisoner 645 violated the rules,' he reported. 'He flew a kite within the prison yard for about ten minutes. Thankfully the prisoners were not agitated and the incident ended upon my suppression.'

Maeda glared at him. 'Thankfully? He flouted the rules in full view of all the Koreans!'

'He did, but I had previously given him permission. Prisoner 645 had requested permission to fly a handmade kite.'

'What were you thinking? How could you allow that kind of behaviour?' Maeda shouted. 'Have you gone mad?'

Sugiyama swallowed hard.

Hasegawa cut in. 'I thought it was fun to watch.'

Maeda wiped his brow, reassured by the warden's mild reaction.

Sugiyama jumped in to explain. 'I thought it would be a good way to control the prisoners. When they're outside, they're scattered in a wide area and they fight. I figured if they were concentrated in one area, it would be easier to watch them and keep them under control. When the kite was flying there were no fights. Everyone was focused on the kite.'

Hasegawa knew that hunger, anxiety and extreme weather aggravated the prisoners, who swung their fists at the smallest perceived insult. Neither torture nor solitary confinement did much to deter them. But this tactic had made them submissive. He smiled approvingly. 'So if we let them fly kites, we'll be able to handle them more effectively.'

Maeda appeared unconvinced. 'But these animals become violent the moment you look away. If their kite ventures beyond the walls, it would just provoke them further.'

'No, it'll be fine.' Hasegawa shook his head. 'No matter what the kite does, the prisoners are still inside the prison. If it becomes a problem we'll just cut the kite lines.'

Maeda quickly conceded. 'Yes, sir. We'll have them fly kites every Tuesday afternoon then!'

'You might want to get them involved in kite-fighting. People always fight, no matter where they are. We'll have fewer incidents if their violent tendencies are channelled that way. Of course, we'll have to keep a close eye on them.' The warden licked his thin lips in satisfaction.

Sugiyama quietly let out his breath. He hadn't realized he'd been holding it the entire time.

The autumn deepened. Cold air burrowed into uniforms. Leaves rustled and rolled around; bare branches brushed against each other. Puffs of dust rose up from the grey yard. Sugiyama had more work to do, constructing a big, strong kite that would be able to fly high. He prepared small scraps of paper, glue made from boiled rice, bamboo shafts and cotton thread for the kite lines. He kept the white kite in his office until Tuesday afternoon, when he handed it to Dong-ju. The prisoners gathered in the yard. The kite line twinkled as it unravelled. The kite flapped like a white flag above the walls. The men stared at it, recalling a time when the high walls and thick barbed wire didn't block every-thing from view. Now they remembered running freely through fields and rice paddies, feeling the breeze in their faces. The kite shot up, staggered, plummeted and circled dizzily; their wishes flew up and their dreams breached the walls. They shouted and laughed, seeing not the kite, but themselves. Free.

With the tips of his fingers, Dong-ju read the capricious wind as it changed direction and speed with every second; with his eyes, he followed its movement. Once, a gust of wind snatched the kite and made it tilt, triggering a burst of moans from the prisoners. With skilled hands, Dong-ju unwound the line and rewound it and the kite regained its balance. His deft touch made it seem as though he'd made the kite circle the air twice on purpose. Finally Dong-ju let go of the spool; it spun like a top and the line unwound quickly. The kite sank, its tail wafting behind it languorously. The prisoners groaned.

Sugiyama grabbed some line and wrapped it around his bare hand. 'What the hell are you doing?' The line dug into his palm, making him bleed.

'You have to give it more slack to get it up higher. Then the kite can ride the wind and lift up.' Just then, the trembling kite caught the wind and shot up higher than before.

The men shouted, pointing the other way. A large blue kite with a sky-blue tail had risen from the other side of the walls, and it attacked Dong-ju's kite like a shark preying on smaller fish.

Sugiyama murmured, 'A fight. The prisoners are getting too excited.'

Instead of answering, Dong-ju quickly dodged the new kite. The blue kite attacked Dong-ju's, which lost its balance and wavered. The blue kite changed height and direction and persistently tried to tangle its kite line with Dong-ju's. The men, holding their breaths, watched as their sad kite avoided the attack. Finally Dong-ju's kite emerged unscathed, and the prisoners let out cheers. Dong-ju quickly wound in the line; the kite dropped down and came back within the walls. The men let out a loud, wounded sigh.

The siren blared, marking the end of break. The men disappeared one by one into the work area or the cells. The yard returned to its quiet.

'Why did you avoid the fight?' Sugiyama asked.

Instead of answering, Dong-ju finished winding the kite line.

Sugiyama wondered if Dong-ju had decided that it would be better to avoid the battle instead of disappointing the prisoners by losing. Perhaps he figured it would be better to shield the hopes and dreams of the Koreans than risk them being felled by an aggressive kite. It had to be better than losing hope.

# GO GO GO LIKE A FUGITIVE

Maeda crumpled the piece of paper in his hand and threw it on the floor. 'What have you been doing as the censor? Explain how these seditious writings were circulated!'

Sugiyama picked up the ball of paper.

'Look at what's written on it!'

Sugiyama unfolded it. His eyes bulged. The tiny letters were in Korean. His face went rigid, as though it would crack at a soft tap. 'I'm unable to decipher it, but—'

Maeda cut him off. 'The fact that it's written in Korean means it's seditious!'

The coals in the furnace crackled loudly.

'I discovered the Korean prisoners passing it round. You must know who wrote this damn document?' Maeda barked.

Sugiyama felt perspiration running down his back. There was only one person in the prison who wrote with such a neat hand. He swallowed the name on the tip of his tongue. 'Sir, I'll find out who it is immediately!'

'No need!' Maeda opened the confiscated documents log and stepped closer to Sugiyama. 'I already know who did it.' He dropped his voice. 'Who else would do this? It's Hiranuma Tochu. Why weren't his confiscated documents incinerated?'

'Sir, I wasn't able to get to it because there has been too much to do.'

Maeda glared at him. 'You mean you were lazy. Get me all of his documents right away! I'm going to handle this myself. You just give him a good beating!'

Sugiyama gave his superior a stiff salute and turned around.

Sugiyama whacked his club across the prisoner's bare torso tied to the torture rack. It sounded as though something was breaking within Dong-ju. His thin shoulders were bare, his joints bulged. Under the light his pale skin was almost translucent. Sugiyama had been foolish, lazy. Despite knowing what would ultimately happen, he'd been lulled by the arsehole's mellifluous words. He hadn't dealt with the danger lurking within. He'd been practically criminal. He should have burned the confiscated documents at the very beginning. He should have turned Dong-ju into a cripple then.

'You fucked me over,' he panted, his voice cracking. 'Talk! What does this goddamn poem mean?' He tossed a pen and piece of paper on the desk. 'Translate it into Japanese!'

Dong-ju picked up the pen with his swollen fingers. The pen trembled as it pushed across the crumpled paper. Words poured out like river water, words that signified innocent confession, pure anguish and embarrassed guilt. Finally the pen fell on the paper, heavy as a rock. Reading it, Sugiyama felt rejuvenated, as though he'd become a boy again. He threw a glance at the waiting guards. They melted into the darkness, knowing from experience that this was when Sugiyama began the most brutal phase of his interrogation.

Sugiyama picked up the paper with the original Korean

poem written on it. It had been constructed from several different pages, cut into long strips and pasted roughly together with glue. 'Where did you get this goddamn paper?'

With great effort Dong-ju moved his bloodied lips. 'I cut tiny slivers off the bottom of the postcards and pasted them together with rice.'

'The rice is for you to fucking eat, not for you to make paper for your scribbles!'

Dong-ju flashed him a faint smile.

Sugiyama's club trembled in the air. 'What were you planning to do with this dangerous poem?'

'That's not a dangerous poem.'

'Is that so? When Koreans read this poem, it's obvious they'll think about home and get disgruntled. Were you planning to start a riot?'

'There's no proof that this poem makes anyone feel that way.'

'No proof? It's obvious this poem will make anyone's emotions run wild!' Sugiyama hesitated. He couldn't reveal that it had made his own cold, violent heart falter. He threw down his club and lowered his voice. 'When I read your stupid poem just now, I felt dizzy.' Sugiyama paused for a breath. 'This will be the death of you. I'm not going to kill you. But I'm going to wash the inside of your head. You're going to solitary. Fifteen days!'

Two days later, Maeda called for Sugiyama to meet him at the incinerator. The head guard was looking more relaxed. 'We got him quickly, so we were able to stop this document from spreading. You made the right decision, Sugiyama. Two weeks in solitary will either make him a corpse or wipe his mind clean.'

Sugiyama stood to attention. 'He's a writer. Words are branded on his mind. He'll survive just so he can write again.'

'No matter,' Maeda said, smiling, a gold-capped tooth glinting in his mouth. 'A danger that's discovered is no longer a problem.'

He tossed Sugiyama a bundle of papers. Red letters were stamped on the top. *To Be Incinerated*. Sugiyama flipped through them. 'Boy', 'Snowing Map', 'Night Seen from Here', 'Morning of the Beginning', 'Another Home', 'Night Counting Stars'. The words trembled.

'Strictly speaking, this incident wasn't your fault,' Maeda reassured him. 'Really, it's his fault. He's being punished accordingly. You just need to clean up. Go ahead and burn these.'

Sugiyama felt his heart drop. 'I'll finish reviewing them as soon as possible and incinerate them after sorting.'

'Do it now!' Maeda snapped. 'Just throw the whole bundle in. He violated the Maintenance of Public Order Act. Resistance runs in his veins. Just look at this poem here!' Maeda impatiently snatched the manuscript out of Sugiyama's hands and flipped through it until he found the page he was looking for. He shoved it in Sugiyama's face:

### ANOTHER HOME

*The night I return home*
*My skeleton follows and lies down next to me.*

*My dark room leads to the universe*
*And the wind blows on me from somewhere, from the sky.*

*Looking at the skeleton that gently weathers in the dark*
*Is it I who is crying*

*Or the skeleton*
*Or a beautiful soul?*

*The dignified dog*
*Barks at the darkness all night.*

*The dog barking at the darkness*
*Must be chasing me.*

*Go, go*
*Go like a fugitive.*
*Go to another beautiful home*
*Behind the skeleton's back.*
*– September 1941*

'See?' Maeda spat triumphantly. 'Everything from the first line to the last is seditious. This poem contains explicit anti-Japanese themes. What else would it mean for a dignified dog to be barking at the darkness? The dog is the stubborn Korean prisoner, the darkness means the occupation. Another home is a liberated Korea. It's urging the Koreans to fight for the liberation of Korea!'

Sugiyama stared at the poem. 'You're being too generous, sir. He wrote this in September 1941. He visited his home in Manchuria during his studies in Seoul. He was just anxious about the future. These are just a kid's worries. The skeleton and beautiful-soul image are just a fancy way to admonish himself. It's not deep enough to be grandiose nationalism. Sir, it's just emotional drivel.'

Sugiyama's heart quaked. The young man from the poor Japanese colony desperately longed for home, but he wasn't able to hide even there. He was describing an era when he had nowhere to turn to, an era when longing was banned.

Maeda turned the pages to another poem. 'Well, this one's very obviously anti-Japanese!'

### SAD TRIBE

*White towel wrapped around black hair*
*White rubber shoes on rough feet.*

*White blouse and skirt shield sad body*
*White belt ties around thin waist.*

'White towel, white rubber shoes, white everything!' Maeda trumpeted. 'You know that the colour white is beloved by Koreans! Black hair, rough feet, sad body, thin waist – these are complaints! The white garments are a coded suggestion for the Koreans to fight us off.'

Sugiyama swallowed. 'As you said, that poem definitely contains an inflammatory nationalism. He's Korean, so this is of course inflammatory. But not all the poems are like that.' He flipped quickly through the manuscript and began to read another poem out loud:

### BOY

Sad autumn drops like fall foliage all around me. Spring is being readied at each spot left vacant by a leaf and the sky is spread above the branches. The boy looks into the sky and blue paint dyes his eyebrows. He wipes his warm cheeks with two hands and blue paint dyes his palms. He looks at his palms again. A clean river flows along the lines, a clean river; in the river is a face, sad like love – beautiful Suni's face. The boy closes his eyes in bliss. Still the clean river flows and the face, sad like love – is beautiful Suni's face.

His own low voice lingered in his ears. Sugiyama looked down at his palms, at his hands as cold as the river. With those hands he'd beaten people without discrimination. He was suddenly ashamed.

'Nowhere in this poem can you find nationalism or a hint of rebellion. It's just the pure heart of a boy who is in love for the first time.'

Maeda glared at him, suspicious. 'Hiranuma is a careful man. He would have stuck a lyric poem in with the rest just to confuse the censor. He probably knew he would get arrested.'

'That's not true. This poem conveys Hiranuma's true feelings.'

'No, he's hiding his true colours. Suni probably doesn't even exist!'

'Suni is not an imaginary woman!' Sugiyama unwittingly raised his voice.

Hasegawa glared at him.

Sugiyama tore through the manuscript again to the page he was looking for:

## SNOWING MAP

On the morning of Suni's departure large snowflakes fall with unmentionable feeling onto the map laid sadly far away outside the windows.

I look around the room, but nobody is there. The walls and ceiling are white. Is it snowing even inside? Are you really leaving, like lost history? Though I write in a letter what I wanted to say before you left, I don't know where you're going, which street, which village, under which roof; are you left only in my heart? The snow keeps covering your small footprints so I cannot follow them. When the snow melts, flowers will bloom in your footprints; looking for your footprints among the flowers, it will keep snowing in my heart for twelve months a year.

'"Boy" and "Snowing Map" are serial poems written two years apart,' Sugiyama explained, pointing at the dates. '"Boy" depicts the heart of a young boy in love, "Snowing Map" is about a young man's despair at lost love. If the first poem was only here to fool us, he wouldn't be able, two years later, to miss the same character this desperately in the same tone.'

Maeda looked uncertain. 'You're not bad at deciphering poems.'

'I just need one day. I'll select the poems to be incinerated and report back.'

Maeda waved his hands. 'No, there's no point. Just burn them all now!'

'But don't you agree that these two are just lyric poems?'

'Well, that's the problem. They're more dangerous because they're not seditious. Whining about love when the entire citizenry has tightened its belt and is fighting against

American and British aggressors? Decadent poems like these weaken the do-or-die pledge.'

'But after the war, they'll be able to heal people's hearts,' Sugiyama insisted, not noticing that his voice was rising.

Maeda snapped, 'You don't need to concern yourself about that. We will be victorious at the war's end. The Great Japanese Imperial Military will chase the aggressors to the end of the world and exterminate them.'

'After the war our people might need these poems. It wouldn't aid the Empire to burn all of this.'

'I appreciate these aren't ordinary poems, especially seeing how confused they made you. That's why we need to get rid of them. They're dangerous.'

Thoughts he couldn't utter echoed in Sugiyama's mind. He slowly yanked the rusted steel door to the incinerator. It screeched open. The air choked with the smell of smoke as dust and ash billowed up. Maeda gave Sugiyama an impatient nod. The manuscript trembled in front of the flames lungeing to swallow it – it contained one young man's lost dreams and agonized repentance. Sugiyama's hands were shaking.

'What are you waiting for?' Maeda urged. 'The arsehole got you to let down your guard. And all the while he wrote all these banned poems. He fooled you. I won't question your judgement. I know these types always target good guards like you.'

Sugiyama ripped out the first page of the manuscript. The flame from his lighter licked the edge of the crumpled paper, swallowed Dong-ju's neat handwriting and ignited the banned sentences. One word at a time, one line at a time, one page at a time, Sugiyama ripped apart the manuscript and tossed it into the fire.

'Self-Portrait', 'Night Looking Back', 'A Dear Memory'.

He glanced at the piece of paper in his hands, the shadow of the fire looming over the words:

## A DEAR MEMORY

*One spring morning, in a small station in Seoul*
*Waiting for the train as I would wait for hope and love,*

*I cast the shadow of exhaustion on the platform*
*And smoked a cigarette.*

*My shadow let out a shadow of smoke,*
*As a herd of doves flew up without shame*
*their wings reflected by sunlight.*

*The train took me far away*
*Without any news*

*After spring left − in a quiet boarding house room*
*in the outskirts of Tokyo*
*I long for myself on the old streets as I would long*
*for hope and love.*

*Today too the train goes by several times,*

*Today too I will wait for someone*
*Pacing the hill close to the station.*

*− Ah, youth! Stay there a while.*

Dong-ju had written this a year ago, as a lonely student in Tokyo. The world had been cold and grey, filled with the smell of gunpowder. Sugiyama threw the poem into the fire. What Dong-ju had looked for in a small station vanished in the flames. Nobody would ever know that this poem had existed. Sugiyama closed his eyes. He didn't want to witness his actions as he murdered the young man's soul. He found himself wishing that time would pass quickly, that all the poems would disappear without a trace. He wanted to sweep the remnants, bury them and scrub his dirty hands until everything disappeared – the trace of ash on his fingertips, the smell of flame threaded into his clothes, the memory of the dead poems. But his guilt would remain, caked on like soot. Sugiyama opened his eyes and glared into the incinerator. *It was your fault, Dong-ju. You did something you shouldn't have. I won't forgive you for making me do something so terrible.*

'Good! That's taken care of then.' The flames danced on Maeda's face. 'After all that time in solitary, the arsehole won't think about writing a poem again.'

'Yes, sir.' Sugiyama realized then that his throat had closed up and his eyes were wet.

Two weeks later, the poet limped out of solitary. Sugiyama was relieved to see Dong-ju walk out on his own, although he did so on shaking legs. His soul had been forever altered. Though weak, he became aggressive, skulking around gloomily. He picked fights with everyone and threw sloppy punches, even though he couldn't actually beat anyone up. He limped towards solitary again, covered in blood.

A week later, he crawled out and became ghost-like. His blank gaze was fixed on the horizon, and he looked lost in time. The blue kite that had floated hopefully outside the prison walls every afternoon stopped appearing. Dong-ju's depression tugged the entire ward into a deep slump. Sugiyama missed the young man with a ready smile. He remembered one of Dong-ju's poems that he'd read in front of the incinerator before turning it into smoke that snaked up to the sky:

ROAD

*I lost it.*
*Not knowing what I lost where*
*my two hands feel my pockets*
*as I go out onto the road.*

*The road snakes along the stone wall*
*Endlessly linking stone and stone and stone.*

*The wall's steel doors are firmly closed*
*Casting a long shadow on the road*

*And the road goes from morning to evening*
*And from evening to morning.*

*When I look up after shedding tears along the stone wall*
*The sky is embarrassingly blue.*

*I walk down this grassless road*
*Because I'm on the other side of the wall,*

*I remain alive*
*Only because I am searching for what I lost.*

It was a desperate confession. What had he lost? Sugiyama knew Dong-ju had lost everything – his country, his language, his name. Had he known long ago that he would be imprisoned, that he would be incarcerated on the other side of the wall?

Every night Sugiyama sat at his desk in his office, unable to sleep. He wanted to force the frail young man to write poems again. He wanted Dong-ju's poems to survive these terrible times. Even if only a single person were to survive this war, he wanted the poems to be able to provide relief. It was all he thought about. He looked down at his desk, at the rough paper in his hands, his palms studded with calluses, his bent fingers, his broken nails. An old pen lay on the desk. An urge to write something came over him. He didn't want to be a poet; he just wanted to write. He wanted to express on paper what was roiling inside him. He'd understood the world by seeing, hearing, touching, tasting and smelling. He'd seen bloodied corpses, heard deafening explosions and screams, touched the upturned earth and dust, smelled the smokiness of gunpowder and tasted blood. But his eyes no longer saw, his ears no longer heard. He'd started to decipher the world around him, appreciating the human side of the prisoners through the postcards given to him to censor and obtaining war news from the dailies. The world now existed for him through letters. He'd obtained a sixth sense.

He recalled what Dong-ju had told him: 'The most impor-tant is the first sentence. If you write the first sentence properly, you can write all the way to the last one.' Sugiyama cautiously picked up the pen as though he were handling a sea creature with dangerous tentacles. He dipped the nib in black ink, but couldn't get started. He couldn't even place it on the paper. The blank page in front of him was as bleak as the prison yard. What was he doing? He couldn't write. He was a torturer who knew only how to beat people. He was a half-literate censor who burned the writings of others. He shook his head, but he couldn't put the pen down.

The wind rattled the thin tin roof. The words in his head glinted like pieces of broken china in the dark. He picked up the dictionary and sped his way through unfamiliar nouns, adjectives, verbs. He took the glistening words and carefully strung them together, then revised them. He couldn't tell what his endeavour would become.

Ten days passed. Or was it fifteen? Each night he stared into the darkness. He could hear the waves, the restless sea tossing and turning. He couldn't fall asleep. Dawn neared. A gloomy foghorn sounded from the navy ship in far-away Hakata Bay. Sugiyama folded the piece of paper and slid it into his breast pocket.

Dong-ju was sitting dejectedly at the top of the hill, his arms around his knees. His soul seemed to have burrowed deep inside the shell of his body, and his dark eyes brimmed with despair and resentment.

Sugiyama approached him with the kite and spool he'd made. 'Yun Dong-ju!' he called. 'How long are you going to remain like this? Enough! Get up! Do you want a beating?'

He tried to push away the guilt he felt from knowing that he was the cause of the young poet's sorry state. With his club he prodded Dong-ju to check that he was all right; his forehead was gashed, his eyes were swollen and his lips were badly cut.

Sugiyama's gaze wavered. He felt short of breath. His fingers trembled. This silent communication was the most truthful conversation he could offer, more sincere than an overwrought apology.

'I knew you would walk out of solitary alive,' he said,

pleadingly. 'Now that you're out, you need to write.' He wanted to read Dong-ju's words once again. He wasn't alone; all the prisoners – even the guards – hoped to hear him whistle, fly his kite and write their postcards again.

'How cruel of you,' Dong-ju finally replied, in a voice as arid as though he'd been buried alive. 'What right do you have to tell me to write poems? To risk my life?'

'I don't. That's true. You can say I have no shame. That's true, too. But don't stop writing poems. You have to stop destroying yourself.' Sugiyama was caught off-guard by the sound of his own desperate voice.

'Why?' Dong-ju spat back harshly. 'Why shouldn't I destroy myself, when the whole world is going insane?'

Sugiyama was stumped. That angered him. He couldn't use his club to force Dong-ju to write poetry; nothing could do that. 'Fuck!' Sugiyama spat out. 'Do whatever you want.' He raged silently at the cruel god who bestowed on Dong-ju the talent for refined language while taking away his mother tongue. Dong-ju's gift wasn't a blessing, it was a curse.

Sugiyama knew he should do something about this state of affairs, instead of just hating it. He should try to repair this vulnerable soul he'd wrecked. He rummaged around in his inner pocket and pulled out a crumpled piece of paper. 'Look! Look at this. It's a poem.'

The words pulled Dong-ju's gaze like bait. Sugiyama wasn't quite sure if what he'd written was a poem. But if Dong-ju was right, if the truth could be poetry, then perhaps his scribbling could be a poem, too. His were a few unspectacular lines, but they weren't a lie. He hadn't been a guard or a censor when he wrote them; he had been true to himself. 'I can't believe it either, but I picked up a pen and wrote this. Do you know why?' He spoke urgently. 'I wanted to show that someone like me could write poems. What's your excuse?'

Dong-ju smiled, fatigued, as though he'd just returned from a long journey. He shook his head sorrowfully, with the grief of a poet who could no longer write, the anguish of a singer who could no longer sing.

Sugiyama realized he was breathing raggedly and tried to calm himself. 'Why do you refuse to write?'

'Because we Koreans are only allowed to write in Japanese,' Dong-ju explained heavily.

Sugiyama felt his head splicing in two. So language wasn't simply a tool to convey meaning. It was the charter of a human being that contained a nation's history; Dong-ju's had shattered, been dumped on the bloodied floor of the interrogation room. And it was Sugiyama who'd done that to him.

'It doesn't matter whether your poems are in Korean or Japanese,' Sugiyama insisted. 'Because, in their essence, they're your own.'

'Why should I bother writing poems that nobody will read?'

Sugiyama's eye twitched imperceptibly. 'I'm going to read them. So write!' He grabbed Dong-ju's collar. 'You're a poet. You have to write. Poetry is the only proof that you're alive. If your poems die, so do you.'

Dong-ju clenched his teeth. 'I'm not dying. I'm walking out of this place on 30 November next year, on my own two feet.'

'If you're lucky, you might survive, but you can't count on luck,' Sugiyama urged. 'Prisoners are continuing to die. If you can't walk out of here, the poems in your head will be shut in forever.'

Dong-ju gazed up impassively at the sky. He no longer

seemed interested in Sugiyama. The blue sky was reflected in his eyes.

Sugiyama offered the kite and the spool to Dong-ju. 'Fine. If you don't want to write, at least fly this kite. You liked doing that.'

Dong-ju's eyes sparkled in momentary joy before he was again overtaken by resignation.

'Everyone's been waiting for you to come out of solitary and fly your kite.' Sugiyama lifted his chin towards the yard where the prisoners were gathered around, talking excitedly.

He pressed the spool into Dong-ju's hands. The prisoners looked at him expectantly. With the spool in hand, Dong-ju closed his eyes and gauged the force and direction of the wind. Sugiyama walked a few paces away, holding the kite. The wind picked up and Dong-ju began to run. Sugiyama gently let go of the kite. The spool spun, as though it had been waiting. The kite soared.

The following week the familiar blue kite flew up over the prison walls as the prisoners watched with bated breath. The blue kite circled, jostling for a fight. Dong-ju quickly reeled his kite in.

'Why are you avoiding it?' Sugiyama glared at the fragile young man, who resembled the kite made of thin paper and bamboo. 'Fight till the end!'

Dong-ju thought for a moment before unspooling the kite line. His kite rocketed up. The blue kite followed, its tail swaying. The blue kite changed direction and approached. Dong-ju gripped the spool. The thin kite lines cut into his palms. The blue kite blocked the wind and came close, and Dong-ju's kite stumbled. The spectators let out a groan. The wind billowed again. Dong-ju's kite swooped and circled the blue kite a few times. Now, even if the lines were cut, the two kites would fall, bound together. Suddenly, with a tug, the taut kite line sagged; the blue kite had clipped the white one's line. Dong-ju's kite flew on for quite a while before sinking slowly, the blue kite descending along with it. Dong-ju quietly wound in the line. The men murmured in the yard; there was a smattering of cheering and applause.

'These guys never cared about winning,' Sugiyama said with a faint smile, nodding over at the yard. 'They just wanted the kite to go beyond the walls.' Sugiyama kept looking at the descending kites in the distance.

Dong-ju imagined himself looking down at the ground from the sky, down at the vast ocean, the endless sea-foam coasting in with each wave, the port twinkling in the sunlight, the workers on deck, the children flying their kites, and the wooden guard post, in front of the large dome of the main ward, glistening brassily in the setting sun. Perhaps now he'd be able to write again.

Every Tuesday Dong-ju flew the kite in the prison yard. Through the slender line, he sensed the girl on the other side of the wall – her pink cheeks, her firmly closed mouth. The goal wasn't to win, but to see how long he could endure. The blue kite seemed to cross lines, not to fight but to engage in conversation. When Dong-ju unspooled more line, the girl did too, and when he reeled it in, she did as well. When Dong-ju's kite staggered, the blue kite tugged at its line to give it wind. The two kites crossed lines and detached, reeled down and went back up and teased each other. They approached and stepped back, tangled and fell. If Dong-ju's kite spiralled down, the blue kite flew up, spinning in the opposite direction. If Dong-ju's kite flew sluggishly, the blue one dragged along with it. Their beautiful dance embroidered the clear sky. A gust of wind would carry Dong-ju's kite far away, and the prisoners watching would feel better, imagining their dreams flying far away with it. The two kites' solemn waltz was the only beautiful scene at Fukuoka Prison.

# NIGHT COUNTING STARS

Sugiyama stood against the cold brick wall. He took out a worn piece of paper from his inner pocket and opened it. Winter sunlight fell onto his clumsy handwriting:

> *In the bronze mirror stained with blue rust*
> *my face remains so disgraced*
> *A relic of which dynasty?*

Each word beaded in his heart. Dong-ju's skeletal form blocked the sun. Sugiyama looked up, carefully folding the piece of paper and sliding it back into his pocket.

'Why do you have that poem?' Dong-ju demanded.

Sugiyama didn't know what to say. As he was the one who'd burned Dong-ju's poems, he couldn't tell him that the poem had healed his battered heart. He couldn't confide in Dong-ju that, when he read the poem, he felt as though he'd found something he'd been desperately searching for. He felt that he was the only person who could save the young man's poems; he'd begun memorizing them hungrily, reading as though he were praying, reciting them to himself reverently, fingering the copies deep in his pockets.

'Since these poems helped me, they could help many

others,' Sugiyama managed to reply. 'I know they could make everyone feel better.'

Dong-ju closed his eyes. He could hear crows flapping their wings on top of the poplar trees. His face seemed to be made of thin ice about to shatter. 'It's possible that the book of poems is still around.'

Sugiyama's eyes gleamed. If a copy of the manuscript was intact somewhere, the poems would be, too. His guilt could lessen. He grabbed Dong-ju's shoulders and shook them. 'Where?'

Dong-ju gazed up at the empty sky. 'I don't know. They left my hands a long time ago.'

During Dong-ju's time at Yonhi College, he wrote poems fervently, read books and listened to music. He spent his afternoons going on pilgrimage to used bookshops and music cafes, and on his return to the dormitory he stayed up all night reading. His shabby bookcase was stuffed with literary magazines and books. Between the pages he dried perfect leaves he found on his walks, writing down the place and date he found them. In those days, everything glistened with possibility.

But he wasn't spared the cruel clutches of war. The four years he spent in Seoul were harsh and ruthless; young men were dragged off to war and the citizenry was impoverished by the allocated collections for war goods. He had to leave the dormitory and move into a boarding house run by the novelist Kim Song, blacklisted by the Special Higher Police. Kim's boarders were targets of inspection; detectives watched the students' every move at all hours of the day.

Like clockwork, they burst in every evening to scribble down the students' book titles and confiscate letters from their desk drawers. Dong-ju packed his bags again, but there was no place for him to go. No matter where he went, he wasn't safe from brutal restriction and watchful eyes. Several of Dong-ju's friends were conscripted, a red band tied around their tonsured heads; others were brought into the police station, beaten within an inch of their lives and sent to prison. For Koreans, there was no future. Every night Dong-ju sat before his tiny desk and threw himself into the darkness. Unfinished poems piled up, along with crumpled, discarded pieces of paper smudged with eraser marks and slivers of words.

With graduation looming, Dong-ju made three copies of a manuscript containing nineteen poems. He asked his friend Jeong Byeong-uk to safeguard one copy, kept one for himself and took the final copy to his professor Lee Yang-ha. He explained his desire to publish a couple of dozen copies and asked Professor Lee to write a foreword. His mentor shook his head; the book of poems would be considered seditious. The Special Higher Police detectives would bare their teeth if they saw poems like 'Cross', 'Sad Tribe' and 'Another Home'. Professor Lee suggested that they wait for a better time.

'When would that be?' Dong-ju asked.

His mentor couldn't give him an answer.

Dong-ju wondered if such a day would ever come, and whether his nineteen poems would survive until the day the world changed.

'Are you saying that there are two more copies of the manuscript in Korea?' Sugiyama demanded.

'That was three years ago. Who's to say that someone else could save the poems I myself couldn't protect?' Dong-ju was less concerned about his poems than for Byeong-uk, who'd been enlisted as a student-soldier. He also didn't wish his professor to be put in danger for owning a seditious manuscript.

But Sugiyama wanted to believe that they had protected those poems from the gale.

Dong-ju changed the subject. 'The stars will be in the sky tonight too, right?' He sounded parched.

Sugiyama nodded. Every night, from the eastern sky, Venus rose without fail, and the Big Dipper circled the North Star like an enormous waterwheel in the sky. The Milky Way and the sharp twinkling stars giggled and whispered and fought like children. Stars didn't appear in Dong-ju's sky. Each night he lay in his cell and drew an imaginary constellation on the ceiling. Sugiyama couldn't blame Dong-ju for wondering whether light had disappeared from the world and whether stars no longer twinkled in the sky.

That night at 10 p.m. Sugiyama stood in front of the cells. The steel doors opened with a screech. He walked down to Cell 28 at the end of the corridor on the right. '645! Interrogation! Regarding seditious writings.'

The prisoners turned around in their cots and hurried back into slumber. Men called out in the middle of the night rarely came back whole. The guard on duty unlatched the lock and opened the door, then tied Dong-ju's arms together. Sugiyama signed off on the prisoner log and prodded 645 with his club. He could feel Dong-ju's protruding ribs through the tip of his club. The long, winding corridor heading towards the interrogation room was dark. The two passed the interrogation room. The shackles clacked and shrieked. Dong-ju was afraid. Where was Sugiyama taking him?

They stood in the prison yard, spotted with white light as though salt had been scattered over it. They heard the watchtower machine gun readying. The cool searchlight stopped over them.

'Sugiyama Dozan, Guard Department!' Sugiyama shouted. 'Interrogation of the scene with Prisoner 645.'

The guard above them checked his files; he found paperwork signed by Maeda that had been submitted earlier. The searchlight returned to its normal pattern, circling the premises. Sugiyama and Dong-ju could hear the wind against the branches of the poplar trees as they rose like soft, leavening bread. They sat against a tree, side-by-side. The wind blew cold air on Dong-ju's pale cheeks and temples. He could hear his own heart beating. Sugiyama loosened Dong-ju's ties and took off the handcuffs. The cold night air smelled sweet. Dong-ju inhaled deeply and murmured words Sugiyama couldn't understand; he was reciting a poem in his mother tongue, the same language he shouted in as he played in the mountains and fields of his hometown. The language he'd had to repress now burst out through his lips.

A shooting star raced over their heads. Dong-ju had too many wishes to pick only one. Not Sugiyama; he asked that this poet pass safely through this cruel era. He gazed up at the stars as they traced concentric circles along the sky and wondered if they made a noise as they orbited, or whether they gave off a gentle rustle. He wanted to hear it. The wind blew; his cheek was wet and cold.

Back in the interrogation room, Sugiyama opened the

report form. Dong-ju began to speak, translating 'Night Counting Stars' into Japanese. The poem emerged as fragile as candlelight in a gale. Sugiyama wondered: how could he not blame himself if he couldn't usher these poems past the end of the war? He was the only person who could protect this young man's legacy; there was no one else. Sugiyama dipped his pen in ink and began transcribing the words, which floated like stars on the dark paper:

## NIGHT COUNTING STARS

*The sky of passing seasons
Is filled with autumn.*

*Without a single worry
I think I can count all the autumn stars.*

*The reason I can't count all the stars carved
one by one in my heart is
because morning is coming,
because night will fall again tomorrow,
because my youth is not yet gone.*

*For one star, memory;
For one star, love;
For one star, loneliness;
For one star, longing;
For one star, poetry;
For one star, mother, mother.*

*Mother, I call out one beautiful word for every star. The names of the children I shared a desk with in primary school,*

*the foreign names of girls, Pei, Jing, Yu, other girls who*
*have already become mothers, the names of impoverished*
*neighbours, dove, puppy, rabbit, donkey, deer, the names of*
*poets like Francis Jammes and Rainer Maria Rilke.*

*They are so far away.*
*Like stars in the beyond,*

*And you, Mother –*
*you are in Manchuria far away.*

*Longing for something,*
*On top of the hill under falling starlight*
*I etched my name,*
*And covered it with dirt.*

*The insect that cries all night*
*Does because of its sorrow about its shameful name.*

*But after winter passes and spring dawns on my star,*
*On the hill where my name is buried*
*Grass will stand thick and proud*
*Like green grass blooming on a grave.*

Sugiyama carefully folded the report form and slid it into
the inner pocket of his uniform.

# PART TWO

# HOW DESPAIR BECOMES A SONG

Warden Hasegawa and Director Morioka were immersed in Midori's playing, their eyes closed. Hasegawa began to clap when she finished. 'Wonderful performance, Miss Iwanami! Thank you in advance for your efforts in preparing for the concert. The entire city of Fukuoka is waiting with anticipation.' He laughed loudly, revealing molars capped in silver.

Thanks to the newsworthy concert, the Interior Minister and high-level officials in attendance would be favourably inclined towards him, Hasegawa thought. Reporters from leading newspapers would rush in; he might become a nationwide celebrity. He planned to invite the ambassadors of allied countries, Germany and Italy, as well as the foreign press; his fame might stretch beyond national boundaries. He couldn't keep the pleasant thoughts away or tamp down his gleeful smile.

Midori spoke up, taking advantage of the moment. 'I have one request.'

Hasegawa nodded eagerly.

'I would like to include a chorus at the end of the concert.'

Hasegawa twisted his moustache, looking amused. 'A chorus? Who will sing? And who will lead the practice?'

'This prison is filled with people who can sing.'

'You mean the prisoners?' Hasegawa's face contorted.

'The concert would be more noteworthy precisely because they are prisoners. Their beautiful song would demonstrate how the Empire's incarceration system has reformed them.'

'But it's a solo recital by the respected Professor Marui Yasujiro. You'll ruin the stage for the best singer in all Japan!'

Midori hesitated a moment before taking out a pristine letter from her pocket and handing it to the sceptical warden. 'This is Professor Marui's letter. It arrived yesterday. He's already agreed to it.'

Hasegawa hesitated. A chorus of prisoners couldn't do much harm, could it? He appraised Midori coldly. 'But who would want to sing? And even if we had volunteers, I don't know what the prisoners might do, if we don't watch them carefully.'

Sugiyama jumped in. 'I can take care of that, sir. I'll bring them to practice and guard them.' He would do anything to provide an audience for the piano he had tuned, no matter what everyone else's hidden intentions were.

'The repertoire is "Va, pensiero" in Scene Two, Act Three of Verdi's opera *Nabucco*,' Midori said.

'Verdi . . . Verdi?' Hasegawa looked puzzled.

'Verdi, to our ally Italy, is what Wagner is to Germany,' Morioka explained. '*Nabucco* was a huge success at La Scala. Everything about the opera represents Italy's hopes. It reminded Italians, who were suffering from division and war, of their love for their country. And of all the songs, "Va, pensiero" is in effect Italy's second national anthem – it was sung at Verdi's funeral. It's majestic and powerful, so it would work for our purposes, even if we only have male singers.'

Hasegawa was pleased. To encourage participation, he decided to exempt volunteers from labour and give them an additional meal a day. Morioka excused Midori from her medical duties in the afternoons, to allow her to conduct the auditions and oversee practice.

The auditions took place over a week. Each volunteer was escorted to the auditorium, where Midori observed as the prisoner vocalized. She recorded her opinion on the prisoner's tone, vocal strength and suggested chord-part in a meticulous log, and seventy-odd prisoners were selected. She launched an even more detailed and complex second evaluation, checking to see if the candidates could sing precise notes. Many men's voices cracked on the higher notes; others had no sense of rhythm. Three days later, she had thirty men, ten each assigned to baritone, bass and tenor. Prisoners with excellent vocalization and tone were to be leaders. A Korean, who'd been taking preparatory courses at Ueno Music School before being sent to prison for his ideology, was made the concert master. Hasegawa allowed the singers to change cell assignments so that everyone in the same vocal group was together. On Mondays, Sugiyama went out to the cells, put manacles and shackles on the singers and led them to the auditorium, where he stayed to observe them. He also listened carefully to the piano, in case it needed tuning.

The auditorium erupted into chaos during the first practice – the singers didn't know how to read music and they didn't have even a basic understanding of how scales worked. Verdi's opera was ill-fitted to men who didn't know what sheet music was. They were there solely for the perks. Midori asked the warden to allow the prisoners to shed their manacles. With their hands bound together, she argued, the prisoners were forced to lean forward, compacting their lungs and making it difficult to draw in a breath or vocalize.

Hasegawa scoffed. 'And what will you do if they riot?'

Midori slammed both hands down on the keyboard. The majestic roar of the piano curtailed the jungle of the men's murmuring.

'Fine!' Hasegawa said. 'But not the shackles.'

The singers, their hands freed, stood around looking lost. Midori handed out sheet music to the leaders. She played the melody of 'Va, pensiero' over and over again, familiarizing each part with what they would be singing.

For weeks the auditorium was a crucible of cacophony. Voices cracked, tangled and flipped. Vocalizations were terrible. The prisoners seemed incapable of singing a simple lullaby, let alone the magnificent Verdi. Midori played the piano tirelessly, correcting the prisoners' vocalizations, giving suggestions on how to breathe deeply. Slowly, the mass of noise turned into sound, and the sound into music. The men could hear their own voices, once lost. Singing was no longer performed for special treatment; the prisoners were recovering their lost selves. Their voices told them who they were. After practice, they lined up as tenors, baritones and basses. Sugiyama counted the men, manacled them and shouted, 'Return to cells. Forward, march!' The line of prisoners snaked along the corridor, back to their cells, and now they sang of their own volition. They practiced vocalization and harmonized with others in the adjoining cells. The thick walls couldn't keep their voices apart. Each part began to shine.

Back in rehearsals, Midori carefully regulated the brightness and darkness, forcefulness and frailness, cold and warmth. The prisoners sang bluer than the sky, clearer than the wind and brighter than the stars. They concentrated on extracting the purest sounds from their bodies, like monks in meditation. Watching it all unfold, Sugiyama felt his heart warming; moved by beauty, he realized he was still human.

# SANITATION INSPECTION

Each season brought grave disappointment – spring's blooming leaves pushed prisoners into a deep depression, summer's brutal temperatures and humidity overwhelmed them with sweat and swarms of mosquitoes, autumn's falling leaves and cold wind reminded them of the coming temperatures and every second of winter bared its sharp teeth in attack.

One day in the late summer of 1944 Hasegawa and Maeda escorted Director Morioka and his team of doctors into Ward Three. A parade of white coats filled the corridors; never before had so many medical staff entered the ward.

From one end Hasegawa called out, 'Open all cell doors!'

The guards dispersed with a loud thudding of boots. Keys jangled as locks turned. When the doors opened, the sour smell of sweat and filth rushed out. The guards lined up on each side of the corridor, equidistant from one another. Morioka gave a signal and doctors in masks and rubber gloves entered the cells, followed by the guards. 'Special sanitation inspection!' the guards called. 'Strip!'

The prisoners glanced at one another warily as they took their clothes off. The hesitant were met with clubs. The prisoners lined up on either side of the cells facing each other. The doctors estimated each prisoner's height and weight; with gloved hands they looked into their eyes and examined their mouths. Afterwards the doctors gathered in the corridor and submitted their inspection logs to Morioka, who left, leaving behind a sharp antiseptic smell.

Twisting the ends of his moustache, Hasegawa watched the medical team disappearing down the corridor. 'End of sanitation inspection! Close the cell doors!'

Sugiyama looked on nervously. He knew that everything was a prelude to something else; no single incident existed in isolation. But he couldn't tell what was about to happen, whether it would bring an unbelievable stroke of luck or terrible misfortune.

The following day Hasegawa ordered Ward Three prisoners to line up in the military training grounds. The tight ranks squeezed everyone's freedom; nobody could burst out of line or fall behind. By obeying, the prisoners forced others to follow suit. Hasegawa looked down silently from the platform, appearing to enjoy the prisoners' growing anxiety. Time was on the side of the powerful; the more one delayed, the more worried the powerless became. The prisoners watched the warden's lips. A long time passed before Hasegawa spoke into the microphone: 'You should all be grateful to the medical staff of the Kyushu Imperial University Medical School!'

The prisoners began to murmur.

Hasegawa paused, fanning their curiosity. 'Thanks to the magnanimity of the Great Emperor of Japan, the best medical staff in the nation gave you an inspection. It was revealed that a large number of prisoners are suffering from ill health. The medical staff will provide free medical treatment to those prisoners.'

Hasegawa stepped away from the crackling microphone. A guard tacked a piece of paper filled with prisoner numbers on a bulletin board next to the platform. The prisoners crowded around it, the illiterate openly fretting. As Maeda opened a log and began to call out the numbers, the yard erupted in excited shouts.

Several men who were not selected crowded around Maeda.

A pale man walked up. From the yellowed whites of his eyes, it was clear he was jaundiced. 'I've been suffering for a long time from anaemia,' he said dejectedly. 'Why are you helping people who are fine, but not me?'

'You're disqualified because you have a wound on your forehead,' Maeda said. 'But there will be more chances. The inspection will continue at regular intervals.' He laughed arrogantly.

The prison hummed with cheers and laughter. Only those who weren't selected were unhappy, as was one guard standing in the corner, nervously watching the celebrations.

# TO BE, OR NOT TO BE

Every time I walked into the censor office, I was on the lookout for any evidence of Sugiyama's life. The desk, the bookcases and the boxes of documents weren't illuminating, and the only other furniture in the office was an old wooden cabinet with a broken lock, squeezed in the narrow space between the bookcases and the wall, which Sugiyama used to store his clothes and personal effects. I opened the cabinet. Inside hung a well-ironed dress uniform, a brown winter uniform and two grey summer uniforms. The drawer near the bottom contained worn underwear, socks, gaiters and a few neatly folded handkerchiefs. A large box sat in the bottom, probably filled with dirty laundry. Right after the murder I'd taken an inventory of his things and noticed how everything was in perfect order, revealing Sugiyama's obsessive personality. I closed the cabinet door. Something made me open it again. I took the top off the large box. It smelled sour — sweat and mould. Dirty laundry, like I'd thought. I caught sight of a pair of winter uniform trousers, dirt embedded in the baggy knees. It gave me pause. Come to think of it, the dust in the prison yard flew away easily. I examined the trousers hanging in the cabinet. The knees showed faint traces of having been dragged along damp dirt. I remembered the scratches on Sugiyama's knees. What could that be about?

The heavy doors to the interrogation room opened and Choi walked in. His sunken, glinting eyes glanced at my shoulder, at my new, stiff badge. 'Congratulations. I see you've got yourself a promotion.'

I was embarrassed. I'd got my corporal's badge by making him out to be the murderer.

'Well,' he said, noticing my discomfort. 'People who will die should die, and those who survive should live well. Get a promotion, go on leave.' He sat himself on the chair, looking tired and anxious.

I felt warm. I unfastened a button on my uniform top. 'I have a few more questions about Hiranuma Tochu.'

'Him again?' he snapped. 'That man's a different breed. I don't want to get involved in any way.' His eyes flickered.

'You're right. Hiranuma is very different from you. I know why you and your men kept going to solitary. Why did he?'

Choi rubbed his beard. 'How am I supposed to know? Why don't you ask him?'

I had to trip him up. 'You're lying. Or you're not telling me the whole truth. I know your men beat him up when he got out of solitary.'

'How do you know that?'

'It was written in Sugiyama's daily log. He watched Hiranuma very carefully. So don't bother lying.'

'Don't you find that people usually lie because they're afraid or because they're hopeful? Since I'm neither, I might as well tell you.' Choi drew in a breath. 'We tried to pull him into our plan. Of course, we didn't like him, but we thought he would be someone the other Koreans would look up to.'

Choi kept his eye on Yun Dong-ju from the very beginning. Dong-ju was gentle; he exuded helplessness. Choi was disgusted that the young man had changed his name, as he believed that was equivalent to denying one's country. His men gathered information about the new prisoner. Man-gyo wheedled out Dong-ju's story from the guards – a student from Manchuria who attended the prestigious Yonhi College in Seoul and ended up in Japan. An intellectual, the kind of man Choi despised.

But something shifted when Yun arrived. The Korean prisoners started to crowd around him. Choi couldn't understand it. After all, Yun didn't have either the acumen to rally the men or the brute force to overpower someone. But he seemed to draw people in with spellbinding power, though all he did was listen to their stories, write their postcards and fly a kite. All he had going for him was his talent for writing. But that was how he unified all the Koreans. Choi didn't fully understand how language could move a man's heart, but he wanted to harness Dong-ju's influence for his own use.

It was obvious that they were extreme opposites. Choi considered Dong-ju to be sentimental, and Dong-ju probably thought Choi a boor. But Dong-ju's undeniable magnetism pulled Choi in. So Choi sent his men to set up a meeting with Dong-ju, who claimed he wasn't interested. Finally Choi took matters into his own hands and approached Dong-ju himself.

'Aren't you hard to pin down! We need to talk. I think it'll interest you.'

Dong-ju gazed up at the empty sky without answering, and the others began to turn their heads to look at the two men, aware of the roaring silence.

Choi laughed heartily and stalked off, not wanting his authority to be flouted in the presence of the rest of the prisoners.

After that encounter Choi began to approach Dong-ju daily. It was patently obvious that Choi was desperate to get this inexperienced young man on his side. Finally, one day, Choi revealed his true feelings. 'Don't you want to get out of this place?' he asked. 'Listen to me if you want to leave this prison alive.'

'No, thanks,' Dong-ju said placidly. 'I'm going to walk out through the front gates on my release date, 30 November of next year. No sooner, no later.'

Choi wanted to stab this idiot; he wanted to brandish his metal shaft and force Dong-ju to understand that these were tools with which to break out of prison. He wished he could drag him into solitary to show him the tunnel to freedom. But he had to be careful. He grinned. 'Then you must not realize how terrible this place is. There's no way a puny bastard like you could last until next year.'

'I don't need your protection. God will protect me.'

Everything changed when Dong-ju was sent to solitary. Choi watched anxiously as Dong-ju walked in there with his shoulders hunched. He was worried that the sensitive boy might discover his secret. Choi was on tenterhooks until Dong-ju limped out after a fortnight.

'Glad you made it out alive,' Choi said, smiling nonchalantly.

Dong-ju squinted against the strong sunlight. During his

stay in solitary his face had grown paler. 'It was hard, but not hard enough to die. Agony can't kill a man, not like despair can. People who have hope live, and people who lose it die.'

'What are you talking about? Your poems? Poetry isn't hope. It doesn't help you overcome reality. It just makes you forget it. Sinking into sentimentalism doesn't make the world disappear. Escaping these bars and walls and barbed wire – that's the only way.'

'Yours is an impossible dream. There's no freedom for the colonized.'

Frustrated heat spread inside Choi's heart. He wanted to tell Dong-ju his entire plan; Dong-ju wouldn't talk lightly if he knew. But he suppressed the urge with a deep sigh. 'Don't talk like that. You don't know anything. Behind these walls we have our own rules and secrets.'

'And you might die because of those secrets.'

Choi leaned forward and whispered, 'What do you know? What did you see?'

It was a useless question – their secret was already cracking at the seams.

Choi swallowed. 'You have good eyes, buddy. Okay. You don't have to say anything.'

'How can you be so sure I saw anything?'

Choi's sharp eyes cut to Dong-ju's dirty knees. 'The cell floor is cement. Where else would you have got your knees muddy?' He shot a glance at his men, waiting at a distance.

The group exchanged furtive looks. One hitched his trousers up, grabbing a shaft of metal from inside his pocket. Another began to walk towards the other prisoners. Their movements were in perfect synchronicity – the man approaching the other prisoners would start shouting to draw the guards' attention, while the man with the weapon would stab Dong-ju and disappear back into the crowd.

'I found some dirt around the latrine,' Dong-ju said. 'So I took it out and found a tunnel below.'

'Then you must know that now's the time to make a choice. You either join in on the plan or . . .'

Dong-ju's mind raced. Should he do nothing, or should he act? A rash action could be dangerous, not only for him, but for others. The man with the shaft was approaching quickly.

'For the last six years I've thought up dozens of ideas,' Choi said. 'Before digging the tunnel, I measured the length of the yard with my footsteps and figured out the right direction. I got trustworthy people to help.'

'What will you do when you get out?'

'Go away. Away from this filthy war, from this country.'

'How long do you think you can be on the run for? You'll be caught in less than twenty-four hours and shot. You have nowhere to go. You'll end up getting killed like a dog. That's exactly what the Japs want.'

'So, according to you, the Japs *want* me to escape.'

'Of course. To make you an example. To show everyone what happens when someone tries.'

'If you don't join, you'll be the one killed like a dog.'

The man with the metal shaft was almost in front of Dong-ju, the muscles in his forearms bulging. Dong-ju had intruded on something he wanted nothing to do with, like an insect caught in spider silk. There was no telling to what the strand that tangled him was linked. Everyone was tied to something, but nobody knew what tied him down. Even if he did know, there was nothing he could do. 'Okay, I'll do it!' Dong-ju blurted out.

Choi shot the man with the shaft a look. He whirled around and walked off. Sweat trickled down Dong-ju's back.

'So Hiranuma was in on your plot?' I leaned forward, my forehead almost touching his.

He shook his head. 'I don't know if he did his share of the digging or not. I didn't care, though. All that mattered was that he was with us. He's resourceful and intelligent, and he could rally all the Koreans. That in itself was a huge advantage.'

'He didn't help you at all, though. He just joined your conspiracy to avoid getting killed. He wouldn't have escaped even if you'd managed to complete the tunnel.'

'What does it matter? My secret was safe as long as he was in on the plan. He knew his life would be over if he stayed in prison after we escaped.'

None of it made any sense. According to Choi, Hiranuma wasn't important to the escape plot, so then why did Choi work so hard to bring him into the fold? I scanned his written confession. 'Why is Hiranuma not mentioned here?'

Choi's features darkened. He stroked his beard. 'Because he's not an important figure in the plot.'

Was Choi protecting him? Why? What was he hiding?

Choi stared at the report in front of me. 'Can I have a piece of that paper?'

I was suspicious. 'What for?'

'I don't know when I'm going to die,' he mumbled. 'I should like to write my will.'

I ripped out the last, blank page of the file and handed it to him. He folded it carefully and slid it into his breast pocket. 'Thanks. I owe you one.'

I brushed it aside. What else could a death-row inmate do as he waited for his end in a tiny solitary cell?

# THE PRIVATE LIFE OF A BOOK-WORM

Back in the inspection office, I flipped through the log of incinerated materials. Nothing caught my eye until I got to 18 September. Eighteen books were burned that day, more than the usual ten. They were mostly confiscated items from new prisoners or records that were due to be destroyed, but there was one book without an identification number – *Birth of an Empire*, issued by the Citizens' Education Bureau of the Interior Ministry. I took the log and headed to the tiny library next to the office. The limewashed walls were peeling and giving way to mould. The library contained only two desks, four chairs and rickety bookcases that held guard-education publications distributed by the Public Security Bureau: *How to Make Rounds*, *Prison Administration Regulations* and soldiers' manuals distributed by the Army Ministry. There were some war novels, too: *The Way of the Empire*, *The Cherry Blossom Warrior*, *Cherry Blossoms in the Blue Sky*. It was part of the censor's job to sort the books distributed every month and incinerate older volumes to make room for new ones.

I traced a finger along the spine of each book. I noticed two lines drawn in the dust. Someone had taken out those books. Additional lines, thick and thin, were marked around them, both faint and clear, marking the time when books were removed. These books didn't have identification numbers on their spines. They must have been brought here before Sugiyama became the censor, as he'd created a list of all distributed materials when he took over. I flipped to the back of the books to check the publication dates and found that most of them were much older. I opened the log I was holding in my hands: there was no mention of any publication without identification numbers. A waterwheel began to spin in my heart, creaking, circling, pounding. There was only one conclusion I could draw from all of this: books were disappearing. Dozens of them. They must somehow be related to Sugiyama's death.

I spent the rest of the day in the quiet, cold library, my mind grappling with the dust marks on the bookcases. I was getting tired of chasing secrets. My legs gave way, and I slid down to the floor, leaning against a bookcase. I picked out a book at random. It was about the war; it argued that we would soon be victorious, and it was filled with incitement and the promotion of national sacrifice. I shook my head. Who was victory for, anyway? Countless children were orphans, thousands of women were widows and many more had been imprisoned or lost their lives. The old spine broke in half, revealing long, narrow furrows created by book-worms.

My heart leaped with joy. I wanted to be even more like the book-worms – to be born in books, live among them and die in a library.

'*Oecophora pseudospretella*,' I murmured, looking around.

Then I spotted white powder in the cracks on the shelves and in the corners. I nodded. Sugiyama wouldn't have let book-worms proliferate. But where were they coming from?

There must be a safe haven for them nearby. I stared at the walls, and something wriggling caught my eye; a bug's glistening back and two long feelers seeking the smell of paper and ink. It crawled up the bookcase. Another crawled up from behind, and another. A mature bug must have laid eggs inside the wall. They kept crawling out of the faded grey wall. I walked up to it and heard my footsteps ringing hollow, as though I were walking over empty space below the floorboards. My heart began to pound. I pushed the desk aside and noticed a dislocated square wooden tile. The insects were crawling out of there. I levered up the board and damp, mouldy air washed over me. An old wooden staircase revealed itself, leading underground. I forced my trembling legs into the darkness and descended one step at a time. At the bottom, I took out my lighter. Its tiny flame illuminated the small space. Books. At least fifty volumes were stacked on a makeshift shelf, fashioned from a piece of wood placed on top of two bricks. I ignored my pounding heart and caressed the books' fat spines. Bricks, pieces of wood and planks were piled all around. This narrow, dark and lonely underground space made for a marvellous library, suffused with the smoky scent of dust. I recognized the books with a start. They were the very publications that I'd noticed had disappeared upstairs, but the titles were crossed out and in their place someone had written new ones, both in Korean and in Japanese: *Don Quixote*, *Les Misérables*, *Robinson Crusoe*, Greek mythologies, *Romeo and Juliet*, André Gide, Stendhal, Baudelaire, Rilke and Jammes. I pulled one out, its cover worn and shiny: *German Love: From the Papers of an Alien*. I remembered how the book began: *Childhood has its mysteries and its wonders; but who can describe them? who can interpret them?* But when I opened the book eagerly, I couldn't read it; the pages inside had been blacked out, and new writing was done by hand, in white – in Korean. I closed the volume and returned it to its place. Some books were in Japanese, mostly difficult ones, like Kierkegaard, written in a clumsy but powerful hand – Sugiyama's. Those in Korean were entertaining novels, like Dumas or Stendhal. They were obviously in a different hand. I recognized it. Why would Sugiyama share this clandestine library with him?

I knew I had to report my discovery. Otherwise, I would be a traitor. But this was a perfect little library, with an excellent selection of titles that would satisfy beginners as well as the erudite. The architect of this hidden library knew well how intellectual adventures were shaped, leading uneducated travellers down the path of knowledge, starting with Dickens and Hugo, then to young Werther, and beyond to an even greater city of literature. Adventures, the romances and mythologies, romantic poetry and biographies, arriving finally at the humanities – indeed, this was the very same intellectual path I'd taken.

Should I act? Or should I not? I needed to know more. And there was only one person who could tell me the truth.

# THE SONGS OF VANISHED BOOKS

Dong-ju stepped into the interrogation room, looking spent. His sallow face was tense with nervousness. I untied the ropes binding his wrists. Dozens of questions floated in my head. I didn't know where to begin.

He rubbed his wrists. 'Is this about Sugiyama again? I thought it was all over.' He looked exhausted.

'It might be all over for Sugiyama. But not the books in the underground library.'

'Books? Underground library? Whatever do you mean?'

'Don't bother denying it. I saw it with my own eyes!'

His lips tightened.

I pressed harder. 'You joined Choi's escape plot. But he didn't mention you, even when he got caught. Why is he protecting you?'

Dong-ju's eyes flickered slightly.

'At first I thought he was shielding you from punishment. But that's not it, is it? There's a bigger, more important reason. That secret in the tunnel.'

He looked wary. He finally opened his dry lips. 'What did you find out about Sugiyama?'

'The dirt on his trousers isn't the same dirt found in Choi's tunnel. So that means there was another tunnel. Then I found that there were books in the censor's library that had just vanished. Old government publications and publicity about the Empire.'

He didn't refute my point; his eyes blazed.

'What I want to know is the truth,' I pressed.

'There's no such thing. Even if there is, you won't get it.'

'Well, then I have no choice but to report the missing books to the warden. He'll rip this place apart. It's only a matter of time before they find the hidden library.'

He looked down in resignation.

'Who stole the books?' My voice trembled.

'What's the point of talking about that? Nothing's going to change.'

'Choi's life is on the line.'

He hesitated, then met my gaze reluctantly. 'It was Sugiyama's job to burn books. But – well, he was a craftsman. He actually made them.'

Sugiyama's hatred for books bloomed into a burning admiration; eventually he was moved to steal them. When Sugiyama discovered Choi's escape plan, he marched him and his gang into the interrogation room; they left with swollen eyes and broken wrists. Sugiyama's club had extinguished their hope. They were forced to confront reality – their clumsy escape attempt was doomed, Choi couldn't be trusted and they would never leave this prison. Now they would have to destroy the tunnel they'd dug.

Dong-ju was the last person to be called into the interrogation room. Sugiyama was seething with rage. His facial muscles were contorted, as though each and every one was rebelling against him. But his voice was calm when he began to speak. 'You used to go around reciting poetry and literature. Now you're putting your life on the line for a stupid plot.'

'I might be an idiot, but I've never joined their plot,' Dong-ju protested. 'I knew what Choi's plan was, but I didn't believe it would ever succeed. Even if it did, that's not how I want to leave.'

Sugiyama glared at Dong-ju suspiciously. 'So why did you keep getting yourself sent to solitary?'

'To dig my own tunnel.'

'There's another tunnel?'

'It branches off Choi's tunnel in the middle and comes towards the censor's office.'

'So that's not an escape tunnel.'

'I told you, I'm not leaving this place through a tunnel. I remain oppressed whether I'm in here or outside. Why escape hell for something worse?'

'Then what were you doing?'

'I wanted to escape in another way.'

'Where?'

'Into books.'

Sugiyama snorted, but deep down he knew what Dong-ju was saying. Dong-ju could live in imaginary cities and villages. It suddenly struck Sugiyama that he might actually be insane for thinking Dong-ju made sense. Every night he himself was drawn to the library by an irresistible curiosity, and when he was reading his terror dissolved. 'What do you mean?'

Dong-ju studied Sugiyama, weighing his options. 'Your office and library are the only places with books in the prison.'

Sugiyama shook his head. 'But that's because I burn them here.'

'I was tunnelling towards your office so that I could steal

a book or two when you weren't there. I could smuggle it into solitary and bring it back before you missed it. That way I could read at least a handful of books, if I spent a week in solitary.'

'That's the most ridiculous thing I've ever heard. I would know if someone's creeping into—' He stopped. A thought suddenly came to him. 'If it's the library, fine,' Sugiyama reasoned carefully. 'But don't you dare touch my office! The library has a basement that was used in the past for all interrogations. When the prison expanded, we shut that one down and moved into this bigger room.' His head was reeling; he couldn't believe what he was saying. 'You can make your library there. It's small and damp and smells of dried blood, but it should do.'

Sugiyama wondered if he was committing treason. 'Where would we get our hands on some books?' He knew someone would notice if books started vanishing.

Dong-ju spoke cautiously. 'I would think the government publications slated for incineration are guarded less carefully. If we can get those, I can find a way.'

'You don't have to risk your life for those, you can request to read them in your cell.'

'No, we're going to make new books out of them.'

'How?'

'I know a Korean prisoner on the coal transportation team. If I can obtain a few pieces of coal, grate them down and mix the coal dust with some heating oil, I can make charcoal-black. We can then black out the pages. The paper is old, so it'll take well to colour. The oil will act like a fixing agent, so it won't smear, either.'

'You're going to black out the pages? What's the point of having a black book?'

'You can write on black paper with white ink.'

'Who the hell has white ink?'

'We can make the white ink with coal ash and oil. It won't be ideal, but if we write on the black page at least we'll be able to read it. If you assign me to the work team charged with keeping the guardroom heated, I can make both.'

'Even if you make books and find ink, how will you write them?'

Dong-ju just smiled.

Sugiyama wasn't sure what to do. But he knew he couldn't refuse. He was being sucked in.

'I'm sure there are hundreds of confiscated books,' Dong-ju said cautiously. 'I'll translate the Japanese books into Korean.'

Sugiyama felt himself flush. 'You want to steal confiscated books? It's a death-wish!'

'No, no. I won't steal them. That would be too obvious. I'll just borrow onc a week. I promise to return it, after I'm done translating it.'

'Why would I let you do that? For free? I'm no Jesus Christ!'

'You'll be paid handsomely for your contribution.'

Sugiyama snorted. What could he expect in payment from a prisoner?

'Do you remember telling me that I had to start writing poems again?' Dong-ju asked. 'That's what you'll get. I'll write poems and translate them into Japanese for you. What do you think? Is that fair?'

Sugiyama didn't hesitate. He caught himself nodding fervently.

A sudden worried look passed over Dong-ju's features. 'Why are you trying to help me?'

'I'm not.' Sugiyama stared at him. 'I'm just trying to help myself.'

'You might be accused of being a traitor.'

'You've become as powerful as Choi,' Sugiyama explained. 'My goal is to keep you inside these walls. I'm agreeing to your plan so that I can keep you here.'

Dong-ju let it go. Beauty would yet purify the underground torture chamber, once soaked with Korean blood and tears.

I shook my head in disbelief. Dong-ju had turned against Choi with Sugiyama's help. Choi had killed Sugiyama while also protecting Dong-ju. The three created a labyrinthine tangle. Where to start unravelling the knot?

'Did Choi ever find out about your betrayal?'

Dong-ju nodded. 'At the end of summer he came to me after a stint in solitary. His eyes were burning with rage. He'd discovered my tunnel. He tried to strangle me, shouting, "Why did you dig your own tunnel, you rat?" I told him it was a way to freedom, just like his tunnel. I mean, who was to say that either one would work? And I knew he wouldn't kill me or report me. I don't know how I knew that, but I did. He said, "We're both digging to get out of this place. I guess it's good to have more than one route. All I can do is hope that my tunnel will save me." I said a prayer for our two tunnels to free us in our separate ways. We didn't say anything else about the subject after that.'

'Choi kept your underground library secret this whole time,' I mused. 'He must have known that talking about your tunnel wouldn't help his cause.'

'For all Koreans, Sugiyama was someone who deserved to die. At first, I thought Choi killed him, too.'

'Are you saying he's not the murderer?'

'When Sugiyama died, several Koreans saw Choi in the underground library. He couldn't have killed him.'

'Then why didn't they say anything?'

'Because Choi was going to be executed anyway, for his escape plot. Why send another to his death? I'm sure everyone wanted to protect whoever it was that killed Sugiyama.'

Dong-ju's words struck me as if I'd been winded. Had I accused an innocent man? He was going to die because of me. How would I prove now that he didn't kill Sugiyama? I had to start all over again. 'Then who killed Sugiyama?'

A dark smile appeared on Dong-ju's pale face.

Was that the smile of a murderer wearing the mask of a poet? Suspicion and fear spread like a vine in my head. Was Dong-ju lying to me? He had fooled Choi, after all. 'You blamed Choi to hide the fact that you killed Sugiyama!' I cried. 'Your tunnel led to the inspection ward, which is connected to the central facilities!' My voice trembled.

Dong-ju assumed a cold expression. 'And why would I kill him?'

'Because he found out about the underground library! He knew you stole those books. You silenced him to keep your secret safe. You murderer!' My voice choked with rage. I wanted to punch him. He'd made me falsely accuse another man.

He looked at me sympathetically, as though he understood.

I walked along the dark corridor. My boots were as heavy as lead. Dong-ju's insistence that Choi wasn't the murderer confused me. If Dong-ju had killed Sugiyama, he'd committed a perfect crime. Choi was already accused of it. But Dong-ju went out of his way to insist that it wasn't Choi, even though he must have known I would suspect him next. Or perhaps he was urging me, in his subtle way, to find the real murderer, chastising me for accusing an innocent man. I was back at the beginning, inundated with questions, without a single answer. Titles on those black books swam into my hazy, muddled head. Government publications had been smuggled into the underground space to be reborn as new books – *The Birth of an Empire* became *Les Misérables*, *Regulations for Actions in War* became *The Poetry of Francis Jammes*.

I took the incineration log and a lamp and headed to the inspection library. I lifted the wooden board; dust and the dank odour of mould washed over me. I ran down the stairs. I pushed aside the construction materials and found the waist-high entrance to the tunnel. I examined the wall, bringing the lamp closer. Inside the tunnel I noticed sharp marks from a shovel carved in the hard dirt wall; the way they were cut into the dirt showed that the digging had commenced from the library. So Sugiyama had not only supplied the books. No wonder he had dirt on his uniform. Dong-ju had been telling the truth. Sugiyama hadn't stumbled upon the secret plan; he'd had a crucial role in creating it. Sugiyama Dozan, that feared guard of the Empire, had wilfully betrayed everything it stood for.

Who was he really? And who exactly had killed him?

# THE TRUTH DOES NOT LEAVE FOOTPRINTS

The next day I dragged myself to Maeda's office, feeling embarrassed, fearful and guilt-ridden. Maeda was stirring lumps of coal in the furnace with tongs, his cheeks ruddy.

'I've discovered something new in regard to the murder of the guard,' I announced.

'And what is that?' he asked, bored. 'Did Sugiyama's ghost tell you something?'

I swallowed hard. My lips felt stuck together, as though a spider had spun a web in my mouth. 'I believe we have the wrong man.'

Maeda tossed the tongs aside and turned round to look me squarely in the eyes. 'What are you talking about? You're the one who investigated the murder. You said it was Choi. You've been given a medal and promoted to corporal. And now you're saying you'd reached the wrong conclusion?'

'There was an error in the investigation. Circumstantial evidence pointed strongly to Choi, who, as you know, confessed. But there are still unresolved issues.'

'This prison is filled with unresolved issues! For example, why don't these filthy Koreans disappear from the earth? Why do soldiers of the Empire have to take care of them? Everything is an issue. That doesn't mean there are answers.'

'If Choi killed Sugiyama, there would have been footprints at the entrance to the central facilities. If you remember, it snowed that night. But there were no footprints at the scene of the murder or in the yard leading up to the building.' Of course I knew that the lack of footprints had nothing to do with Choi's innocence, since he could have entered the central facilities through the tunnel leading to the underground library. But I wasn't about to reveal that secret. To get at one truth I had to hide another; I was playing a dangerous game.

'I suppose they could have got erased by the guards' or the prisoners' footprints.'

'That night all the prisoners were in their cells. I have another question.'

'How many goddamn questions do you have?' Maeda snapped.

'Why didn't Sugiyama report Choi's tunnel? And why hasn't Choi been executed for digging it?'

The damp coal in the furnace crackled. Maeda waved his hands impatiently. 'Enough! You intellectuals never know when to put a stop to things. You're over-thinking it. When you're not sure, the very first thought that comes to you is usually the right one.'

'But Sugiyama was so thorough. Why would he look the other way when a prisoner tried to escape? And why would that prisoner be allowed to live? Neither of these things should have happened at a place like Fukuoka Prison.'

Maeda looked uncomfortable. 'So you have a lot of questions. But you're a soldier! Your job is to take orders.'

I straightened my shoulders. 'Sir, I'm not resisting an order. As an investigator—'

Maeda's voice sliced through mine. 'You've wrapped up that incident!'

I forced myself to keep talking. 'But if Choi isn't the murderer . . . If it wasn't Choi, then who killed Sugiyama? Who's the real murderer?' I looked down at my feet.

'Yuichi,' Maeda said gently. 'The investigation is over. Stop picking at scabs. It doesn't matter who killed him. All Koreans are the same. They're not worth being kept alive.'

Although I had begun this investigation only under orders, now I found myself unable to let it rest. I still had no idea what had happened. What was behind Sugiyama's mysterious actions, the secret tunnel and the underground library?

Maeda raised his voice. 'You need to realize how serious the war situation is. Every day young men are dying on one battle-front after another. Sugiyama was just one of them. It's like pouring a small gourd of water into the Pacific. Obsessing over a closed investigation is an affront to their memories. Understood?'

I turned around woodenly and walked out of the office, feeling his gaze burning into the back of my head.

Maeda's voice flew at me like a leather whip. 'By the way, I'm assigning you to take over Sugiyama's other duties. You must censor the sheet music for the concert, escort the chorus and watch over them during practice.'

The grandfather clock rang ten times, like a heavy axe chopping down a tree. I was certain I would begin to fall very slowly, unable to stand upright any more.

# JESUS CHRIST, A HAPPY, SUFFERING MAN

The cells were filled with cold, grey air. Twelve men were crammed in a space five metres wide by five metres long. Their breath formed tiny water drops that clustered on the walls. The stiff, frozen men waited impatiently for the beginning of labour; it was easier to live with the cold when they moved their bodies. They were starving, freezing and dying. Before falling asleep at night, they stared into the face of the person lying next to them. Nobody knew what would happen overnight; an invisible hand silently yanked souls away in the dark. In the morning the prisoners woke with moans, starting a new nightmare all over again. Lying on the frosted floor, their blood frozen, the men would turn their heads to check that their neighbours were still breathing.

One day, as a man ate his meagre ration of rice, he announced, 'If I die, don't move my body until spring. My body won't start rotting because it's so cold. And you can have my share of the rice.'

Indeed, nobody told the guards when someone died. The prisoners would rather sleep next to a corpse, if they could fill their hollow stomachs with a few more frozen balls of rice. They wished they were living a nightmare; at least they wouldn't feel pain if they were dreaming. The men who were still alive ate the meals of the dead, then paid the price by digging graves in the frozen ground when the guards found out. They all believed they might be next.

Soon, even the healthy men started to die. The prisoners liked to say that one could survive the year if one lived through the winter. As the season deepened, more and more men were assigned to receive medical treatment every week. The prisoners felt protected and cared for as the doctors listened to their hearts, measured their blood pressure and drew their blood. Depending on the results, the doctors prescribed infusions. The men entrusted their bare arms to gentle nurses in white masks. They hoped the warm solution entering their veins would invigorate their tired bodies and strengthen their feeble heartbeats. Their fellow cellmates eagerly waited for their return to hear every last detail. The men who'd received treatment exaggerated what they'd experienced, creating a fantastical infirmary, a place filled with bright light that wasn't hot in the summer or cold in the winter, a paradise where angels in white caressed their wrists. Everyone wanted to be chosen, to revel in that special privilege. Weak, sickly men were treated as heroes. Before long, though, their dreams and fantasies crumbled. Those who were called into the infirmary saw no visible changes to their health. They became more subdued and talked less, but it wasn't clear what the cause was. The patients began to tire of going to the infirmary. Eventually some of them wanted none of it, but it wasn't in their power to decide.

Dong-ju was selected to receive treatment at the beginning of winter. I discovered this one Monday morning when I didn't see him in his work area. I felt a sense of foreboding. It began to snow as I ran across the yard. I didn't believe in God, but I prayed that nothing had happened to him. As I ran into the main corridor of the central facilities I heard a guard shout authoritatively, 'Step to it!'

The solemn guard was leading thirty-odd prisoners. Dong-ju stood out among the grey faces. He smiled as always; his smile was luminous against the other pale faces, lustreless skin and muddy eyes.

The guard spotted me. 'I'm escorting prisoners to their medical treatment. What is it?' He was a seventeen-year-old boy, but as he'd been conscripted even younger than I, he was at a higher rank. He should have been eating his lunch in a classroom or trying to stay awake while reading a grammar book or learning trigonometry or calculating the distance to the moon. But war made him a soldier. The youth became taciturn, learning how to destroy a man's dignity before he could realize what dignity was.

I approached Dong-ju. The escort guard cocked his head disapprovingly. While he paused, wondering if he should stop me or not, I grabbed Dong-ju's elbow and tugged, forcing him to stumble out of line. He smiled faintly and shrugged as though to ease my worries, moving his parched lips. 'I'm fine. I have a cold, but it's nothing serious. It would be a cause for worry if you don't get a cold or two in this kind of weather.'

I looked him over, but he did seem fine.

'I don't know why I was chosen, but it's a good thing,' he said. 'If I get treatment I'll feel lighter and it'll be easier to get through winter.'

The escort guard shot Dong-ju a tense look. He limped

back into line. The escort guard reported to another guard manning the gates the reason for the transport and the number of prisoners, and the line slowly passed by.

The red prisoner's garb looked like a baggy coat on Dong-ju because of his emaciated physique; he soon became invisible among all the other pale faces.

I recalled a poem he'd sung out last night in the dark interrogation room, now cradled in my breast pocket like a ticking time bomb:

### CROSS

*The sunlight that used to chase me*
*Is hanging on the cross*
*On top of the church right now.*

*The steeple is so tall*
*How did it climb up there?*

*The bells aren't ringing.*
*I pace, whistling,*

*If a cross were allowed to me*
*Like it was to*
*Jesus Christ,*
*A happy, suffering man,*

The poem still gave off warmth, as though Dong-ju's breath was lingering over the words. I quietly recited the last stanza to myself. He wasn't yet twenty-five when he wrote it, but he was already grappling with his death:

*I would bow my head*
*And quietly let*
*Blood blooming like flowers*
*Trickle under the darkening skies.*

The previous night I'd ripped the poem out of the file. 'There's one stanza that doesn't make sense to me.'

'Which one?'

'"Jesus Christ, a happy, suffering man." It is surely contradictory.'

Dong-ju gave me a faint smile. 'Life isn't always logical. Everything is contradictory.'

'How can you say that?'

'Life is like that. It's filled with falsehoods and filth and evil. But life is made up of these contradictions. Contradictions aren't falsehoods. They're a way to strengthen the truth. Jesus Christ's suffering absolved mankind of its sins. That's why he could be happy at the same time.'

It did make sense. With shame I remembered the way I thoughtlessly treated the people closest to me. Perhaps a brutal era like this forced you to grow. Reality might appear gloomy, but life was even more valuable because of it. Still, I was troubled. 'You're not Jesus Christ!' I shouted at him. 'You're going to die like a dog!'

He just looked at me sadly.

The next day I stood waiting in front of the auditorium. A line of prisoners shuffled over from the other side of the corridor. Their pallid faces were cast with powerlessness and dejection. One man had ringworm from the top of his head down to his temples, another had red, chapped skin and blistered lips, and yet another had pale, cracked cheeks. They limped along, their shackles rubbing against their ankles. The sour smell of unwashed bodies wafted over. I stepped up to the guard, the same one who had escorted these prisoners to the infirmary the day before. The chains stopped clacking.

He looked uncertainly at me. 'What is it?' he barked.

'I am requesting your cooperation, sir.'

He tensed at my use of formality. I assumed a gentle expression, but continued stiffly. 'The chorus is nearing the end of rehearsals. They are improving, but they have stage fright. If they are thrown onstage like this they'll be nervous. It'll ruin their singing.'

'And what does that have to do with me?'

'If the chorus could practise singing to an audience before getting onstage, it would help ease their fear.'

'So what do you want?'

'These prisoners walk through this corridor every day for medical treatment. If they could stop and listen to the chorus practising even for five minutes, they'll be able to perform better.'

His eyes sparked with curiosity, but soon dulled again. 'I have to bring these men to the infirmary on time.'

'You know how important this concert is,' I pressed. 'Everyone will be in attendance, from the Interior Minister and the heads of police, to foreign ambassadors and consuls and their families. If something were to go wrong . . .'

He shook his head, fear crossing his features.

'After the successful conclusion of the concert, those who helped will be recognized for allowing the chorus to have a real practice run.'

He relaxed a little. 'Fine. Only for five minutes, though!'

I looked through the window into the auditorium, where sunlight streamed in like a white curtain. Midori was sitting at the piano and the singers were lined up according to voice part. She caught my eye and nodded. A growing vibration cut through the heavy silence: the beginnings of 'Va, pensiero'. Like the way a stream coursed towards the sea, the men dragged their shackles to the window, one by one. Heavy, sad, but powerful singing reached us. The music coasted towards us like a golden carpet, glowing and smooth. Five minutes flew by, at once over in an instant and an eternity.

The escort guard lobbed a command. 'Turn right! Proceed!'

The men shuffled along, looking softer, as though they'd just been awakened from a sweet dream. I sneaked a glance at Dong-ju. In the silence we exchanged joyful looks, then the men went on their way.

I crossed the auditorium to Midori. 'It was marvellous. Even the escort guard was fully immersed in the music.'

'I'm glad. They're slowly getting better.'

'The one flaw is that I can't understand the lyrics. I can definitely feel the emotion. But it's too bad that we don't understand what the chorus is singing. I know the prisoners have spent days memorizing the Italian, but – what about translating the words into Japanese?'

'True emotion transcends language,' she said. 'Whether it's in Italian or Japanese, everyone can understand the true yearning inherent in that song.' Her hands brushed the keys to pick out 'Va, pensiero'. She started to sing along in Japanese:

> *Fly, thought, on wings of gold;*
> *go settle upon the slopes and the hills,*
> *where, soft and mild, the sweet airs*
> *of our native land smell fragrant!*

*Greet the banks of the Jordan*
*and Zion's toppled towers . . .*
*Oh, my country, so beautiful and lost!*
*Oh, remembrance, so dear and so fatal!*

*Golden harp of the prophetic seers,*
*why dost thou hang mute upon the willow?*
*Rekindle our bosom's memories,*
*and speak to us of times gone by!*

*Mindful of the fate of Jerusalem,*
*give forth a sound of crude lamentation,*
*or may the Lord inspire you a harmony of voices*
*which may instil virtue to suffering.*

I was stunned. I wasn't sure what it was about the lyrics that made them seditious, but I knew that they were. It made me even more nervous. I feigned nonchalance. 'You know, because of the majestic singing, I thought it was an account of the brave exploits of soldiers. I see now that it has a different meaning.'

Midori gave me a wry smile. What was she scheming?

'Va, pensiero' hung over me for the rest of the day. I couldn't work out why it bothered me so. I walked into the inspection office and carefully scanned the log of confiscated materials. I found what I was looking for in the fourth log: *The Titans of Classical Music*, at the very bottom of box number 645. I opened the book and ran my finger down the table of contents – introductions to classical composers' lives and works, from Bach and Handel to Beethoven, Schubert, Chopin and Schumann. I finally came across an entry for Verdi on the sixth page: 'Wagner and Verdi, A Two-Horse Carriage of European Opera'. I turned to that page as though I were under a spell:

The chorus 'Va, pensiero' appears in Act Three, Scene Two of the opera *Nabucco*. Nabucco is another name for Babylon's King Nebuchadnezzar, who appears in the Old Testament, specifically in the Second Book of Kings, the Book of Jeremiah and the Book of Daniel. His powerful kingdom defeated Syria and Egypt and he was thus venerated as the absolute monarch surpassing Hammurabi. King Nebuchadnezzar felled the kingdom of Israel, which had been divided into Judah in the south and Israel to the north after King Solomon's death, and took the captured Hebrews to Babylon. The enslaved Hebrews were forced to construct the embankment of the Babylon River. Psalm 137 in the Book of Psalms contains the story of the Hebrews who sang longingly for their home along the river bank.

After losing his wife and son, Verdi sank into despair and gave up music, confining himself at home. Merelli, the impresario of La Scala, gave the story for *Nabucco* to the depressed Verdi. Verdi was moved by the story of the Hebrew slaves who led their lives with resolve, without losing hope of returning to their homeland, and he began to compose again. *Nabucco* brought Verdi immense success. When it premiered at La Scala on 9 March 1842, the Milanese were moved to tears. The performance fanned nationalist fervour in the hearts of all Italians, who were suffering from the repression of the Austrian Empire and saw parallels in the plight of the enslaved Jews of Babylon; they sang this song all over Italy. 'Va, pensiero' injected despairing Italians with a new passion for freedom.

Italians revered Verdi as the nation's composer and 'Va, pensiero' was treated as the second national anthem. Thirty years after the premiere of *Nabucco* in Milan, Italy became a united country under General Garibaldi. At Verdi's funeral, 'Va, pensiero' was sung in honour of the great man.

I closed the book and returned it to the box. I recalled the lyrics to 'Va, pensiero':

> *Fly, thought, on wings of gold;*
> *go settle upon the slopes and the hills,*
> *where, soft and mild, the sweet airs*
> *of our native land smell fragrant!*

And suddenly I remembered another song:

> *Carry me back to old Virginny,*
> *There's where the cotton and the corn and taters grow,*
> *There's where the birds warble sweet in the springtime,*
> *There's where the old darkey's heart am long'd to go.*

Something shifted, and everything started to fall into place. The Babylonian Hebrews had lost their country, the Italians had suffered under the Austrian Empire's repression, and the Negroes had been enslaved in America – these were people whose homes were torn from them, and many became captive far away. And the men who would be singing this chorus were Korean prisoners, whose homeland had been wrenched away from them, too. Dong-ju habitually whistled 'Carry Me Back to Old Virginny', Midori played 'Va, pensiero' and she defended the violent, despicable Sugiyama, while Sugiyama was moved by Dong-ju's poems . . . They were all linked. Somehow Dong-ju was involved in the selection of 'Va, pensiero'. After all, *The Titans of Classical Music*, which I'd found in his box, mentioned Psalm 137, and Dong-ju was the only person in this prison with a Bible.

Dong-ju settled on the chair in the interrogation room shivering like a withered leaf. I took off his manacles. His wrists, scraped by the metal, were swollen and red. He placed his Bible on the desk and folded his thin, rake-like hands on top. I glared at the Bible like a cat eyeing a fish.

Dong-ju's eyes flickered. He looked nervous; he was probably wondering why I'd told him to bring the Bible with him. Would it be burned?

I spoke first. 'Nothing's going to happen to your Bible. I'm not going to inspect it or burn it.'

He looked at me doubtfully.

I tried to assume a gentle expression. 'I just want to read one part of it. You're the only person with a Bible here. Can you lend it to me? It'll just be for a moment.'

With both hands Dong-ju quietly pushed the Bible towards me. My heart began to pound when I got to the Book of Psalms. The pages rustled as I turned them. I swallowed. Psalm 137:

By the rivers of Babylon, there we sat down, yea, we
    wept, when we remembered Zion.
We hanged our harps upon the willows in the midst thereof.
For there they that carried us away captive required of
    us a song; and they that wasted us required of us
    mirth, saying, Sing us one of the songs of Zion.
How shall we sing the Lord's song in a strange land?

These verses were underlined in pencil. I looked up.

Dong-ju pressed his lips together. 'So you've read *The Titans of Classical Music.*'

I nodded.

He nodded, too. 'The Hebrew slaves who were taken captive sang their old songs by the rivers of Babylon and wept, longing for Zion. The Babylonian keeper taunted them and demanded that they sing a Hebrew song. The Hebrews were in a trap. If they disobeyed, they would be killed; but if they obeyed, they would be dishonouring their homeland. This was what inspired Verdi in composing "Va, pensiero". With this song, he was giving hope to the Hebrews that they would return to Zion with golden wings.'

I nodded slowly. 'Midori isn't the one who chose "Va, pensiero", is she?'

'Who, if not her?'

I stared at him steadily.

'It doesn't matter who chose which song. The sincerity of the song — now, that's important.'

'It looks like everything will unfold as you planned it. The singers will sing of returning and retaking their homeland. But the audience will be filled with high-level government officials and military leaders. What do you expect will happen, if Korean prisoners start singing about longing for their country?'

Dong-ju shook his head. 'My only concern is for the best possible performance.'

I couldn't believe my ears. 'How naive you are! Or are you clever? You know they'll figure out what this song means! "Va, pensiero" is a resistance song! You're giving voice to the Korean independence movement!'

'Whether you're Korean or Japanese or Italian, the listener will feel the same sentiment.'

'Using music and art to push for the independence of Korea is an overt rebellion!' I cried. 'In front of all those people! If they find out what you're up to, everyone is going to be in serious trouble. What about the singers? What about everyone else involved in the concert? Are you trying to fuck with the warden and Maeda? Are you trying to get me and Midori into trouble?'

'This song won't harm anyone. I just want to hear a truly sincere song. Especially now.' He looked at me listlessly, spent.

'This is a mistake.'

'Why would you say that?'

With a heavy heart I remembered the job the Empire had entrusted me with: censorship. 'This seditious song will not be performed in front of distinguished guests.'

'Will you cancel the concert?' Dong-ju asked.

I couldn't breathe, it was as though a cobweb were covering my face. I knew I had to stop this concert. But I couldn't answer him. I dropped my head in despair. The choristers had put everything they had into their singing. They hadn't realized they could produce such beautiful sounds; now music was their religion. Midori was practising late into the night. Everyone was content and carefree during rehearsals, even the other prisoners, who craned to listen to the singing that drifted faintly through the infirmary corridor, the work areas, the cells and the yard.

Dong-ju looked at me knowingly. I hated him for putting me in this position.

He smiled. 'The old man in Cell 38 said to me, "If you have to bet on something, bet on hope." He says you always reap more profits if you throw yourself behind a business that's going well.'

I wanted to punish him for his brashness. If I allowed the concert to go ahead, everyone involved in it might face serious trouble. But maybe, just maybe, the audience would be moved and would applaud. Maybe the concert would be a success. I wanted to see for myself whether the Koreans' singing could move a Japanese audience. Could I pin my hopes on something that foolish? I was a soldier; I didn't want to go along with this precarious plan, putting Dong-ju and Midori in danger. I suddenly grew frightened. I realized I'd done everything Sugiyama had done until he died: I was now the censor, I escorted the chorus, I kept the underground library hidden; I was accomplishing everything he'd secretly wanted to. Would I get killed for my efforts, just like him?

# ENDLESSLY SINKING PROMETHEUS

Dong-ju's eyes appeared sunken in the dim light of the interrogation room. His face was dirty; he had been pulling a cart since dawn.

'You look tired,' I offered.

'I'm no old man,' he said, giving me a wide smile. 'I'm only twenty-six and I'm still all right. I'm due at the infirmary tomorrow. I'll feel better after an infusion.' His eyes twinkled expectantly.

He was completely different with me than when he'd pulled the cart, covered in grime; when he'd stood blankly on the poplar hill; and when he'd crouched under the wall basking in the sun. Speaking of poetry reanimated him, like Lazarus from the grave; his voice was vibrant and his eyes emitted light.

He launched into a poem. '"Liver." On a sunny rock on the shore / I will lay my damp liver flat to dry, / Like a rabbit fleeing the Caucasus mountains / I will circle around and guard my liver. / My pet eagle! / Come peck at it, without a single worry. / You will fatten / And I will lose weight, but, / Turtle! / I will never again fall for the sea god's seduction. / Prometheus, poor Prometheus / A stone around his neck for the crime of stealing fire / Endlessly sinking Prometheus.'

This poem was shockingly different from his others. Violent emotion and condensed rage sprang from every line, taking the place of mild contemplation and private musing. Fire leaped in Dong-ju's eyes, but when he addressed me his voice was calm. 'I tried to publish a book of poetry just before graduating from Yonhi College in 1940. I collected nineteen poems, but as the poems were written in Korean, they wouldn't have passed the Japanese government's censorship. My mentor persuaded me not to publish the volume, for fear of my life. *The Sky, the Stars, the Wind and Poetry*', he continued, sighing. 'That's what it was supposed to be titled.'

I sat up straight. 'Did you say *The Sky, the Stars, the Wind and Poetry*?'

He nodded.

'Not *The Sky, the Wind, the Stars and Poetry*? And didn't you graduate from Yonhi College in 1941, not 1940?'

'What does that matter?' He gave me a puzzled look.

None of it would matter if he were anyone else. But this was Dong-ju. And these were seminal moments in his life that he couldn't possibly forget.

'You can't really trust your memory anyway,' he remarked, flashing me an easy smile.

I was troubled. Was it lack of nutrition? Was it the hard labour? Or had he been beaten too much? I could only hope that his confusion was temporary. Something was definitely wrong. Something was gnawing away at him. His face was thinner and his physique even gaunter. Even the smallest wounds didn't heal quickly and he spent more time staring blankly up at the sky. Once he confused Caesar and Augustus, and on another occasion he mixed up Stendhal with Hugo.

He coughed into his uniform sleeve: it was wet with

blood. I pushed his sleeve up and saw a long cut that was mottled with blood.

'It's nothing,' he said. 'Near the end of the day my cart tipped and I got scratched by an ammunition case. It won't stop bleeding. Maybe because I'm not eating well?'

'Why haven't you said anything?' I shouted. 'It's been over two hours!' I undid my gaiters and used them to bind his forearm.

Dong-ju gazed at me with murky eyes. 'It's because of the weather. I'll get better when spring comes. At least I'm getting medical treatment.'

'I can't wait for this awful winter to end.'

His eyes regained their focus. 'Spring comes only after brutal cold and fierce snowstorms. Just as a rainbow appears only after a shower, beauty comes after hardship. Beauty without suffering is meaningless.'

'When you go to the infirmary, tell them exactly what your symptoms are,' I ordered. 'Hopefully they'll be able to prescribe proper medication or give you a shot.'

He coughed. 'I'm not the only one. Everyone's eyesight and memories are failing, too. The doctors say all of these are temporary reactions because the infusions are a shock to our systems. They told us we'll get better if we continue with the treatment.'

I looked him over carefully. His once-handsome face was unrecognizable from ringworm and the constant beatings by my fellow guards.

His eyes glazed over again, like a dusty sheet of glass. 'Don't worry!' Dong-ju said, smiling. 'I'm going to survive. I'm walking out of this place on my own two feet.'

A thought flashed through my head – I knew who could help us. Midori. I got Dong-ju to his feet. At the steel gates that led to the infirmary corridor I told the guard that I was escorting an emergency patient. He opened the gate. The noise of clanking shackles preceded us in the dark corridor. We could hear the piano. Midori stopped playing and turned to look at the source of the disturbance.

I was breathing hard from the effort of bearing Dong-ju's weight. 'I'm sorry to bother you during practice,' I said, panting. 'It's an emergency. He won't stop bleeding.'

She motioned for Dong-ju to sit on the piano bench and opened the emergency kit she kept next to the piano. She cleaned the wound with alcohol. 'It's only a superficial cut. It won't require stitches. But it's odd that it won't stop bleeding.' She placed gauze on the wound and wrapped it with a bandage. Gradually the blood stopped seeping through the gauze.

Dong-ju turned round in his seat and placed a careful finger on the keyboard. The note lingered, continuing on like a delicate thread. He closed his eyes, feeling the note with his entire body.

I asked Midori to step outside. 'Thankfully the bleeding is under control now, but I'm still worried. He'll keep getting injured during hard labour. Besides, the bleeding might only be an indication that something else is wrong.'

'Does he have any other symptoms?'

'He's definitely changed. He's sluggish. He falls asleep during interrogation. He has a chronic cough and his memory is getting worse.'

'We're seeing plenty of patients with colds, since the temperature is freezing right now and the cells aren't heated. And we've started seeing other prisoners who wouldn't stop bleeding, mostly from Ward Three.'

'Ward Three? Well, they're getting nothing to eat and

their cells aren't heated, but they're assigned to hard labour. It makes sense that their immunity would be compromised.'

'There's another notable thing about the Korean prisoners,' Midori said hesitantly.

'What's that?'

'Most of the patients assigned for medical treatment were chosen from Ward Three.'

I froze. 'The medical treatment was for those who are unwell, right?' I stammered. 'And that's why the Koreans were chosen. But then why would they be getting worse?'

She shook her head. 'It might be the infusions. If a weak person is infused with strong nutritive medication, they might experience side-effects.'

'We need to find out what's going on.'

'These are doctors from the best medical school in the Empire. If they see any side-effects they'll be the first to take action.'

'They should have done so already!'

'We're going to have a research meeting in three days. The doctors will go over the treatment plan and research questions for the week. I'll report the side-effects and suggest remedies. Would you look into the prisoners' symptoms?'

Her calm tone reassured me to some degree. But I was nevertheless deeply troubled by an unidentifiable nervousness.


A few days later, I was called into Director Morioka's research lab. The air was filled with the cool, clean smell of dozens of medications and, on one wall, bookcases were lined with numerous foreign-language medical texts.

The director offered his hand eagerly. I took it stiffly.

'Yuichi!' the director cried. 'I heard that you recently

volunteered to escort the prisoners to the infirmary for their medical treatments. I commend you for that. I understand that you put together Nurse Iwanami's report at the research meeting. It seems there was a small misunderstanding about the medical treatments.'

At the meeting Midori had presented a chart of prisoner numbers and the side-effects each suffered. Almost all the patients experienced headaches, fatigue, weakness and indigestion. Vomiting and diarrhoea weren't uncommon. They also experienced loss of memory, dizziness, bleeding and bruising at the smallest impact. Almost all the prisoners showed several symptoms.

'I merely reported the results after receiving complaints from the prisoners,' I said, somewhat defensively.

'Oh, I'm not reprimanding you. The medical team has decided to review the report and come up with an appropriate plan. It was a wonderful report, except for one fatal flaw.'

'A flaw?'

'You relied too heavily on the patients' statements. These kinds of symptoms have to be determined through careful medical examination.'

I felt cowed by Director Morioka's gentle expression and melodic voice. 'Sir,' I began hesitantly. 'The symptoms weren't false. The prisoners who received infusions are in pain. What the patient is feeling has to be the most accurate documentation of his pain.'

Director Morioka smiled. 'Will you be my guest tomorrow in the infirmary? Your misgivings will be put aside when you see for yourself how scientifically and hygienically we conduct the medical treatments.'

I nodded, mute.

*

The next day, at two in the afternoon, I escorted thirty prisoners to the infirmary. We stopped, as always, in front of the auditorium. Dong-ju's gaunt cheeks were flushed with vitality as he stood listening to the singing. At the end of the song I led the prisoners down the corridor, their shackles dragging behind us.

In the infirmary a doctor wearing silver glasses motioned for me to follow him. He opened the door to the infusion room, revealing six cots shielded by white curtains on either side of the room. 'The infusion room is the height of hygiene and convenience,' he explained.

In a clear, high voice a nurse called out six numbers. Prisoners filed in and each took a cot. Nurses approached them and, with precise movements, found the veins and inserted the needles in their thin arms. After the treatment the men rested. The doctor explained to me that they might experience dizziness or muscle spasms if they moved right away. I tagged along behind him as he moved slowly between the cots.

'This medication will give them more vitality and help prolong their lives,' he said and opened the door at the other end of the room. I followed him in, feeling like Alice hurtling down the rabbit hole. He sat down at the desk, which was stacked with medical files, and nodded at the young prisoner, an interpreter, sitting stiffly in a chair in the corner.

The doctor flipped through the list and shouted, '531! Enter!'

The interpreter followed suit in Korean.

A man with sunken eyes walked in.

The doctor didn't look up from the chart. 'Any uncomfortable symptoms?' he snapped.

The patient blinked his eyes, waiting for the interpreter

to finish translating. 'Nowhere in particular,' he replied nervously. 'I'm always uncomfortable. My head feels foggy and I'm tired, but I can't sleep at night. I haven't eaten much. I can't digest anything, anyway. I have the runs, you see.'

The doctor wrote down the symptoms on the chart. He laid down his pen and took out a stopwatch and a piece of paper from the desk drawer. He turned to me and explained that he would conduct a mental-agility test that would reveal any damage to brain function. Apparently, performance of arithmetic was the most effective neurological test, as it required instant recall, strong focus and accurate maths skills.

He handed the piece of paper to the prisoner and pressed a button on the stopwatch. 'Begin!'

The patient started on the problems. They were mostly double-digit additions and subtractions. The stopwatch ticked through the silence. One minute later, the doctor told him to stop. The patient put down the pen with a tired expression. The doctor checked the answers, recorded the number of questions solved and the number of accurate and inaccurate answers.

'What's the date today?'

'January 1945.'

'Where are we?'

'Fukuoka Prison . . .' The patient was speaking hesitantly now.

The doctor cocked his head and wrote something down on the chart. 'Where are you from?'

'Uiju, on the Korean peninsula.'

'When will you be released?'

The prisoner paused. '1946?'

229

The doctor wrote, 'Doesn't clearly remember when he will be released.'

The questioning continued. The prisoner hesitated a few times and then the doctor compared the results with those of a previous test.

'How am I, Doctor?' the patient interrupted. 'Am I getting better?'

'You know that things get worse before they get better. You're getting a special infusion, so it'll take some time for you to get used to it. You'll improve gradually, so be patient.'

The doctor looked at him sympathetically as the prisoner left the room. 'He answered twelve problems in a minute. He got nine right. He completed one less than last week and he got one more wrong. On the memory test, he answered two fewer than last time and hesitated twice more. It's not good. Like you said, it must be the side-effects of the infusions.'

'Then shouldn't we halt them immediately?'

The doctor shook his head in exasperation. 'Look here, Soldier! Do you even understand what we're doing? The medical team will take care of this, so just concern yourself with your own job.' He then explained that the infusions were part of a larger research project – they were aiming to ameliorate the fatality rates of soldiers and air-strike victims – and they were testing this new medication on the prisoners, which would make them feel stronger. They were also doing all they could to eliminate side-effects. He concluded by saying that there would be no need for research if medications didn't have side-effects and never failed.

Dong-ju entered the room. His cheekbones protruded starkly over his gaunt cheeks, and his pale skin was stretched grotesquely over his skull.

The doctor opened his chart. 'Prisoner number!'

'I don't remember.'

'Name?'

'Yun Dong-ju.'

The doctor looked up at him in surprise. 'Your Japanese name!' he snapped.

'I don't remember.'

The doctor gave Dong-ju the arithmetic test. Dong-ju took the pencil and started working on the problems. One minute later, the doctor pressed the stopwatch.

'Home town?'

'Mingdong village in Jiandao Province, Manchuria,' Dong-ju replied. 'It's a lovely little village surrounded by mountains. In the spring, azaleas, cherry blossoms and peonies bloom and soft catkins cover the river banks.'

'That's enough,' the doctor said, cutting him off. 'This is not the time to reminisce about your birthplace. When will you be released?'

'30 November 1945.'

'Who is the Emperor of Japan?'

'I don't remember.'

The doctor's mouth flickered with a tiny spasm. 'What words can you recall?'

Dong-ju closed his eyes. Smiling, he answered, 'Sky, wind, stars, poetry.'

The doctor wrote the words down. 'What is the multiplication table for nine?'

Dong-ju slowly recited the numbers with a blank expression: '9, 18, 27, 36, 45, 54, 63, 72, 81, 90, 99 . . .'

'Enough. You may leave.'

Dong-ju turned round slowly, his thin, stooped back as unsightly as his gaunt face. His body was slowly betraying him.

The doctor turned to me. 'His memory and his arithmetic are perfect. He solved many more questions than anyone else and he didn't give any wrong answers. This is an example of someone adjusting well to the infusions. He's had no side-effects to worry about.'

I couldn't believe my ears. 'But his memory is faulty. He couldn't remember his Japanese name or his prisoner number.'

'Ah, that. You, of all people, should know that you have to be alert and to sort out made-up answers when examining prisoners.'

'Made-up answers?'

'I mean an intentionally wrong answer, or an answer that has nothing to do with the question posed. He didn't tell us his Japanese name because he didn't want to. Not because he couldn't remember. And it was the same with his prisoner number.'

'Why would he conceal what he remembers?'

'You must be well aware of this tactic! It's a way to deny his crime. He's avoiding acknowledging it by erasing his prisoner number from his memory. He's not admitting to the fact that he has a Japanese name. It's typical of an intelligent mind.'

'Are you saying he was trying to trick you?'

'Obviously! He's realized that the patients suffer from one or two side-effects. He's using memory loss, which is fairly common. If he really couldn't remember his prisoner number, he would have looked down at his uniform. But he didn't. And he remembered his release date and even recited the multiplication table. You saw that yourself!'

'But he didn't recite the multiplication table the way most people do. He didn't say nine times one is nine, nine times two is eighteen. He just blurted out the answers directly.'

'So?'

'What I mean is, he didn't recite the table. I think he had to calculate it. He wasn't multiplying; he was adding nine to the last number.'

'It doesn't matter. If he can add in his head, it's clear that his brain function is good. I think we're done here. You can escort the prisoners back.'

I wanted to say something else, but my lips wouldn't comply. I spun on my heel and left the room.

The prisoners were lined up in two rows in the dark corridor. As I called out the prisoner numbers one by one, hoarse voices wheezed out in reply. 'Forward, march!' I called out, spitting out my resentment. The men's shackles began clanking on the cold, hard floor. I wanted to turn around to make sure that Dong-ju was fine, but I stopped myself. I didn't want him to see the sorrow in my eyes.

# IF SPRING CAME TO MY STAR . . .

The air strikes became more frequent. Japan turned into an enormous barracks and Fukuoka was the front yard for the US Air Force. The bleak warning of the urgent air-raid siren always came as the prelude to death and destruction. B-29 bombers were turning the city into ash. The sirens blared on, a requiem both for the burning city and for the people who were buried under it. Women with buckets scurried through the bombed streets to stamp out fires. People tried to forget the sirens, the buzzing of aeroplanes, the explosions and screams, recalling instead the other sounds that had once filled these streets – the laughter of children, jazz music coming out of record shops, women's delighted laughter. War had transformed everything. Streets resonated with the sound of heavy boots, shops were shuttered, military trucks filled with terrified young male conscripts. People were weighted down with terror. Death had become a routine affair and survival was the only goal. Hard labour continued in lockstep with the war. More and more military uniforms were needed; the prisoners washed, mended and re-dyed military uniforms that were soaked in blood and torn by shrapnel. Dong-ju's job was to pull carts piled high with blood-stained uniforms. When the siren sounded, signalling the start of the prisoners' outdoor break time, Dong-ju stood in the yard and looked up at the grey sky, whistling.

I approached him one afternoon. He smelled sour. Strangely, it was a welcome odour; it meant that his body was still functioning. I followed his gaze up to the sky, which stretched low over the yard like a faded piece of grey fabric.

Dong-ju looked at me. 'It's been three days. I haven't seen the blue kite that usually flies up around this time.'

'Well, I'm sure someone flew that kite out of curiosity,' I said. 'He had fun cutting your line, but when we banned kite-flying, he got bored and left.'

'That girl didn't fly the kite just to cut my line. The way she flew the kite — it was delicate. Sophisticated.' He explained that it had been like a waltz. The girl gently tugged at his line like a shy girl at her first ball. He would lead her kite, like a young man wrapping an arm around her waist. They had performed a beautiful dance in the sky. He could sense her careful consideration through her line.

'Why would she do that?' I asked.

'Maybe she was lonely,' he said. 'She would often put the weight of her kite on my line, as if she were a puppy cavorting on her master's lap. Her purpose wasn't to boast how well she could fly, but to lean against someone.'

I didn't know what he was talking about. How could anyone show their feelings through kite lines?

Dong-ju looked up at the sky beyond the walls, searching for the blue kite again.

'She probably lost interest in flying it,' I said.

He looked at me hopefully, but quickly grew dispirited. It was then that I finally understood what he was concerned about. Three days before there had been terrible bombings.

Dong-ju told me that he'd stood in the middle of his cell, listening to the explosions. The Korean prisoners had loved it; they'd prayed for the B-29s to turn the city into a fire pit, even if it meant that they, too, would be swept away by the carnage. He rounded his shoulders. 'I just want to make sure that she's alive. I wish I could fly a kite . . . If I could fly mine, I know she'd definitely fly hers . . .'

'Kite-flying has been banned,' I said, feeling suddenly anxious in the face of his despair. 'I'm sure there's another way to confirm that she's safe.' I hoped he wouldn't press me. The siren blared from the speakers on the roof, signalling the end of break; Dong-ju jumped up and went back to his cart.

The next day, after rehearsal, I cautiously brought up the matter with Midori. I asked if she could find out about a young girl who flew a kite near the prison, even though I didn't know her name or what she looked like. Midori didn't answer. Instead she placed her hands on the keys. I shouldn't have asked; it was presumptuous of me. Two days later, I saw Midori again, and light returned to my life. We walked side-by-side on the frozen snow, our shoes crunching. I stole a look at her delicate profile, feeling anxious.

'I know where she lives,' Midori said. 'Her house is on the outskirts of the city, closer to Fukuoka than Hakata Bay, in a neighbourhood with about twenty shanties clustered together.'

'How do you know that?'

'I've gone to her house before. On behalf of Sugiyama-*san*.'

'What happened to her? According to the paper, the road linking Hakata Port to downtown Fukuoka suffered the most damage.'

'The bombs dropped along the road and destroyed the neighbourhood. I could still smell gunpowder in the air.

Because it's a poor neighbourhood that's out of the way, they didn't have any bomb shelters.'

My blood chilled. It would have been better if I hadn't found out.

She continued, her voice cracking. 'I managed to find her mother in a temporary ward at Fukuoka City Hospital. A beam fell from the roof and broke her leg.'

'And the girl?' I almost couldn't bear to ask.

'Thankfully, she left Fukuoka before the attack. Following the government's recommendation for evacuation, she was sent to her grandmother's house in the countryside. It's a farming town an hour away from here, so they wouldn't have been bombed.'

My body surged with relief, as though a furnace had been lit inside. All I needed was for the girl to be alive. It didn't matter where she was.

Midori handed me a white bundle and nodded for me to open it. Inside was a battered, yellowed paper kite. The rounded stake in the middle was broken.

'Her mother was asleep when she woke to the sound of bombs exploding,' Midori continued. 'She was running down the stairs when it occurred to her that she should take her daughter's cherished kite. When the girl left for her grandmother's house she took all the kites she'd won in battles, but she'd left this one hanging on the wall in the attic, telling her mother to look at it whenever she missed her. There was an explosion, and her mother lost consciousness. She was found clutching this kite to her chest.'

Midori told me that this had been the first kite the girl had won, and that her mother had told her that flying the kite had been her lonely daughter's sole source of happiness.

In my mind's eye, I saw a girl carefully working on her

blue kite, grinding bits of china to embed onto her line, in the afternoons when she was left home alone. While the other children rushed to the hill near the shore to catch the marine wind, the girl headed to the empty lot near the prison. There, nobody teased her and no bully entwined his thick line with hers. One day, from within the high prison walls, a kite flew up. With it came faint shouts from the other side of the walls, cheering her on. The girl approached the white kite, danced with it and circled the air. She eventually cut the white kite's weak cotton line and watched as it spiralled to the ground. She hung her first prize on her wall.

Dong-ju's reclaimed kite smelled faintly of ash and gunpowder. The shaft had broken and the bottom was torn. I flipped the kite over and saw traces of black ink. I could decipher a familiar, careful hand:

To the best kite-fighter in Fukuoka,

Congratulations! Today, you won.

If you're reading this, you clipped our kite. We tried our best, but we couldn't beat your power and speed. Or your surprising talent. Since you won, you can take this as your prize. But we'll make a new kite. Tomorrow we'll stand off again. Maybe tomorrow we'll be able to take your kite. Or maybe the next day.

After the winter is over and kite-flying season ends, I'm sure your room will be filled with our kites. Keep them safe. They're proof that you're the best kite-fighter in all of Fukuoka.

Who would have known that gentleness was hiding behind Sugiyama's hard, metallic voice? I wondered how he'd been with those he loved, like the woman he tuned the piano for.

Did he listen with all of his being as she played clumsy jazz? Did he drink coffee with her? Did he dream of having soft, peachy babies with her? Could he have been a good husband? A wonderful father? Who had killed him in the end?

I raised my head, realizing that I hadn't asked the most crucial question. 'How did you even know all of this was going on?'

'When the poet gave up writing poems, Sugiyama-*san* came to me for help. Tuning the piano was only an excuse.'

The golden sunset outside the windows pooled on the piano's shiny black surface. Midori looked down at Sugiyama's rough hands, at the knife wounds and the twisted knuckles. She wondered if his hands remembered their victims, then decided that they wouldn't; they couldn't produce such beautiful sounds with such brutal memories.

Sugiyama asked her to play something. She began the opening bar of 'Carry Me Back to Old Virginny'. He closed his eyes, frowning and smiling, revelling in the colour and vibration of each lingering note. He opened his eyes only after the last note disappeared completely. His rough hands came together to clap. 'Much better. Almost moving.'

The sunset drew red shadows over Midori's face. 'The sound?'

'No, not the sound – the playing. Your playing has become so natural.' Thick veins bulged in his neck.

To Midori, he seemed angry, but actually Sugiyama was embarrassed. He was ignorant of most emotions. The world had never been gentle to him and he didn't expect kind treatment; he had wrapped himself in the armour of fury.

When he hated something he got mad. He expressed his love and embarrassment in anger, shouted to express sympathy and was brusque when he was showing interest. He was most comfortable with silence.

He placed a hand on the piano and swallowed. 'I have a favour to ask. I have to find someone outside the prison . . .' He trailed off. As a soldier he had to maintain barracks life, but a nurse was free to come and go as she pleased.

She widened her eyes and looked round. 'Who?'

Sugiyama couldn't bring himself to speak for a long time. Then he spoke hesitantly. 'I don't know whether it's a man or woman, or their age or address. Or what they look like. But I know they must live somewhere around here. Every Tuesday someone flies a kite outside the prison walls. Might be young. Supposedly thirteen or fourteen, and lonely.'

'Who told you that?'

'Hiranuma Tochu. I mean, Yun Dong-ju. You must know him?'

Midori's eyes flickered in fright. She not only knew Dong-ju, having met him in the infirmary, but she'd grown to know about his poems and his favourite music. She respected him. She had included 'Va, pensiero' in the concert at his suggestion. She hesitated. 'Has he – done something wrong?'

Sugiyama shook his head. The more he got to know Dong-ju, the more he was convinced that the prisoner had done nothing wrong. He looked down at his thick, calloused hands. 'He hasn't written a single line since he got back from solitary. Makes sense. Solitary destroys your body and soul. And while he was in solitary the child flying the kite disappeared.'

'What do you want me to do?'

'Tell her to fly her kite again. Tell her she'll be able to fight us if she flies it right outside the prison.' He looked out of the window at the golden sunset that was listening in on their clandestine conversation.

'And a few days later the girl's kite flew up. This must be the one she cut down that time.' Midori touched the mangled kite, whose broken shaft and ripped tail contained beautiful memories of soaring in the sky against the wind.

'So now we won't be able to see the kite again.'

'When the war's over and the girl returns, the kites will fly again.'

'It was smart of Sugiyama to bring her back into kite-fighting. It enabled him to control the prisoners effectively.'

'Sugiyama-*san* didn't bring her in for that,' Midori shot back. 'What he sent over the walls weren't kites. They were poems.'

A stray cat came up to the window. I could hear its footsteps crunching on the snow. 'What do you mean?'

She explained Sugiyama's ruse. He'd had Dong-ju write poems and fly kites; he brought the girl into the fight as part of an intricate plan to smuggle Dong-ju's poems out of the prison. 'Sugiyama-*san* had a deal with Dong-ju. He would allow Dong-ju to write poems in Korean if he recited them in Japanese. Sugiyama-*san* became his audience. When Dong-ju recited his new poem in Japanese, Sugiyama would write it down and then use that paper to make a kite. Dong-ju didn't know that. But his kites would often fall outside the prison, releasing his poems into the world.'

All winter Dong-ju read his poems out loud in the interrogation room and Sugiyama wrote them down as though
he were taking down a confession. The poems Dong-ju
recited were dark but glorious, steeped in sorrow but brim-
ming with joy – they sang of a wanderer's thoughts as he
walked down a dark snow-covered road, a man suffering
in a strong tempest, a young scholar betrayed by the times.
His poetry illuminated the darkness briefly, line by line.
Sugiyama copied it all down. He was the first to hear the
young poet's new work, poems that had formed in Dong-
ju's head over weeks or months, poems previously unknown
to the world.

The poems flew up like doves on the belly of Sugiyama's
kites. They leaped over the walls with the breeze. The kite
danced and circled in the blue sky in tandem with the girl's
kite waiting on the outside. The prison's feeble kite, cut by
the girl's glass-studded line, tilted in the wind and sank.
The girl chased after the kite as it took off sluggishly over
the fields. Often the kites disappeared from the girl's sight
and became stuck inside a thorny bush, fell in mud or
ended up in a narrow, dirty alley. The girl looked all over
for the missing kites until, late in the evening, she found
them impaled on an electric pole in the harbour or torn
and wet on the sandy beach. She discovered clumsily
written poems on the back of the creased kites and, upon
returning home, hid them deep in her cupboard.

# OUR LOVE WAS MERELY A MUTE

Dong-ju often entered the interrogation room looking grey and pallid, as though he had been doused in ash. But he regained his vitality as I began to question him. He talked about things that didn't exist but could be perceived, that couldn't be seen but could be inferred, that vanished from earth but remained in memory, that he couldn't possess but longed for. We sat facing each other. We talked not as a guard and prisoner, but as equals. We discussed writers and their tales, conversed about poets and novelists, philosophers and artists.

But the very fact that we were in this interrogation room enraged me. 'Poetry?' I spat out once. 'Hope? It's ridiculous. We're in a barren prison.'

'We're waiting for spring, but maybe spring is already here,' Dong-ju insisted, ever optimistic. 'One realizes that spring has come and gone only when it's summer. There's happiness even behind these cold bars.'

'No,' I argued. 'There's nothing in this forsaken hell. There's no beauty or virtue or intellect in this place.'

'But we can look for it.'

'There's no point.'

'If we look and we can't find it, I guess we'll just have

to create hope and happiness and dreams and beautiful poetry. The poetry we both long for isn't on paper. Look around you! It's everywhere; in the narrow cells and behind the thick bars. Thanks to the thick steel that imprisons me, I can write even more heartfelt poems.'

I hoped that was true.

'After I came here, I gave up on poetry for a while,' Dong-ju confessed.

'How were you able to write again?'

'Sugiyama – I had Sugiyama,' Dong-ju said, looking pained. 'Without him, I wouldn't have been able to write again.' He suddenly looked very old.

I wanted to lighten the mood. 'I have a question about your poem "The Blowing Wind". You say, "I haven't loved a single woman." Are you saying you've never loved anyone?' Although I'd read many of Dong-ju's poems, I hadn't come across a single poem about love. Had he truly never loved anyone? There had to have been a happy period in his life, when he'd been able to laugh, sing and love.

'Everyone has secrets,' he answered obliquely. He frowned, gave me an embarrassed smile and began to recite a poem. '"The Temple of Love." Suni, when did you come into my temple? / When did I enter yours? / Ours is / A temple of love steeped in old customs. / Suni, lower your crystal eyes like a doe. / I will groom my tousled hair like a lion. / Our love was merely a mute. / Ah, youth! / Before the weak flame on the holy candlestick extinguishes / Suni, run towards the front door. / Before darkness and wind slam into our window / I will carry my eternal love for you / And disappear through the back door. Now / You have a cosy lake in the woods, / And I have steep mountains.'

I stopped transcribing the poem and laid down the pencil stub. 'Is it still love if you can't say "I love you"?'

I thought of Midori. In front of her I was a mute. She didn't know of the passionate feelings roiling in my heart. Or maybe she knew, but pretended not to.

Dong-ju's voice broke me out of my reverie. 'No, that's still love. It may even be deeper love than the one you can talk about.'

I quickly changed the subject. 'Suni – do you know where she is now?'

He smiled bitterly and shook his head.

For a moment I was worried that I had brought back unpleasant memories. But I realized that there was no such thing as a bad memory. All memories are precious, and even a painful one is formative. That meant that my time at Fukuoka would also become a formative part of me. When time passed, would I think of Midori in the way Dong-ju was now thinking of his girl?

He recited two more poems: 'Boy' and 'Snowing Map'. 'Boy' depicted a boy's passionate love for the beautiful Suni, and 'Snowing Map' drew a boy's pain as he said farewell to his beloved Suni one winter morning. All three poems traced the tale of meeting a girl, falling in love and parting. Did Dong-ju really love a girl named Suni? Was she real? I couldn't ask. I was afraid Dong-ju wouldn't remember. I didn't want to confirm that his memories were rusting, crumbling, vanishing.

He looked famished, not from his physical starvation, but from a deeper hunger in his soul. 'Can I read *The Notebooks of Malte Laurids Brigge* just once?' His voice broke.

I understood. Some books had the power to heal illness and provide the essence of life. I had experienced that myself when I took comfort in the bookcases in our bookshop. Would *The Notebooks of Malte Laurids Brigge* make Dong-ju stronger and help him recover his memories?

I ran to the inspection office and retrieved the book from his box. The yellowed pages were so faded that they might crumble at a mere touch. I returned to the interrogation room and placed the old book on the desk. With a trembling hand Dong-ju caressed the old cover, as if it were the face of a woman he'd once loved. He turned the pages slowly and stopped. I stole a glance at the page he was reading:

I think I should begin to work on something, now that I am learning to see. I am twenty-eight, and just about nothing has happened. Let's summarize: I have written a study of Carpaccio, which is bad, a drama called *Marriage* that tries to prove something false by ambiguous means, and poems. But alas, with poems one accomplishes so little when one writes them early. One should hold off and gather sense and sweetness a whole life long, a long life if possible, and then, right at the end, one could perhaps write ten lines that are good. For poems are not, as people think, feelings (those one has early enough) — they are experiences. For the sake of a line of poetry one must see many cities, people and things, one must know animals, must feel how the birds fly, and know the gestures with which small flowers open in the morning. One must be able to think back to paths in unknown regions, to unexpected meetings and to partings one long saw coming; to childhood days that are still not understood, to parents one had to hurt when they brought one a joy and one did not understand it (it was a joy to someone else); to childhood illnesses that set in so strangely with so many profound and heavy transformations, to days in quiet, muted rooms and to mornings by the sea, the sea altogether, to nights travelling that rushed up and away and flew with all the stars; and if one can think of all that, it is still not enough. One must have memories of many nights of love, none of which resembled another, of screams in the delivery room and of easy, pale, sleeping women delivered, who are closing themselves. But one must also have been with the dying, have sat by the dead in the room with the open window and the spasmodic noises. But it is still not enough to have memories. One must be able to forget them, if they are many, and have the great patience to wait for them to come again. For it is not the memories themselves. Only when they become blood in us, glance and gesture, nameless and no longer to be distinguished from ourselves, only then can it happen that in a very rare hour the first word of a line arises in their midst and strides out of them.

Rilke's sentences brimmed with passion. I knew that the same poetic passion thrummed within Dong-ju. Perhaps he understood this book intuitively because he was now close to Rilke's age when he wrote it. I hoped I, too, would be able to comprehend it in that way at twenty-six.

Dong-ju stroked the page. And that was when it happened. The book might not be able to recognize me, but I recognized the book. I snatched it out of Dong-ju's hands and hurriedly flipped through the pages. When I found what I was looking for, I felt as though I would faint. A barely visible line was drawn under a sentence I had read a long time ago:

At first he did not want to believe that a long life could be spent forming the first, short, false sentences that are without meaning.

One long-ago autumn day, crouched in the corner of our dust-filled bookshop, I was caught by a raging fervour for literature that I had not been able to shake off. That night, as we walked home, my mother had told me about a young Korean man who'd asked her to reserve for him a copy of *The Notebooks of Malte Laurids Brigge* if it came in. Thinking about the copy I had hidden deep in the bookshelves, I felt a small pang of guilt and a slight relief. After I enlisted in the military, my mother, finding that copy, would have remembered the Korean student. And she would have handed him the book that carried her son's fingerprints. This old book linked us. It was an implausible coincidence; we loved the same poet and the exact same book, almost as though we were in love with the same girl.

Dong-ju pushed it towards me. 'You can have it.'

I turned the pages one by one. This book had come to me from some stranger and stayed with the young poet before returning to me. Rilke's words had wandered through the world, embracing and healing damaged spirits. That night, the world became a little more beautiful.

Dong-ju's memories were fleeting. He murmured to himself in Korean as we walked towards the interrogation room. He was trying his hardest to cling to the words that were attempting to desert him. Snow fell silently outside.

'Can I rest for a while?' he asked.

'Certainly,' I said.

He looked into his reflection in the window. 'The snow blankets everything in white.' He started walking slowly again, murmuring in Korean.

The heavy chain dragged along, pressing down on my soul. Dong-ju accidentally took the wrong corridor. Had he forgotten this familiar route? At our destination I had to grab his shoulder to stop him; he would have continued to walk past the interrogation room. The room was freezing. It didn't seem to bother him, though; he opened his mouth as soon as he sat down, perhaps fearing that the words in his head might die there and vanish without a trace.

'"Another Morning at the Beginning of the World." The snow blankets everything in white / And the telephone pole weeps / conveying God's words. / What revelation is forthcoming? / When spring comes / Quickly / I sin / And eyes / Are bright. / After Eve finishes the hard work of delivering a baby / She will hide her nakedness with a fig leaf and / I will have to sweat, beading on my forehead.'

I was struck dumb – original sin was reflected against a pure sense of self and a bleak situation. I could feel Dong-ju's powerful will for life, the will to construct his own reality. His emotive poem drew out deep feelings within me; perhaps the more so because he recited the words in a calm, low voice. I put down the pen and lobbed my nightly questions at him. 'What's your name?' 'Where is your home town?' 'What's the date today?' 'When will you be released?' 'What words can you think of now?' I didn't ask for his prisoner number or his Japanese name and I didn't make him recite the multiplication tables again. Those questions polluted and ruined his memories. He deserved to recall happier times.

'In the winter, white snow covered the village, and the deer and boars came as if they were guests, looking for food. The children flew kites that filled the sky, and the adults hunted falcons. I lived in a large, traditional tile roof house near the school. We had a plum tree in our yard, an orchard of apricot trees in the back, and a large mulberry tree and a deep well outside the east gate. Oh, the mulberries were so sweet! I would shout into the well to hear the echo and raise my head, and see the sunlight on the far-away cross atop the church belfry. I took long walks, crossing the stream into the forest, climbing the hill towards the village, on paths that were lined with dandelions, where magpies flew overhead, where I passed young ladies, feeling the breeze . . .' His eyes were dreamy.

I remained quiet, unwilling to break his reverie. Memory had to be like a muscle: the more it was used, the stronger it must become.

He struggled to raise his eyes to meet mine. 'Yuichi — Watanabe Yuichi!' he called out.

'Yes?'

He smiled. I realized he'd just wanted to utter my name before it, too, disappeared, before he ceased to recognize me. He was fighting a fierce battle in a war he would end up losing. He recited Shakespeare and Tolstoy and Rilke and Jammes constantly. He began talking ceaselessly, about his home town, his school days, literature, music and artists. Before, I used to ask him questions and he would answer, but now he talked and I listened. Watching him desperately cling to the last of his memory sent pangs through my heart. Since he no longer trusted his own mind, he was trying to move his memories into mine. 'Have you seen Van Gogh's paintings? *Starry Night* or *Cafe Terrace at Night*?' he suddenly asked.

I had seen pictures of those paintings; I'd cherished a book of Van Gogh paintings in colour that we had at the bookshop. 'Van Gogh was the artist of stars,' Dong-ju said. 'He loved stars and loved painting them. He wrote to his brother Theo about them, too. Listen to this.' He took a few shallow breaths. '"But the sight of the stars always makes me dream *in as simple a way* as the black spots on the map, representing towns and villages, make me dream. Why, I say to myself, should the spots of light in the firmament be less accessible to us than the black spots on the map of France? Just as we take the train to go to Tarascon or Rouen, we take death to go to a star. What's certainly true in this argument is that while *alive,* we *cannot* go to a star, any more than once dead we'd be able to take the train . . . To die peacefully of old age would be to go there on foot."' He looked anxious.

I knew he was having difficulty sleeping; his insomnia made him more agitated. I led him to the underground library, hoping it would lift his mood.

Dong-ju looked around the dimly lit space. 'I'd hoped you wouldn't find out about this. It's too dangerous.'

'But I did,' I said, my voice crackling with fear. 'I don't know what to do. If anyone finds out, none of us will be safe.' I regretted not running to Maeda the minute I'd discovered that dank underground space. It was too late, though, and now I could only live with the anxiety. Dong-ju grabbed my shoulders. 'Even if it's discovered at some point, you don't know anything about it.'

'You're not going to implicate me?'

'Even if I wanted to tell everyone, I won't remember. Soon enough I won't even remember this moment.' He smiled bitterly and traced a finger down the spine of each book, as though to engrave the title forever in his head. 'Soon these titles will vanish from my mind. As though I'd never heard of them. At some point you'll have to tell me that I once read such beautiful books.' His breath, visible in the cold, drifted around his pale face.

Each time he let out a breath, it was as though his soul were escaping.

Dong-ju recited another poem from memory. '"Hospital." Shielding her face with the shadow of the apricot tree, lying in the back yard of the hospital, a young woman reveals her pale legs under her white gown and sunbathes. Not even a butterfly visits this woman suffering from tuberculosis. There is not a breeze against the not-unhappy tree. // I came to this place for the first time after suffering for a long time from an unknown pain. But my old doctor does not know the illness of my young self. He says I am not ill. This excessive hardship, this excessive fatigue; I must not become cross. // The woman gets up and straightens her clothes and picks a marigold from the garden to place on her breast and disappears into the hospital. I wish for her health – as well as mine – to recover quickly; I lie down where she lay.'

'You'll be fine,' I said, more to reassure myself. 'The doctors said your side-effects will disappear. You'll leave this place on 30 November and write poems and publish books. After the war, when the world becomes a better place, countless people will read your poems.'

'That'd be nice,' he said, smiling faintly; he, too, must have been hoping for a happy ending.

Secretly, I was afraid that I already knew this story would end differently.

# THE NAMES OF IMPOVERISHED NEIGHBOURS AND FRANCIS JAMMES, RAINER MARIA RILKE . . .

The New Year brought nothing new. The winter deepened; there was no sign of spring. Something had tipped; the war wasn't going as well and Japan was starting to lose. Nobody said it out loud, but everyone could tell. Citizens sank into torpor and anxiety infected everyone with lightning speed. An angry voice on the radio promoted a final battle to defend Japan; flyers were plastered all over the city, urging us to defend our country with our lives. I wasn't convinced that victory would bring us anything other than more death and shattered consciences.

The prison was no longer a safe zone. In the middle of the night an immense shadow covered the city. Explosions overshadowed screams, blanketing everything in silence in their aftermath. The streets were engulfed in a sea of fire and later settled into ruin. Everything – love, belief, hope, dreams – burned. That January twenty metres of the northern prison wall collapsed under heavy bombing. Ensuing attacks cratered the yard, and two poplar trees on the hill were burned to a crisp. When the loud siren blared, the frightened guards dashed into bomb shelters; sometimes, the enemy planes flew in ahead of the warnings.

Everything hung on the abilities of the nation's air defence. Warden Hasegawa ordered a review of the prison's facilities; the newer Wards Four, Five, Six and the infirmary were fine. Stairways in the corridors led directly to the solid underground bomb shelters. The problem was the old central facilities, which didn't have an underground shelter. Fearing retaliation after Pearl Harbor, the warden had tried to build one, but it had been determined that digging under the building would risk collapse. As a last resort, a bomb shelter was built outside, about thirty metres away, but it was too far to run to when sneak attacks were launched.

One early morning I finished my shift and left my office, rubbing my eyes. A group of guards pushed past me, heading down the corridor. I wondered what was going on; the inspection ward was usually deserted. Cold sweat pricked my spine as I watched the guards enter the library. Would they discover our secret? I sprinted after them, the sound of my footsteps whipping my back. I reached the door to the library, which had been flung wide open. The guards were talking among themselves in the doorway; they looked at me oddly and let me by. I stepped inside, willing my trembling legs not to buckle.

The desks and bookshelves that lined the wall were gone. The floor had been ripped out. The darkness below spread open its maw, with a faint trickle of light shining out. I slowly approached the opening and went down the narrow stairs. At the bottom I involuntarily closed my eyes. All the shelves had been smashed; the books had been flung onto the floor.

Maeda, his expression deadly serious, was down there,

surrounded by guards. He grabbed a black book. 'These Korean arseholes dug their way into the heart of the prison,' he spat out. 'As if this is their playground!'

I looked around, shell-shocked.

'Take everything out of this rat hole and put it in the yard!' he shouted. 'It's going up in flames! In front of all of them! Find out who did this!'

I froze.

Maeda whacked his thigh with his club in anger as he went up the stairs. The others began to gather the torn books and haul them upstairs. I picked some up, too. *Gulliver's Travels*, *Great Expectations*, *Sonnets of Shakespeare*, *Poetry of Jeong Ji-yong*. I couldn't believe that these beautiful stories would soon be destroyed in the flames.

A senior guard followed me up. 'I guess we need to thank the damn Yankees. If it weren't for the bombings, this rat hole would never have been discovered.'

I must have looked puzzled.

'Maeda examined dozens of blueprints from when the central facilities were constructed,' he explained. 'So that we could build a bomb shelter under this building. That's how he discovered this basement. It used to be an interrogation room. Since this space already existed, we could save time and money. We could just expand and fortify the space, instead of digging somewhere new. So we came down here to see where the non-load-bearing walls and beams stood. And then we found this shit!'

My heart rattled like a worn-out cart. What if Maeda discovered my involvement? I thought of my mother, and my eyes clouded over in sorrow and fear.

The senior guard spat in disgust. 'The Japanese handwriting is clearly Sugiyama's. Can you believe he was in cahoots with those Koreans? He should have known better. But that's what happens when you get mixed up with them. You get yourself killed.'

So I wasn't a suspect. I was safe. I wiped my eyes furtively. 'Why would a Korean kill Sugiyama, if he helped them?'

'They're like that. They pay back a favour with revenge. Or maybe he tried to reveal their secret.'

Just then a loud siren screamed, signalling prisoners from Ward Three to assemble in the military training ground. The prisoners lined up, trembling from cold and fear, avoiding the guards' vindictive gazes.

'We have granted excessive special privileges to you seditious, delinquent Korean prisoners!' Maeda boomed. 'But you abused our goodwill. This morning we exposed yet another plot. Now you'll watch what happens.'

A guard wheeled a cart to the front of the platform. Another cart came out, and yet another; the pile of books grew. A senior guard poured a steel can of petrol on the pile. I stood to attention nearby, nearly overwhelmed by the noxious fumes.

'Watanabe! Incinerate!' Maeda's voice was chilling.

My heart flipped. Perhaps he wouldn't notice my anxiety. I knew I had to demonstrate how deeply I despised these banned volumes. I flicked the lighter and its blue light danced. Maeda's eyes glinted coldly. I picked up a book with a trembling hand; it smelled of oil and the pages were practically transparent.

I remembered a passage from *Crime and Punishment*:

'Where is it,' thought Raskolnikov. 'Where is it I've read that someone condemned to death says or thinks, an hour before his death, that if he had to live on some high rock, on such a narrow ledge that he'd only room to stand, and the ocean, everlasting darkness, everlasting solitude, everlasting tempest around him, if he had to remain standing on a square yard of space all his life, a thousand years, eternity, it were better to live so than to die at once! Only to live, to live and live! Life, whatever it may be! . . . How true it is! Good God, how true!

I could never write something that examined life with such deep, thought-provoking insight. But as I read that passage, I'd become convinced that I was in conversation with Dostoyevsky. We existed in different eras and places, but we dreamed the same dreams and understood the same truth. At this moment, the very moment I was forced to burn his masterpiece, I was seeing the clearest vision of his soul.

The prisoners watched the spark at my fingertips. I spotted a pair of clear, deep eyes amongst the blank gazes; Dong-ju's face lit up when our eyes met. I wanted to think that he was telling me, 'Yuichi, light it. The books won't die.' Just then my grip loosened and the lighter slipped. The oil-soaked paper sucked in the flame and burst into an immense column of fire. Planks crackled, the wind fanned the flames, and black smoke rose, heat pushing against our faces.

'Watch carefully!' Maeda shouted as he became enveloped by smoke. 'This is what happens when you betray the Empire!'

The prisoners inched closer to the blazing fire, lifting their frozen feet surreptitiously to warm them. Dong-ju watched the fire blankly, as though he didn't have the energy to be sad or enraged. Perhaps this was the best outcome; everyone could chase away the cold for a moment while the books burned. But after they were rendered into ash, the last spark died and the remnants fluttered away with the wind blowing along the blackened ground, what would be left to give comfort to these barren souls?

We assembled in the warden's office. Hasegawa was looking out through the gauzy curtains. 'It's loud out there,' he said, sounding placid and annoyed at the same time.

'The Koreans instigated an incident involving banned books,' Maeda said pompously. 'Fortuitously I discovered their plot and destroyed it before they could do much damage. Even better, the important task of building a bomb shelter under this building can proceed.'

Next I gave a short report, as the crime had happened in my territory.

Hasegawa puffed on his pipe. 'Good. Find out who did this. Punish them as a warning to the others. The shelter must be completed as soon as possible!'

Maeda had already ordered a senior guard to ferret out the leader of the plot and his co-conspirators by beating all the literate Koreans. 'We'll find out who did it and hang 'em,' he said confidently.

The warden took his pipe and tapped it against the ashtray. 'There's no point. All Koreans are the same. Everyone's the leader and everyone's a co-conspirator. They're all pigs. A pig is a pig, no one any better-looking or uglier than any other.'

Maeda licked his lips. 'You're right, sir, they're pigs. I'll bring in a few who are responsible, and we won't have any more problems.' His eyes gleamed expectantly as he waited for the warden's consent.

The warden sucked loudly on his empty pipe. 'There's

no point, anyway. The bomb shelter is strictly for us. Those vermin won't be able to survive the Yankees' attacks now.'

That night, in the interrogation room, Dong-ju and I stared at each other across the desk. I could tell he wanted to revisit what had happened during the day, but we were too tired.

After a long silence Dong-ju asked, 'Can you take me to the underground library?'

'There is no point,' I cried, springing up from my chair. 'The books were burned. They're all gone.'

Dong-ju stood up slowly. 'It doesn't matter. The books may have been destroyed, but their essence still remains. Their voices are still there.'

'It's all over! I burned them with this very hand!' I began to tremble as emotion took hold of me. Everything poured out of me – regret, guilt, powerlessness and the emptiness of losing everything.

'It's not your fault, Yuichi.' Dong-ju patted my back. 'Yuichi, you can't blame yourself. We all have to survive. We have to survive so that we can see the end of this war. Remember, surviving is winning. A corpse cannot cheer.'

'But I can't survive unless I become evil.'

'If these times make us evil, fine, let's become evil. But let's keep a human heart. Like Sugiyama.'

'I can't bear to see what I ruined.'

'You burned only paper. You didn't ruin anything. The words are more vivid than ever.'

I wiped my eyes with the sleeve of my uniform. I didn't know what he was talking about. He helped me up this time, and I followed his clanking shackles. We went down the stairs through the gaping hole in the ground. I lifted my lamp. The room was empty, but still fragrant with the smell of paper. Dong-ju paced, dragging his shackles. He stopped and picked up a page from a book. Somehow it had been spared. He held it gingerly, as though he were cradling a bird with an injured wing. '*The Sorrows of Young Werther.*'

My heart began to pound. Young Werther's story began on 4 May 1771 – *How happy I am that I am gone! My dear friend, what a thing is the heart of man!* – and ended with a letter he sent to Charlotte on 22 December: *They are loaded – the clock strikes twelve. I say amen. Charlotte, Charlotte! farewell, farewell!*

There is a melody which she plays on the piano with angelic skill – so simple is it, and yet so spiritual! It is her favourite air; and, when she plays the first note, all pain, care and sorrow disappear from me in a moment.

I believe every word that is said of the magic of ancient music. How her simple song enchants me! Sometimes, when I am ready to commit suicide, she sings that air; and instantly the gloom and madness which hung over me are dispersed, and I breathe freely again.

When I'd read it before, these lines hadn't meant a thing to me. But now I understood Werther; we were the same. Werther thought of his beloved Charlotte playing the piano, just as I listened to Midori.

Dong-ju reread those lines a couple of times, before carefully folding the piece of paper and placing it in his pocket. 'There are so many books I want to read. It worries me that I'm getting slower. Even a few pages into a story, I can't remember what preceded it. I can't seem to make a connection. I don't quite remember the meaning of some words, and I can't decipher long sentences. Words and phrases get mixed up and plots get tangled.'

'That's normal,' I said, trying to brush aside his worries. 'I sometimes think that Tolstoy wrote *The Brothers Karamazov* and André Gide wrote *The Red and the Black*. A man's memory isn't perfect. We have the ability to remember, but also an ability to forget.'

Dong-ju looked around. Perhaps he was thinking about his own incinerated poems, pieces of him that perished without ever having touched another being. 'Once, Sugiyama asked me why Koreans talked so much. He wanted to know what we talked about during our breaks.'

I'd always wondered about that, too.

Dong-ju glanced at me. 'They talk about Jean Valjean, Jammes, Shakespeare.'

I must have misheard him. Was it possible? 'How? Most of them don't even know how to read.'

'The men who went to solitary were literate, but they weren't reading just for themselves. In one week they would memorize as much of a book as possible. They'd go back to their cells and tell their friends what they'd memorized. And the men who heard the stories remembered them. A few pages or a chapter or a poem at a time.'

Dong-ju smiled.

'Cell 113 has Jammes's book of poetry, Cell 115 has *Les Misérables*, Cell 119 has *The Count of Monte Cristo*. Our breaks were the marketplace for tales. Men would take turns telling others what they remembered. The men who heard those stories would repeat them. They shared and gave each other hope this way.'

So books were still alive, having laid down roots in

someone's heart. They were living and breathing inside this brutal prison.

Ten prisoners were assigned to transform the underground library into a bomb shelter. They built reinforcing beams and laid thick planks against the walls. The space quadrupled in size in a mere three days, so that it could comfortably shelter the forty-odd guards working in the central facilities.

Air raids continued daily. Death became even more commonplace. When the siren went off, we ran down to the basement. I would crouch against the dirt wall, imagining what was happening above ground. But the prisoners who actually built the bomb shelter were not only unprotected; they weren't even told what to do in the air raids. They would hear everything – the propeller approaching in prelude to death, the wail of the siren, the explosions – without any means of escape. They could only pray that the bombs would fall elsewhere. Even as I waited out the bombings, I felt a deep shame; we'd left these men to die while we'd scurried into safety.

One day, while we were hunkered in the bomb shelter, we heard a loud explosion. The light bulb overhead flickered. Dirt rained down on us, but we all survived. We left the shelter, and my fellow guards were laughing and talking, thrilled to be alive, as though we were boys returning home after a game of hide-and-seek. I pushed through them and sprinted up to Ward Three, which had sustained minor damage. I found Dong-ju. He was alive, his head covered in white dust. His lips trembled when our eyes met.

# EXCESSIVE HARDSHIP,
# EXCESSIVE FATIGUE

Dong-ju dragged his feet as he made his way towards the chair. His white ankles showed under his threadbare trousers. He creaked when he moved, like a shuttered window. He placed his interlaced fingers on the table. His thumbnail had cracked from the cold. His deep-set eyes watched mine. I'd brought him to the interrogation room because I wanted to know more about Sugiyama. Dong-ju's memories were fading. I had to get all the information while I still could.

'You must know who killed Sugiyama,' I said bluntly.

'Yes. This terrible era. Everyone goes insane. Everyone's dying off.' He didn't sound like his usual self.

I didn't say anything.

'Being alive is the most beautiful thing,' Dong-ju said, regaining his customary optimism. 'Surviving this hell, Yuichi, means being cowardly. It's better than meeting a hero's death. You need to see this war through and witness the end of all the atrocities. Promise me that.'

'Do you think Sugiyama wore the mask of evil to survive?' I asked, changing the subject.He shook his head. 'No, no. He was evil. But he was ashamed of being that way, which was why he was so brutal.'

'What do you mean?'

Dong-ju glanced down at his hands, hesitating. 'He wasn't a war hero, you see. He was only a survivor. He hated himself for that.'

'What does that have to do with how violent he was?'

'He was punishing himself. He destroyed others, which ruined his soul. He closed his eyes to humanity and encouraged his own hatred and rage.'

That didn't make any sense. The person who deserved sympathy was the victim of torture, not its perpetrator. I'd known Sugiyama – he was unfeeling towards another man's pain. In fact, he seemed to enjoy it. 'Brutality is simply immoral. It's not a way to punish yourself,' I shot back. 'Your theory might make more sense if he harmed himself or committed suicide.'

Dong-ju mulled over my words before nodding agreement. 'That's right, but you should know that he was a very sensitive soul. He was wounded and broken.'

'And you're wrong, by the way,' I countered. 'He was a war hero. He was surrounded by a Soviet mechanized brigade with dozens of tanks. At night, he attacked the enemy base. He dodged shells for two weeks before returning to headquarters.'

'That's not true,' Dong-ju insisted. 'The Army Ministry fabricated that story. They made him a hero because they needed to hide the fact that they had been defeated. He wasn't a hero. He was a human being, just like the rest of us. He was someone who wanted to run away.'

'What are you saying? He was never surrounded by the Soviets?'

Dong-ju paused. 'Well . . .'

Actually, he had been surrounded. Sugiyama's search party of nine had broken off from the rest of the unit in search of a retreat route. That was when the Soviets attacked. Four of the party died on the spot and Sugiyama was captured. Later, he couldn't remember the details of the ten days of brutal torture he'd suffered. As evil ate away at his soul, he gradually turned evil, too. That was the only way to fight against it. As he had known only pain since birth, survival to him was winning; death was defeat, abandonment, shame.

The Soviets were insistent. They kept him dehydrated, then demanded that he tell them where his platoon was hiding out. When he refused, they taunted him, pouring iced water on the ground in front of him. He wouldn't break. They kept him awake for three days straight; soon he wasn't sure how many days had passed or even who he was. He fervently wished he could forget where the platoon was and its plans and signals, so that he wouldn't accidentally say something. He fainted, came to, fainted again. Everything smelled like blood. His consciousness eroded; he spat out smashed fragments of words, not realizing what he was saying.

When he opened his eyes, he smelled something fresh instead of blood. He thought he'd died. He figured he was in hell. But when he looked around, it was as though he'd gone to heaven. There was a cup of water and a bowl of watery gruel by his bed. He was in a Soviet field hospital.

He touched his legs. His knees were skinned and parts of his flesh were burned, but nothing was broken. He looked out through a gap between the tent flaps. A soldier was standing guard at each of the four large tents of the field hospital. He had to escape. There was still hope. Even if they knew where the platoon was, his comrades would have moved by now. If he followed the signs they left behind, he might be able to rejoin them. Sugiyama pulled a tent stake out of the ground. He considered stabbing the guard and stealing his gun, but changed his mind; his goal was to escape, not to kill. He stretched his weak legs and looked around. A thick forest of birch trees began about a hundred metres from the tent.

He counted to three, closed his eyes and dashed out, kicking one leg out before the other leg touched the ground. A bullet might shatter his spine at any moment. The breeze rushed at him and whistled past his ears. Soon it was quiet. It smelled of fallen leaves. He opened his eyes. He'd made it into the dark woods. The forest embraced him. He couldn't tell in which direction he was going; the thick branches slapped his face, the thin rays of light stabbed his eyes, roots grabbed his ankles and vines tangled his limbs. His tired legs trembled and he felt nauseated. Each time he was close to collapse, the thought of his platoon members kept him going. He walked all day and night, and another day and night until he arrived at the platoon's hiding spot. There was no sign of his friends. They had already moved on to their next location, as planned. Two days later, he'd almost caught up with them. He hoped he would be forgiven for revealing their location. If he were fated to die, he wanted to die with them. He had just one more hill to climb before he could be reunited with his brothers. He was crawling up the steep slope when he heard the long whistle of death: a shell flying overhead. The forest erupted into chaos, with explosions, gunshots and screams.

Sugiyama hauled himself over the hill, pulling himself up by rocks and roots. Sweat and dirt clung to his body.

When he got up to the top of the hill, he saw what had transpired. The Soviets had attacked his platoon. They'd been one step ahead of him. The trees were columns of fire. He practically rolled down the hill. The forest had burned to a crisp. The heat from the explosions warmed the bottom of his feet. He shouted the names of his friends. There was no answer. He was looking up at a far-away hill when a flash blinded him. He heard a gunshot that shattered the quiet and was knocked off-balance as though he had been clubbed. Hot blood trickled down from his shoulder. He laid his cheek against the ground, listening to the burning trees crackle; it sounded like music. He remembered the long, white fingers of the girl he once loved. This wasn't a bad way to go.

When he woke again, the forest was cold. He opened his heavy eyelids. He saw the gaiters that were part of the Japanese military uniform. They belonged to a search squadron of the Kwantung Army mobilized to rescue the isolated platoon. They were too late. They'd only found one dying soldier. Sugiyama's eyelids slid shut. He heard someone shouting, as though through a tunnel, 'A survivor! Let's evacuate!' He heard urgent footsteps; his body was hoisted up. He'd performed his duty; he'd survived. For the rest of his life he wondered if he should have died in that forest. For a long time he couldn't forget what he'd seen. In the meantime, a demon entered his soul and settled there.

I heaved a deep sigh. 'So you're saying Sugiyama was violent because he felt guilty. He was trying to atone for betraying his comrades.'

Dong-ju ran a hand through his bristly hair. 'He might not have thought about it that way, but yes, that's what happened.'

'That doesn't make any sense.'

'I believe he thought the torture he experienced caused everything that happened. If it weren't for the torture, he wouldn't have told them anything.'

'What does that have to do with how he treated the prisoners here?'

'Becoming evil might have been the only way for him to survive. Judas hanged himself after betraying Jesus,' Dong-ju said cryptically. 'But Sugiyama survived.'

I pondered Dong-ju's words. So every time Sugiyama felt guilty, he remembered being tortured, and then he thought about his dead friends. An awful memory bred another evil; it was an unbreakable chain. 'How could you possibly atone, if you keep doing bad things?'

'I think he had to see with his own eyes that man is powerless in the face of pain. He had to assure himself that nobody could stand up to cruel treatment.'

I was having a hard time wrapping my head around all of it. 'Did Sugiyama really tell the Soviets the location of his platoon?'

'Nobody knows. He didn't know. But he was still destroyed over it.' Dong-ju shook his head.

'I don't think Sugiyama talked,' I said quietly. 'He should have realized that the Soviets were tricking him. They would have let him escape precisely because he didn't talk. They must have followed him. And then, when he had led them there, they destroyed the platoon.'

'What makes you think so?'

'If he had told them, his platoon would have been killed

much sooner. Then he wouldn't have witnessed the attack. His remorseful conscience is what destroyed his soul.'

I still wasn't certain if Sugiyama had been a good man, and I still didn't know what to make of his death.

# THE CHORUS OF THE HEBREW SLAVES

It was February. Dong-ju's release date inched closer. But now he often forgot when he would be released.

Some time after Sugiyama's death, Dong-ju stopped writing letters for the prisoners. One day I pulled aside a friendly Korean prisoner who'd frequently sent out postcards, to ask him why they'd stopped.

He sighed. 'We need good news to send out a postcard. If it's bad news, it's better if our friends and family don't know.'

But then why had all those Koreans asked Dong-ju to write postcards for them in the first place?

'That man has a talent for writing the worst news in the most beautiful way. It could be so cold that it might kill you, and he would write: Thanks to the cold, I'm feeling invigorated. Even though there are so many of us crammed into our cells, he would write: Thanks to the tight quarters, we can survive the winter. He never lied. He just framed our truths in warm, kind words that reassured the reader. He helped us think about terrible things in a good way. That's why so many of us went to him. I wonder if he'll ever help us write postcards again.'

I didn't have an answer.

The war limped on. There was nothing to eat, nothing

to wear and nothing left over. People starved; fear suffocated them. But the prison was roiling with excitement. In a week there would be a concert; it was the biggest event in the history of the institution. Warden Hasegawa rushed about, from the auditorium to the yard to the administrative offices, while Maeda prepared to host high-level officials from Tokyo, the choristers focused on final rehearsals and Midori fine-tuned their voices. Some officials declined to come to Fukuoka amid the continuing air raids, but the Interior Minister and an army general would still be attending.

Dong-ju seemed revitalized as the concert approached. He knew it would be impossible to hear anything from his cell; it was too far from the auditorium. The noisy machinery in the work area would drown everything out.

Two days before the concert he came up with an idea. 'Yuichi,' he said, his eyes sparkling, 'I know how I can hear it.'

'How?'

'The concert's on Monday. I'll volunteer to receive medical treatment that day!'

The infusion room was on the same floor as the auditorium, so he might be able to hear something. But his plan was dangerous; he might only become weaker.

I shook my head firmly. 'Your medical treatment schedule is Tuesday and Friday. It can't be changed.'

'Yuichi! Please!'

I couldn't refuse him. His memories were slipping away like sand pouring through open fingers. He would do anything to fill his failing mind with music. The next day, after I escorted the choristers to the auditorium, I headed to the infusion room. I kept stopping in the long corridor, wondering whether to turn back. Finally I opened the door to the room and reported to the puzzled doctor that a prisoner wanted additional infusions. 'It appears that the medication is starting to work. The patient has recovered and he does not tire during labour.'

A look of disbelief flashed across the doctor's face. He excitedly asked for the prisoner number. Three numbers circled my head. It took me a while to spit out the numbers. '645.'

'Wonderful!' the doctor cried. 'Bring him here at two on Monday! We'll conduct a careful observation.'

I turned to leave. Had I finally become a murderer?

I woke up on the morning of the concert to a blanket of snow that had fallen silently overnight. The prison yard looked like a piece of white paper. As the sun rose, I escorted the singers across the yard to the auditorium. Inside, dozens of guards were scurrying about under Maeda's direction. The stage was carpeted in red. There were enough seats for 300. I lined up the choristers backstage and finished the head count. I looked at Midori. She led the final rehearsal, starting with simple individual vocalizations and organizing the men to then practise by voice part.

Some minutes past noon, a black car pulled up to the gates of the prison. Professor Marui, wearing a black tuxedo, got out. He immediately headed to the auditorium to inspect it. After the final stage check, he went into make-up. Black cars drove up to the main gates, spilling out men in tuxedos and dress uniforms and women in finery. They appeared uneasy about the unusual setting, but seemed oddly excited, too. Warden Hasegawa greeted each guest, smiling widely. Senior guards in well-ironed uniforms and nurses ushered the guests to the auditorium. The empty seats gradually filled. Then the concert began with everyone singing the 'Kimigayo'. The stage lights were turned off and the curtain rose. Professor Marui, wearing tails, walked into the spotlight.

A guard checked the shackles around Dong-ju's ankles before leading him out of the cell. They slowly proceeded towards the infirmary. The snow underfoot made angry grinding sounds and fluttered in the wind, but silenced the clanking of the shackles. As soon as they entered the infirmary building, Dong-ju could sense the expectation in the air. His footsteps became lively. A doctor greeted him with a smile in front of the infusion room and, as Dong-ju entered, he could hear a clear, sorrowful voice singing from far away:

> Am Brunnen vor dem Tore
> Da steht ein Lindenbaum:

Dong-ju closed his eyes.
The doctor spoke. 'Prisoner number!'
'645.'

> Ich träumt in seinem Schatten
> So manchen süßen Traum.

'Name?'
'Hiranuma Tochu.'

> Und seine Zweige rauschten,
> Als riefen sie mir zu:

'When will you be released?'
'30 November 1945. In 298 days.'

Applause broke the short silence. Professor Marui wiped away the sweat on his forehead. The applause continued. He bowed deeply and disappeared backstage. The unceasing applause brought him out again. Backstage, I closed my eyes.

The nurse attached the tube with skilful hands. The cold needle pricked Dong-ju's arm and clear liquid entered his body. The singing and applause swelled and receded like the tide. Then a long silence ensued.

Onstage, the prisoners dragged their heavy shackles to line up. The audience looked tense. Midori, in her white nurse's uniform, stepped onstage to a smattering of applause. She walked over to the piano and sat down. Blank eyes watched her. She drew in a deep breath and nodded, her fingers grazing the keys.

Dong-ju closed his eyes. His breathing was calm, but his mind was sluggish. It seemed as though he were submerged in deep water. He could hear the piano from far away. As the clear liquid slowly infused his bloodstream, the solemn, sad voices rushed into his ears:

> *Va, pensiero, sull'ali dorate;*
> *va, ti posa sui clivi, sui colli,*
> *ove olezzano tepide e molli*
> *l'aure dolci del suolo natal!*

*Del Giordano le rive saluta,*
*di Sionne le torri atterrate . . .*

Strong but sorrowful voices hurtled forward, shoving me aside. The sad beauty of the song made me wonder if I had the right to enjoy it. I was shaken awake by the joy for life. My heart heaved in turmoil; I was human, I was still alive.

*O, mia patria, sì bella e perduta!*
*O, membranza, sì cara e fatal!*

The song careened from tautness to softness, from speed to languidness, like a grand love-affair. The different notes and the varying timbres of each person's voice melded together, howling sorrowfully and pounding majestically like a rainstorm. Midori pushed, suppressed and urged the voices on. They blended with the piano, then exploded in bliss:

*Arpa d'or dei fatidici vati,*
*perché muta dal salice pendi?*
*Le memorie nel petto raccendi,*
*ci favella del tempo che fu!*
*O simile di Sòlima ai fati*
*traggi un suono di crudo lamento,*
*o t'ispiri il Signore un concento*
*che ne infonda al patire virtù.*

The song ended, but the final chord remained ringing in the cold air. The last note dissipated, leading to a short silence. Dong-ju's eyes were still closed as he held on to the lingering notes. The silence burst into thunderous applause and cheers. Dong-ju opened his eyes. His lashes were wet; he looked content, like a boy waking up from a happy dream. As the nurse pulled the needle out, the doctor exclaimed, 'Good. You look more alert than usual.'

The following day Warden Hasegawa summoned me. Had he discovered my role in the underground library? Had he found out about the girl flying the kite? Frozen stiff, I perched on the chair the warden offered me. He held several newspapers aloft. The large letters danced in front of my eyes. Fukuoka Prison. Concert. Moving. Beautiful. 'The concert was a huge success,' he said, overcome with emotion. 'Even the national press covered it! You contributed greatly by escorting the prisoners and watching over the rehearsals.' He put the papers down and twisted the ends of his moustache. 'By the way, you should know that Prisoner 331 was executed two days ago.'

Everything suddenly went dark.

'Good job. You have successfully completed the investigation and resolved the murder.'

Choi was dead? I hadn't even begun to figure out who the real killer was. I felt powerless. 'Did he have any final words?'

'No. He refused to say anything.'

'Was his family notified?'

'According to his file, he didn't have any family. So I had no choice but to oversee the execution and then the burial.'

I nodded slowly.

Hasegawa thumped my slumped shoulders and congratulated me on a task well done, telling me that, as a reward, he would grant me leave in the spring. None of what he said registered. I left the warden's office and walked mechanically down the long corridor of the administrative wing into the snow-covered yard. I felt that I was floating, as though the ground beneath my feet had collapsed. Choi's death wasn't an out-of-the-ordinary event at this prison, but I was racked with guilt. He shouldn't have died. He'd risked his life to get out of this prison; his endless escape attempts and the resulting stints in solitary were the two true pillars that had supported his life. He was brought close to death, and yet he'd survived each time. But he'd failed to leave Fukuoka, even as a corpse.

I headed to the cemetery. I spotted a new marker inscribed with his number. I'd strung the noose around his neck. While I was lost in a maze, searching for the truth, he'd died alone. There was nothing I could do.

Or maybe, just maybe, there was something – I could find the man who had really killed Sugiyama.

# WHAT IN THE WORLD HAPPENED?

Darkness fell over the frozen ground. The faint sounds of a piano could be heard outside the infirmary. The ivy snaking up the red-brick walls rustled in the wind. White frost nibbled at the edges of the clear window as warm light spilled into the darkness. Sitting at the piano, Midori was focused on the sheet music in front of her. She paused and turned round to look at me.

'I want to see the charts of the patients who received treatment in the infirmary,' I blurted out. 'You see patients from Ward Three. You must oversee those records.'

'I need a note from the head guard and to obtain permission from the head doctor.'

I paused. 'Those records would help me figure out how Sugiyama died.'

Her forehead furrowed.

'What do the charts have to do with the murder?' she asked.

'If I could see what he was involved in before he died, I'll be able to find clues. Who he injured, when and how.'

'The charts merely have simple entries about how the injury occurred and how it was treated. What could that possibly say about a murder?'

'Records are living documents. Just as your sheet music becomes beautiful music, charts might be able to tell me more about Sugiyama's life.'

Midori stared out the window for a long time. 'Come back here at my next practice session.' She turned back to the piano. Her beautiful music began once more.

Midori took out a black, hardcover file from in between her sheet music and handed it to me. As the sun set and left gold streaks across the keys, I started to read through the chart. From January to August, no Korean prisoner was treated. The mention of a Korean name was always followed by a note of the cause of death. Ward Three was lethal; at least three to four died every month. In January, a prisoner was sucked into the dye-baths and drowned, one fell to his death while repairing the ceiling and another died from a heart attack in his sleep. In February, two fell to their deaths, another suffered cardiac arrest and one suffocated. In the summer, incidents of aneurisms and heart attacks increased.

I noticed that at the end of August, the injured prisoners began to be treated. The number of Korean patients increased markedly in October. They were treated by the on-duty nurse, mostly for head injuries from falling during labour or slipping on stairs. The same prisoner names appeared repeatedly: Choi Chi-su, Kim Gwing-pil, Hiranuma Tochu. My eyes pricked. Choi and Dong-ju had received treatment once a month for head injuries and lacerations on their calves, shoulders, biceps and forearms. But the reasons for the injuries were different from what I knew to be true. I took the open file to Midori, who stopped playing.

'I'm not sure whether this file is accurate,' I said. 'Sugiyama regularly beat up Ward Three prisoners. I probably brought a handful of them to the infirmary myself. There isn't a single mention of that in here.'

Midori avoided meeting my eyes. 'These are merely records. They differ from reality.'

'Are you saying the treatment logs are falsified?'

'When a Ward Three patient comes to the infirmary, I treat them. Afterwards I report the type of wound and the severity of the injury, and the doctor records the information in the log, usually as being caused by falling during labour or being struck by a falling object.'

'Why would a doctor make things up?'

'The warden doesn't want to have unpleasant facts live on in official prison records.'

'But the doctors are supposed to take care of the patients. They have a duty to record why and how their patients got hurt.'

'The injuries of a few Korean prisoners mean nothing to them.'

I glared at her. My voice cracked. 'What's going on? Tell me what you know.'

She stared down at the keys. 'The Korean patients began to come to the infirmary starting around August. When I asked them what happened, they usually mentioned Sugiyama. He was a butcher, he was going to kill all the Koreans with his club. All of the wounds were caused by a blunt object. But I noticed something odd about all the prisoners' injuries.'

'What?'

'Most of the wounds were lacerations about two to three centimetres long. They were deliberate – the skin was very precisely cut, probably with the tip of a whip.'

'Hmm,' I murmured, 'we're supposed to be careful not to create marks on the body.'

'Once I was treating a prisoner for a shallow cut when I noticed that his left little finger was bent. It had broken, but hadn't properly healed, so it was twisted. He told me he'd blocked Sugiyama's club with his hand, and that was how he broke it.'

'That's odd,' I said. 'When a forehead is busted open, it looks like a major and bloody injury, but it actually heals quickly. A broken finger is much more serious. He wasn't treated for that?'

'No. And that was how it was with the rest of the prisoners. Even those with serious wounds weren't sent to us, and then all of a sudden prisoners with minor cuts came flooding in.'

It didn't make any sense. Sugiyama had been violent for a long time, but he had never referred anyone for medical treatment. And then, in August, he began to send people with minor cuts to the infirmary. What happened in August? 'Choi and Hiranuma went to the infirmary once a month. But, starting in October, they began going once a fortnight. What was going on?'

Midori's eyes flickered almost imperceptibly. Was she hiding something? 'I remember Choi being investigated for his tunnel around that time. Hiranuma—'

My eyes fixed on hers. 'That was when Sugiyama was communicating with Hiranuma through poetry. He was still violent, but he was almost the man's guardian. So then why would he injure him?'

The sun turned purple before disappearing in a reddish black. Darkness watched us through the window.

'August 1944,' I said to myself. 'What happened then?' My head was spinning with thoughts.

But Midori said nothing. She slid the file back into the leaves of the sheet music, crossed the auditorium and disappeared into the darkness.

I dragged myself back to the guard office, and the guard on duty looked up. I told him I would take over, as I had to catch up on reports anyway. He flashed a dazzling smile, handed me the ring of keys and scurried off. I opened the cabinet where we kept all the files: the Disinfection and Sanitation Log, Air Raid Evacuation Training Report, Ward Three Prisoner Interrogation Log, Assignment of Workers and Review of Work. I found what I was looking for on the third shelf – Diagnostic Referrals and Autopsy Requests.

Guards filled out diagnostic referral forms when a prisoner needed treatment, and gave them to Maeda for signature. The two-page form had carbon paper underneath, which was submitted to the infirmary; the original went into the file. The same procedure was followed for autopsy requests. I noticed that the forms were the same as those in the file Midori had shown me. The only difference was that we kept the two forms in separate files, while they filed them both in one. In our file, too, the referrals increased, starting on 22 August, mostly by Sugiyama. Various reasons were listed as the cause of injury. Another file, the Infirmary Inspection Results Report, drew my gaze like bait to a fish. I opened it. It didn't start in January; it began with 24 August. So the inspection programme had begun in August. I flipped the page. There were twelve patients identified, along with their symptoms and suspected illnesses. The symptoms were listed as malnourishment, weakness, weakened eyesight, insomnia, haemorrhoids and emotional instability. These were all common; none was worthy of study by Kyushu Imperial University doctors. Why didn't they select Japanese prisoners with more critical illnesses? I knew that many suffered from diabetes, glaucoma, hepatitis and arthritis. But these Korean prisoners seemed relatively healthy, and they were all young, in their late teens to early thirties.

Could it be that the best medical team in the nation had made a grave mistake? I laid the Diagnostic Referrals, Autopsy Requests and Infirmary Inspection Results Report files side-by-side and started to cross reference them by date. Kaneyama Tokichiro, Korean name Kim Myeong-sul, age twenty-nine, was selected during the first infirmary inspection on 24 August. He suffered from malnourishment and insomnia. I was puzzled. Even we guards experienced those conditions. Food was becoming scarce, rations were dwindling and air-raid sirens blared in the middle of the night. I found Kaneyama in the Autopsy Request file for 17 November. What had killed a healthy twenty-nine-year-old man in three months? I flipped through the Diagnostic Referrals carefully, but didn't spot his name. He'd never received treatment for any ailment. I went back and compared the Autopsy Request forms with the Infirmary Inspection Results Report. Since October, five out of seven autopsied bodies had been selected for medical treatment. The causes of death were listed as an aneurism, abnormality of heart function and disturbances of metabolism.

I heard a loud bang and felt suddenly cold. I spun round. The wind was rattling the old doorframe. Freezing air burst through the gap in the windowsill. I looked out the window. Goosebumps prickled all over my skin. Prisoners who had been referred to the infirmary by Sugiyama hadn't been chosen for medical treatment during the inspections. Prisoners who had been chosen died. Why did they keep dying? What was happening during these medical treatments?

*

The next morning I walked into Director Morioka's office. The antique brown carpet muffled my footsteps. Next to the glistening hardwood desk stood a model of a skeleton. An anatomical diagram, a muscular model and a model of the human body hung on the walls; I could see the shoreline of Hakata Bay outside the window.

'How are things, Yuichi?' Morioka asked kindly. 'Was it helpful for you to observe the medical treatment procedures?' His smile was white and sparkling, almost blinding.

'Yes, sir,' I said, my voice cracking.

'Very good. I'm sure your misgivings were put to rest. I will give my recommendation to the warden that you be granted leave. I hope you will be able to visit your family with your mind at ease.'

I couldn't wait. I wanted to flee this place and its bars and fall asleep between the dark, narrow bookcases in Kyoto, inhaling the scent of old paper and dust. But I forced myself to speak up. 'Thank you, sir, but unfortunately, the side-effects are continuing.'

Thick furrows creased the director's brow, but he continued to smile. He coughed. 'I know. They're not side-effects. We had fully anticipated these symptoms.'

I was stunned. 'You expected that your patients would lose their memories and keep bleeding? So why are you continuing the treatment?'

The director's face stiffened incrementally. His eyes glinted, cold and ruthless. 'You're Japanese, aren't you?' His voice was chilly.

'Yes, sir.'

'Then you must know what a great war we are waging. And how important it is to Japan's legacy.'

'Yes, sir!' I'd heard this my entire life. After all, we'd been at war from the day I was born. With Russia, with China, with Mongolia, with Korea, with America, against regular armies and Communist forces and guerrillas. When one battle-front was vanquished, we moved on to yet another.

The director nodded. 'My medical team is devoted to research. Just as you are devoted to our country. You handle prisoners for the glory of the Empire, and the doctors handle patients for victory.'

I felt nauseated, as though I had swallowed maggots. 'How can that be for the victory of the Empire?'

'We've been working hard to develop new treatments for our soldiers. We're on the brink of developing great, life-changing medicine.'

'I'm sure you're right. But I know for a fact that the patients are experiencing side-effects from those treatments.'

'Enough about that!'

'People are dying off. What is going on in this infirmary?' I shouted, unable finally to restrain myself.

Morioka's gaze grew flinty.

I pressed on. 'One record might be false. But the truth is disclosed by many others. I'm talking about the Diagnostic Referrals, the Autopsy Requests and the Infirmary Inspection Results.'

His face drained of blood. 'You're actually quite intelligent. Fine. I knew you were persistent, but if you figured that out, you'll understand what we're doing. I'll tell you what you want to know.' Morioka lowered his voice, as though to soothe a cranky child. 'My medical team is in the process of developing revolutionary medical techniques. If we succeed, we can drastically lower casualty rates on the battle-field. This will be a new era for medicine.'

'What are the techniques?'

'We're looking for a new substance that will replace blood. The war is getting more serious. Blood is what the injured need most. So many good soldiers haemorrhage to death on the battlefield. Even if they're transported to the hospital on time, we have a severe shortage of blood for them. So we can't operate. If we can substitute blood with something else, we can save thousands of soldiers' lives. As well as civilians'.'

'There's a substance that could take the place of human blood?'

'Blood is largely composed of plasma and blood cells. Of those, there are white blood cells, red blood cells and platelets. Plasma is mostly liquid and various proteins and blood-coagulation factors.'

I nodded.

'Like I said, we don't have enough blood. If the platelets, which are the most important component, could be manufactured, we can change the direction of the war.' Morioka's voice trembled.

My heart pounded. 'So you've created blood?'

'We're in the process of developing a saline solution to substitute for platelets. It has similar sodium levels to bodily fluids and is composed of similar substances to platelets. Currently it's used to replace fluids for patients who are ill or injured. We're tinkering with the concentration of the saline. That's what we're using to develop a platelet substitute.'

'But saline solution is basically salt and water,' I murmured, frowning. 'How can that take the place of blood?'

'If one isn't knowledgeable about medicine, like you, one would think that we are killing people, not saving them,' the director said breezily. 'That's why we work under high security. Don't worry. We're reviewing all side-effects as we conduct experiments on human adaptation to varying saline concentrations, resistance to sodium concentrations and infections.'

'But the side-effects are not diminishing.'

'Well, I told you we're still working on it. And we're conducting detailed diagnostic checks to ensure that abnormal reactions are treated. You saw how we give arithmetic tests, right? That's the best way to determine overall neurophysical function. We can instantly determine the effect of foreign substances in the subjects' bodies.'

I finally understood everything. They were experimenting on people. I'd led unsuspecting Koreans to a laboratory of death. I could tell my face was flushed. 'The Kyushu Imperial University medical team is conducting human experiments that kill healthy men! Now I get it. You came here because you needed people to experiment on.'

Morioka smiled. 'I understand what you're saying. You're still young. Why, you're not even twenty years old! Look, Yuichi. The world isn't black-and-white. It's tough and complicated. This research could save the lives of many, many soldiers. All the women and children dying in air raids.'

Tears coursed down my cheeks. I was ashamed and enraged. This wasn't right. However lofty the cause, we couldn't do this. We couldn't toy with one person's life, even if it benefited many more. I squeezed my eyes closed.

The director patted my shoulder gently. 'Listen carefully, Yuichi. The people we need to save are the Empire's soldiers and civilians. The people you're crying over are Koreans who have committed very serious crimes. They've set fire to police stations. They have thrown bombs at the Emperor. They've cut Japanese throats. You know what I mean?'

I didn't. How many people had to die? When would this all come to an end?

Morioka continued. 'They're evil spores growing in our society. Cancerous tumours taking over our bodies. They'll eventually take our lives. Do you know what the treatment for cancer is? You cut it out. You remove it surgically. But the cancerous cells keep growing, damaging healthy cells and ruining the entire body. Who do we need to save? Should we let countless Japanese die, just to save some cancerous fellows?'

Time clattered into the deserted space around me. The golden pendulum of the grandfather clock swung mechanically, wrenching my heart with it. 'Who are we to decide who gets to live and who ends up dead?'

'You know this place is a graveyard for Korean prisoners anyway. So many die before they finish their terms. Don't you think their lives would be put to good use if they could teach us something in death?' Morioka smiled. 'There's no difference between a dying man and a dead man. I'm telling you, the prisoners are on their way to the grave anyway.'

Was he right? Could this terrible situation be even more complex than I thought?

# FRIGHTENING TIMES

It was loud inside the fabric workroom. The washing machines spun manically, the sewing machines clattered, the guards shouted, the prisoners grunted and moaned. Here, prisoners mended tattered military uniforms with bullet holes; their owners were probably no longer alive. I'd searched for a way to get Dong-ju out of the medical treatments, but as yet I hadn't found a solution. The best I could do was move him to the dye-team, in charge of dipping cloth into the dye-baths. At least here he was indoors. As Dong-ju pulled a cart heaped with faded uniforms, a loud siren sliced through the shriek of steam; it was time for break. Dong-ju backed away slowly and squatted near the dye-bath. Other workers were collapsed in exhaustion near the window on the opposite side. The guards stood to one side, smoking and laughing.

Dong-ju dipped a finger in a can of dark-navy paint under the dye-bath. He scrawled something on the dirty wall, before wiping his finger on his uniform. He looked at me with relief. He stood awkwardly in front of the wall, hiding the words. A guard was watching suspiciously from the other side of the room. I took out my club, approached Dong-ju and whacked him on the thigh. He winced and lost his balance. The guard turned around and started talking with the others again. Dong-ju whispered to me what he'd written for my benefit. 'Sky, Wind, Stars, Poetry.'

I nodded in unspoken promise. If he lost all his memories, I would bring him here to these words. Even if he couldn't remember, I would tell him that he *was* a poet, and would always be one. That I remembered his poems, that I was safekeeping that part of his soul. A smile bloomed on his face, unsullied and strong. I stood in front of him, facing out, so that the guards wouldn't see his face. That was the only kindness I could offer.

Dong-ju's health deteriorated rapidly. During our time in the interrogation room he spoke less and less, uttering only half-formed sentences and tangled thoughts. Our conversation was like Morse code: a long silence interrupted by a short dialogue, leading to an even longer silence and an even shorter exchange. His spark was vanishing, like the last breath of a dying man. Eventually our conversation ceased entirely – silence, longer silence and, finally, endless silence. I wasn't sure if he was choosing not to talk or if he couldn't. His memories had scattered like fallen leaves; thin winter branches were all that were left, leaving behind a barren tree yearning for a bygone summer. Dong-ju no longer recalled his brilliant past; he merely suffered through empty time.

On what would end up being our last day in the interrogation room, we shared a silent conversation. I felt his exhaustion and his pain as though they were my own.

Suddenly, his lips opened. '"Frightening Times." Who are you, calling me? / In a shadow of green oak leaves, / I am still breathing. / I who have never raised my hand / I who don't have the sky to greet with my hand / Why are you calling me / I, who have no sky to put my body under? / On the morning of my death, after my work is done / Oak leaves will fall in peace . . . / Do not call me.'

I scribbled down his halting words. Was this the last light emitted by his pale soul, lightning tearing through darkness one last time? The words blurred. Why was it this poem that he remembered now?

Suddenly it reminded me of one of his favourite poets, Francis Jammes, and one of his poems that I'd come across in Dong-ju's box of confiscated documents:

## IT WAS TERRIBLE

*It was terrible to see that poor struggling little calf being
dragged
just now to the slaughterhouse,*

*and who tried to lick the rainwater
on the grey walls of the sad little town.*

*O my God! he seemed so gentle
and so good, he who had been the friend of the holly-lined
lanes.*

*O my God! You who are so good,
tell us that there will be a pardon for us all*

*— and that some day, in golden Heaven, we shall no longer
murder precious little calves,*

*and, instead, having become kindlier,
we shall wreathe their little horns with flowers.*

> *O my God! Don't let that little calf*
> *Suffer too much as he feels the knife enter . . .*

I looked away; I didn't have the courage to look Dong-ju in the eye. We were the ones who started this horrible war, we were the ones who put him behind bars, we were the ones who had destroyed him. Whether we wanted it or not, we had all consented to this terrible war waged in the name of our country. Could we be forgiven for that?

Dong-ju continued performing hard labour, his body frail and doe-like. I didn't know where he was going; he may not have known, either. The workroom was hot, filled with smoky dust, the dizzying clatter of the sewing machines and the strong smell of dye. The prisoners' faces glistened, blackened by sweat, dust and dye. We urged them on, swinging our clubs. Dong-ju went between the sewing machines and the dye-bath like a dung beetle, pulling the cart piled with uniforms behind him. He pulled that heavy cart with all his might.

The siren rang out loudly, signalling break time. Men collapsed like blades of cut grass. Dong-ju put the handle of the cart down on the ground and sank to the floor. Sweat glistened on his forehead.

'You okay?' I asked, taking care to tamp down the trembling in my voice.

He looked at me blankly. Then he smiled in recognition. 'Ah!'

That was it. He didn't know who I was. I could tell he was analysing my features, noting my short hair and brown uniform, considering whether I knew him and, if so, how. He knew he was a prisoner, but he didn't know why he was there. He knew he was a poet, but he didn't know what he wrote. He knew he read books, but didn't know their contents. Did the times we spent together remain in his memory? Our quiet literary conversations in the interrogation room, the secret underground library, the black books that had lived there, the postcards he wrote, the sound of singing that he listened to, as he trembled in the corridor of the infirmary ward? I hoped so, even if they couldn't be recovered. I wanted to help him – to tell him who he was.

I grabbed his thin wrist. He followed me placidly. We walked through the groups of resting prisoners. I tightened my grip when he lost his balance and let go only when we got to the dye-bath. I turned him towards the wall marked with the words – Sky, Wind, Stars, Poetry. A smile bloomed on his face, the same one I'd seen the first day I met him. But now, everything had been taken away from him. I was the only one who knew the man he used to be. He was a child born into a lost nation; a boy who lived in a house with a plum tree, who ate mulberries and revelled in the blue sky reflected in the well; a child who looked up at the cross on the tip of a high steeple, sad that his country was no longer; a teenager who loved Tolstoy, Goethe, Rilke and Jammes, bringing a precious book he bought at a used bookshop to his boarding house, feeling as though he'd conquered the world; a studious young man who read that book all night; a writer of brilliant poems that nobody ever read; someone who liked to walk along a winding path; a boy who loved a girl without telling her so; a colonized man whose soul had been shattered by the dark era, but still created sparks; a traveller who boarded a boat and left home, studying in a six-mat *tatami* room in a foreign country; a young man awaiting the dawn of a new era; an offender shackled for writing poems in his native tongue; a son longing for his mother in far-away Manchuria; a prisoner awaiting the bugle signalling dawn in this cold prison, flying kites on windy days; a man who always had a smile on his face.

Dong-ju was staring at his own handwriting; he had missed those words dearly. They remained a promise, telling him who he was, how pure his soul was, how he wrote beautiful poems. He reached out with a trembling hand to touch the words.

In a low voice I recited 'Night Counting Stars'. 'The sky of passing seasons / Is filled with autumn. // Without a single worry / I think I can count all the autumn stars. // The reason I can't count all the stars carved one by one in my heart is / because morning is coming, / because night will fall again tomorrow, / because my youth is not yet gone. // For one star, memory / For one star, love / For one star, loneliness / For one star, longing // For one star, poetry / For one star mother, mother. // Mother, I call out one beautiful word for every star. The names of children I shared a desk with in primary school, the foreign names of girls, Pei, Jing, Yu, other girls who have already become mothers, the names of impoverished neighbours, dove, puppy, rabbit, donkey, deer, the names of poets like Francis Jammes and Rainer Maria Rilke. // They are so far away. / Like stars in the beyond, // And you, Mother − / you are in Manchuria far away. // Longing for something, / On top of the hill under falling starlight / I etched my name, / And covered it with dirt. // The insect that cries all night / Does because of its sorrow about its shameful name. // But after winter passes and spring dawns on my star, / On the hill where my name is buried / Grass will stand thick and proud / Like green grass blooming on a grave.'

Dong-ju's face brightened. Perhaps he was thinking of the night sky he and Sugiyama had watched, of the stars scattered above, of eternity glimpsed beyond the hazy constellations, of the voice singing of those twinkling lights. Perhaps he would gather his scattered memories and once again write poems and discuss Tolstoy, Dostoyevsky and Rilke. But it was more likely that he had no idea he once couldn't sleep because of those shining words, or that his own head had been filled with such beauty, or that he had written this poem himself.

I was losing a friend. I couldn't bear it.

Break was over. The prisoners rose to their feet, moaning and grunting. Dong-ju hurried to his cart, his legs shaking under him. I shoved my club under his armpit to help him up, hoping it would look as though I were prodding him to hurry. He was astoundingly light. He murmured his poem that I had just recited. 'Mother . . . Longing for something, on top of the hill under falling starlight I etched my name, And covered it with dirt . . . but after winter passes and spring dawns on my star—' He suddenly stopped as his ankles gave way.

'645! Hiranuma! Yun Dong-ju!' I cried.

He was unconscious. He must have hit his head on the way down. Or maybe he had fallen because he'd lost consciousness. The prisoners rushed forward and surrounded us, glaring at me. Dong-ju was sprawled on the ground. His eyes were closed, but he was still smiling.

# AFTER WINTER PASSES AND
# SPRING DAWNS ON MY STAR

The doctors checked Dong-ju's vitals every hour, gauging his blood pressure, temperature and pulse. They weren't trying to save him; they were simply observing the process of death. The doctor on duty granted me special permission to visit Dong-ju, and led me down the narrow hallway lined with dancing white curtains. That was where patients awaited the end of their lives. The doctor showed me to a cot and pushed aside the thin curtain. I could sense the presence of death; Dong-ju was slipping in and out of consciousness. I shot a resentful look at the needle in his arm, through which clear liquid was flowing into his body. The doctor explained that it was a nutritional supplement. Was that even true? I wanted to yank it out. Each time Dong-ju came to, the doctor rattled off a series of questions. 'What's your name?' 'What's today's date?' 'Where are we?'

Dong-ju cocked his head. He struggled to open his mouth. 'I don't know. 14 July 1943. I'm at . . . is this the Shimogamo Police Station?'

That was the date he was arrested by the Special Higher Police.

The doctor frowned. 'His memory's completely shot. Do you remember anything? Tell me whatever you can think of.'

'Sky, wind, stars, poetry,' Dong-ju murmured. 'Memories and love and longing and poetry and mother . . . One star and a beautiful word, impoverished neighbours' names, and puppy, rabbit, deer, donkey, Rainer Maria Rilke—'

The doctor shook his head. He motioned for me to follow him out. Dong-ju stared through me as though he were looking into another world.

That was the last time I saw him.

A few days later, I was in the censor office when I came across a form signed by Dong-ju's doctor. *Requesting posting of prisoner 645's death notification.* I felt everything turn black. It was my job to send telegrams notifying deaths. I pulled the phone on the desk towards me. I turned the handle to call the operator, but I couldn't speak. The operator's annoyed voice cut through my muteness.

I managed to dictate the telegram. 'Dong-ju died 16 February. Collect body.' My hand – no, my entire body – was trembling. I returned the receiver to its cradle. I opened my hand to count out the days that remained until his release.

I paced the frozen prison yard like a caged animal. Ten days later, Dong-ju's father and cousin arrived to gather Dong-ju's remains. I approached them as they headed out of the prison. I bowed my head. I wanted to say something. I wanted to convey his appearance, his last words, something that would allow his father to remember his son the way he was. After a while I raised my head. 'It's unbelievable – Dong-ju has died. That beautiful person . . .' I quickly turned round and walked away; my own tears were inappropriate in the face of their grief.

# BLESSED ARE THEY THAT MOURN

Time stopped for me, but it somehow kept ticking away for everyone else. Snow fell, piled up, drifted and melted, and new grass sprouted. On frozen branches spring flowers bloomed and died. I didn't notice the winter fading into spring, which heated into summer in turn. I was a small, unmoored boat on an empty ocean, my sail torn, my oars broken. I was haunted by the men no longer here; Sugiyama's face and Dong-ju's voice dogged me wherever I went. My memories flashed back to the guard's corpse hanging in the main corridor. I heard the plangent strokes of *Die Winterreise*, saw the poet's long, pale hand opening the door to the interrogation room and Sugiyama's rough hand writing on coarse recycled paper, and recalled Dong-ju's eyes as he recited poetry under the stars. I thought often of the underground library, the long, narrow tunnel, Midori's fingers flying across the piano keys like birds on the wing and the way she said, 'He was a poet.' My memory swam with poems that withered into a plume of smoke, books that transformed into a handful of ash, conversations in the interrogation room and Dong-ju's words: 'A book that takes root in someone's heart never disappears.'

Everyone was leaving this world, especially the innocent.

The war wrought violence on my soul. People left even when it wasn't death that took them. Midori was suddenly transferred to a military hospital in Nagasaki. Perhaps she wanted to get out of here, knowing what nightmares were happening in this place. She left in a swirl of dry wind, without leaving behind even the shortest smile. Her departure made the prison feel emptier. I thought of her every moment I was awake. To push her away from my thoughts, I brandished my club with fervour and harassed the prisoners brutally, like Sugiyama used to. I thought I could understand him now, the guard who couldn't help but become a monster, walking arrogantly to conceal his limp and turning brutal to hide his guilt. The prisoners began to avoid me, which is exactly what I wanted. I wanted to stop thinking about Midori; she was a good person, not like me. I could stand to be alive only if I could become even more brutal than the war.

I wanted to be invisible, to get out. I holed up in the inspection office, reading books and postcards, consoling myself that I wasn't the only person bruised by the times. With the excuse of my censorship duties, I skipped meals and didn't show up for the soldier-guard assemblies. Whenever I thought about Dong-ju, I went to the bookshelves, even though his box of confiscated materials was long gone. In those moments, I took out his black leather-bound Bible from the bottom of my drawer. This was the only thing that still proved his existence to me. I flipped through the pages his fingers had touched and opened it to a passage I'd read so often that my lips moved almost by rote:

Blessed are the poor in spirit: for theirs is the kingdom of heaven.

Blessed are they that mourn: for they shall be comforted.
Blessed are the meek: for they shall inherit the earth.
Blessed are they which do hunger and thirst after right-
eousness: for they shall be filled.
Blessed are the merciful: for they shall obtain mercy.
Blessed are the pure in heart: for they shall see God.
Blessed are the peacemakers: for they shall be called the
children of God.
Blessed are they which are persecuted for righteousness'
sake: for theirs is the kingdom of heaven.

— MATTHEW 5:3—10

Dong-ju had made peace with unfathomable despair, even in his brutal, barbaric death. Now, these calm sentences that had meant so much to him soothed me.

One day, I opened the back cover of the Bible and a small piece of paper, covered in neat, familiar handwriting, fluttered out like a feather.

### Eight Blessings

*Blessed are they that mourn*
*Blessed are they that mourn*
*Blessed are they that mourn*
*Blessed are they that mourn*
*Blessed are they that mourn*
*Blessed are they that mourn*
*Blessed are they that mourn*
*Blessed are they that mourn*

*For they shall mourn forever.*

I felt an immense despair. The repetition seemed to fore-shadow the acceptance of his fate, but the last line empha-sized that the pain would go on for eternity. Had Dong-ju resigned himself to this? I shook my head. That wasn't like him. He would have looked squarely at the hardship he faced; his poem was a promise that he would accept and survive it, no matter what happened. I couldn't give up now. I had to face these times courageously, just as he had done.

With renewed energy I headed to the post room every day, filled my mailbag and brought it back to my office. Once in a while there was a big package. But my duties bored me; all I was doing was snooping into other people's correspondence. Postcards flew in and out of my office like a flock of swallows, gliding over the prison walls and on-wards to the mountains and the ocean.

One day at the end of May I came across a letter addressed to Warden Hasegawa. I hadn't seen the warden receive personal post; he usually only got official documents sent from the police department or the Interior Ministry. I flipped through the logs to see how Sugiyama had dealt with similar letters, but the warden had never received private letters under Sugiyama's watch, either. I held the brown envelope under the light and noticed the foreign stamp. It was from Manchuria. The warden had never been stationed in Manchuria, and if he'd had a friend in the Kwantung Army, he would have used the military post, which was cheaper and faster. Who sent this letter? There was no return address, and the sender's name consisted of uncommon Chinese characters: 泊光 壽 太郎. Hakuaki Jutaro? Hakuteru Jutaro? Or was it Hakumitsu Jutaro? What kind of name was this? All of a sudden, the letters began to regroup before my eyes.

The first character, 泊, could be divided into two: 三白. 300. That meant that the next character, 光, might not be *aki* or *teru*, meaning bright, but a number as well – *mitsu* meant three. Hakumitsu. 壽, which I'd read as *ju*, could be 十, meaning ten, which had the same pronunciation. The numbers revealed themselves in front of my eyes. 三百三十! 330? With wide eyes I stared at the last character. I suddenly remembered the first time I'd brought Choi into the interrogation room. When I asked him for his Japanese name, he'd replied, 'Call me Ichiro (一郎).' Taro (太郎) was, like Ichiro, another name to refer to the eldest son of a family. 三百三十一. 331. Choi Chi-su. Could it really be? Was he still alive?

My need to see what was in the letter overruled my hesitation; my hands were already ripping open the envelope. I justified it to myself that I had a duty to review all incoming post. I pulled out a brownish piece of paper, the same paper we used here. What was it doing in an envelope from Manchuria? I shouldn't open this letter. But it was too late.

Dear Warden Hasegawa,

I apologize for not sending news earlier. I hope you understand; I returned to Manchuria after such a long absence that I had many tasks to do. I realize I wouldn't be writing this letter if it weren't for you. So, thank you. If you hadn't helped me, risking everything, I would never have been able to escape Fukuoka Prison.

Here, I am leading a platoon of 460 soldiers for the independence movement. Seven days ago we destroyed three Kwantung Army platoons. Now the Kwantung Army stationed in Manchuria is powerless. All of that is thanks to you.

First, the news that you have been waiting for: unfortunately, the three men you sent along with me are dead. They weren't as smart or intelligent or strong as you'd thought, though they did protect me on my way to Manchuria through Vladivostok. It was a miscalculation on your part to think that a few rule-abiding men would be able to deal with me in this rough part of the world. Because of our longtime affection, I buried them deep so they wouldn't be eaten by wolves.

I have another piece of news. Unfortunately, I haven't been able to obtain the gold bullion. I know you smuggled me out and sent those three secret agents with me for the gold, but it was all for naught. I didn't take your share; the gold bullion never existed. But you shouldn't think that I tricked you. What I told you was true – I was indeed the only one who knew of an enormous amount of treasure hidden in Manchuria. What you didn't know was that I was talking about my leaving prison, that priceless freedom. But the greedy, like you, took that statement to mean that I was referring to the Kwantung Army's gold, and you let me escape so you could get your hands on it. I found my treasure, but you didn't. You must know Hiranuma Tochu. Yun Dong-ju, the poet? He calls that a metaphor – a truth hidden in a false sentence.

I have a request. I would like you to keep my promise to Watanabe Yuichi, the soldier-guard. I promised to tell him about the life and death of Sugiyama Dozan, but I won't have the chance now. He's probably figured out what was going on in the prison by now, but I don't think he knows about our deal. Tell him for me. Even if you don't, I'm sure he'll keep digging until he finds out.

I have another request. I suppose you could call it a warning. I hope nothing bad happens to the Koreans you're holding hostage. If anything happens to them I will send a copy of this letter to the Interior Ministry. I'm sure you wouldn't want to see the Special Higher Police rushing to the prison.

Thanks for feeding me and clothing me and giving me a place to sleep for all those years.

Number 331

What was going on? Choi clearly knew I would read his letter. In the end he'd kept his two promises: he'd repaid me for the paper I'd given him, and he was making sure I'd hear the truth about Sugiyama's death. But I was afraid. What was the point of mining for truth in this godforsaken place? What did it matter that a guard had been killed? I could take the easy route and burn the letter. It was wartime; no one would question post from Manchuria going missing. Hasegawa certainly wasn't expecting a message like this from Choi. The letter, trembling in my hands, awaited its fate. Finally, I stamped it: *Censorship Completed*. The letter would be delivered to Hasegawa, who would know that I'd read it. I might have done something I shouldn't have. I might regret it deeply. But there was no turning back now.

# RABID DOG DAYS

I was summoned to the warden's office. I stood at attention in front of his desk for an eternity, but he didn't look up from his newspaper blaring the headlines 'All Schools from Primary School to University Will Become Military Schools', 'Army Ministry Reforms Military Service Law Regarding Early Conscription'. They'd lowered the conscription age once again; it was now fifteen. All people talked about was national resistance. Finally Hasegawa folded the newspaper and placed it on his desk. He looked at me with the dignity of a lion. 'I received the letter from Manchuria.'

I was trembling like a frail antelope. 'I had no choice,' I murmured defensively. 'I am to review all incoming and outgoing post.'

Of course, we both knew that exceptions existed for all regulations; I should have sent the post addressed to the warden without opening it. This time the performance of my duties was tantamount to a declaration of war.

Hasegawa maintained his calm with effort. 'I'm not finding fault with you. You were right to be faithful to your duties.'

I'd expected him to shout at me; now I felt all the more nervous.

Hasegawa slowly added tobacco to his pipe and tamped it down with his thumb. 'I called you here because there's something you need to know.'

My heart thumped. He wouldn't hide or avoid anything now; I wanted to be done with all of this. 'Yes, sir. There are things I've been seeking to understand.'

He lit his pipe. He sucked in loudly a few times; smoke curled up to the ceiling. 'Well, what is it that you want to know?'

'All I know is that there's something going on in this prison that shouldn't be.'

His features stiffened. I felt an eerie chill.

'Nothing's going on that shouldn't be happening,' he said. 'What are you referring to?'

'The doctors in the infirmary are conducting human experiments on healthy Korean prisoners. They—'

'What is it that you really want to know?' he barked.

'Is Choi still alive?'

Hasegawa's eyebrows furrowed. He sucked deeply on his pipe and let out a plume of white smoke. He nodded.

Dozens of questions collided with one another in my head, but I managed to bleat out only one. 'How?'

The warden gazed at the smoke trailing upwards. He tapped his pipe on the ashtray. He sucked a few more times on the empty pipe. 'For the Empire. I kept him alive for the Empire.'

When Choi arrived at the prison, rumours about the man who'd hurled a bomb at the Emperor raced around the prison. But Choi kept to himself, his mouth sealed. He paced the prison yard like a caged wild beast. The very day the warden arrived at Fukuoka, he watched Choi from behind the white curtains in his office. Hasegawa could tell that Choi still reeked of conspiracies, even when he didn't say a word and was just sitting in the sun by himself. Hasegawa wanted to know what Choi was plotting. He tasked Kim Man-gyo with watching Choi and ordered him to report back. The following day Choi was moved into Kim's cell. Outgoing and affable, Kim gained Choi's trust quickly by procuring hard-to-find goods and providing him with information from the guards.

Soon Kim relayed a rumour that Choi had left an enormous treasure in the hills of Manchuria. Eyes glinting, he reported that the prisoners claimed that Choi, who had led a fairly large brigade of independence fighters before coming to Japan, had attacked a Kwantung Army supply unit that held the military chest for Manchuria. Choi had apparently hidden the gold in a secret location before smuggling himself into Japan. Hasegawa laughed. It was preposterous. A ragtag bunch of bandits couldn't possibly defeat a Kwantung Army supply unit. And why would this Choi bury mounds of gold and leave his riches, to go back into the danger of war?

But then Choi attempted to break out of prison. Already a regular in solitary, he pushed a guard aside in the yard and sprinted towards the wall. Hasegawa took it upon himself to interrogate Choi personally, after he'd been beaten beyond recognition. Hasegawa looked greedily into his swollen eyes. 'It's General Choi, I hear? Why did you try to escape?'

'Escape is the number-one duty of a soldier in captivity.'

Hasegawa struck Choi's cheek angrily with his baton. 'You're not a soldier or a prisoner of war. You're just a criminal. You weren't trying to escape, you were trying to die.'

'It doesn't matter. If dying is the only way I can get out of here, then that's what I'll do.'

'Fearless, aren't you? Why is that?'

'There's something I need to do.'

Hasegawa suddenly remembered the rumour. What if Choi actually had stolen the Empire's military chest? If he recovered it, that achievement would be truly unsurpassed. Hasegawa's temples began to throb. He couldn't be impatient; he had to bide his time until he was certain. He twisted his moustache. 'I should execute you for attempting to escape. But just this once, I'll look the other way. You're going to solitary for a fortnight. If you do something stupid like this again, I promise you'll be riddled with bullets next time.'

But soon after Choi was released from solitary he attempted another escape. This time, he'd lain in the drain along the wall. A guard on his rounds discovered him immediately. The warden interrogated him a second time. It was the same thing all over again. Choi insisted there was something he had to do. Hasegawa sent him back to solitary. Choi escaped and tried to climb over the wall. Again, Hasegawa sent him to solitary. The two men continued this endless game of cat-and-mouse. The fourth attempt resulted in Choi hiding in the back of a lorry scheduled to ship out bricks made in the prison workroom. Hasegawa stopped the lorry and had all the bricks unloaded; Choi, covered in dust, rolled out and sprinted desperately towards the gates. The guard positioned at the watchtower aimed the machine gun at his back, watching the warden's hand. If the warden lowered his hand, he was to shoot. Hasegawa instead gave the guards around him a look. The guards took out their clubs and went after Choi. Practically a corpse, he was now dragged yet again into the interrogation room. Hasegawa looked down at him. Why did this prisoner keep trying to escape in such desperate ways, when he knew his life was on the line?

'Why do you keep doing this?' Hasegawa asked.

Choi didn't answer.

Hasegawa looked round to make sure they were alone. 'You won't say it yourself, so I'll say it. The reason you're trying to escape so desperately is not because of a prisoner-of-war's duty, or for the independence of your sorry country.'

'Then why?'

'Because of money. The enormous amount of gold you hid somewhere in Manchuria.'

Choi raised his swollen eyes. 'What are you talking about?'

'I looked through some files at the Army Ministry. There is a record of an anti-Japanese surge in Manchuria in the mid-1930s. In 1936 some Korean independence and Communist elements attacked the supply unit of the Kwantung Army. We beat them, but suffered significant loss of life and goods.'

'Are you saying there are records about gold being stolen?'

Hasegawa shook his head. 'It was wartime. The military wouldn't have revealed the amount of loss. If they had lost a large portion of the military chest, the person responsible for the platoon and several others would have been shot dead. It's the basics of war propaganda. You diminish setbacks as much as possible and exaggerate any victory.'

'What makes you think that the gold was stolen?'

'That year the Ministry sent 8,000 troops to the Kwantung Army, including regimental-level supply troops, 700 guard troops and 300 recon troops. They sent sixteen separate orders to round up Korean insurgents and Communists in Manchuria. That had never happened before or since. That means that around that time they had suffered immense losses. They had to reconstruct the platoon, strengthen vigilance and go after the anti-Japanese elements.'

'And what was the result?'

'It was a partial success. They destroyed those elements armed against us throughout Manchuria, more than 2,000 of them.'

'Why was it only a partial success then?'

Hasegawa smiled meaningfully. 'There's no record anywhere that they found the stolen military chest. Had we got the money back, it would certainly have been recorded, in celebration of such an enormous defeat for our enemies.'

'So where is all that gold?'

'That's something I should ask you.' Hasegawa smiled suggestively. He saw Choi's lips purse involuntarily. 'I know the rumour is true. You're risking your life to get out of this place to recover that hidden gold. Because you're the one who attacked the platoon.'

Hasegawa unfastened the top button of his uniform. He was ready to make a deal. First, they had to establish the rules. Choi was the only person who knew where the gold was. He had to leave the prison to get it. Hasegawa would look the other way. They would split the gold in half. Hasegawa would send armed guards with Choi, so he couldn't get away. His secret plan was to order the guards to kill Choi the moment the gold was recovered. But now they needed a convincing escape plan. They discussed various options and came to an agreement on the best one. Choi would dig his way out and the warden would look the other way. It might take months, even years, but it had to be done perfectly.

Choi began to get himself sent to solitary and brought in other prisoners. The solitary cells were always at capacity as he and his gang began to dig. When they only had fifteen metres left, they encountered a problem: Sugiyama. The guard had been watching Choi and had sniffed out the plot. Sugiyama reported the incident to Hasegawa, his eyes emitting righteous fire.

'Sugiyama!' Hasegawa soothed. 'I know what's going on. Thank you for your efforts, but this is not something to get worked up about. There's a bigger plan in place. So forget you know anything about this.'

Sugiyama didn't understand. All he could think about was stopping this prisoner from escaping. He brought Choi to the interrogation room and beat him to a pulp. If Choi filled up the tunnel, Sugiyama would forget it ever happened. That was the best Sugiyama could do to obey Hasegawa's order and still stop Choi from escaping. Choi couldn't flout Sugiyama, who now checked on the tunnel daily. Hasegawa became frustrated; Choi was unable to do anything.

That was when Sugiyama died.

'Who killed Sugiyama?' I asked, voice trembling.

'As you know, it was Choi. But it doesn't matter who actually committed the deed. Sugiyama's death created a way out for the stalled plan.'

I shook my head. 'You used a guard's death to further your plan?'

'That's how important it was. A dead man is a dead man. If he knew his death would contribute to the victory of the Empire, Sugiyama would have been happy, too.'

'How could that possibly happen?'

'It was too late to continue digging the tunnel. With the war effort faltering, there was no time to hesitate. So we changed our plan. Choi's execution would be the best way for him to get out of prison. And to do that, Choi had to be

Sugiyama's murderer.' Hasegawa grinned. His self-importance was nauseating me.

My chin trembled with rage and resentment. 'So you assigned me to the murder investigation so that I would accuse Choi? Was it also part of the plan to promote me for solving it?'

Hasegawa looked bashful for a moment. 'I'm sorry about that. Really, I am. But you were the perfect person to be assigned that task. You are both adequately naive and well-meaning. I couldn't tell you what was going on. Anyway, you did your best in the situation. You found the murderer and contributed greatly to the plan.'

That was why Choi had confessed so readily when I interrogated him. I was merely a puppet. I had worked so hard for nothing; the countless sleepless nights, the time I spent racked with guilt – all was meaningless. I was the only one who'd been kept in the dark.

'As I said, you did a good job,' Hasegawa said gently. 'Your job was to be completely fooled.'

'You made me a fool and a puppet!' I shouted.

'Maybe you're right. But sometimes a puppet is necessary. We were able to get Choi out and recover the imperial gold.'

'But your plan failed! The three guards protecting Choi died. And there's no gold.'

'No, no. I checked all the records. He did attack the supply unit and stole immense amounts of gold. I'll have to dispatch special service guards to capture him. We have to find that gold!' Hasegawa's face was flushed.

'Forget it, sir. You were tricked. You know why? You weren't trying to get the military chest back, you were coveting the gold for yourself. If you were going to recover the military chest, you would have reported it to the Ministry or the Special Higher Police. But you plotted everything in secret. If it hadn't been for your greed, you would have seen through Choi's trick.'

'What do you mean?'

'Choi made his first ridiculous escape attempt so that he would be personally interrogated by you. He made up a rumour about the secret gold and then attempted to escape. He knew he wouldn't succeed. When he was sent to solitary instead of being shot, he was certain that you believed the rumour. He was the only person who knew where the mythical treasure was, so he was certain that you wouldn't kill him. After that, he attempted many more escapes. He demonstrated that he would risk death to escape, proving that there was something he had to do on the outside. He slowly got you to believe him.'

'That's not possible.'

'You might think you would never be tricked, but you were begging to be fooled. You wanted to believe him. You believed Choi's story because of your greed.'

'Greed?' Hasegawa glared at me and slammed his baton on his desk. 'Is it greed to show my loyalty to the Empire, to return stolen gold to the nation?'

I froze in place. I'd said too much. I had to choose: I would be safe if I took the warden's secret to my grave; time would pass uneventfully, and I would survive if I buried all of those things deep within me. 'Sir, was it your plan all along to kill Sugiyama? Did you need a victim to make Choi a murderer?'

Hasegawa shook his head. 'Sugiyama wasn't part of the plan. He just got in the way. Nothing would have happened to him if he hadn't discovered the tunnel, or if he'd listened to my advice. But he was persistent, and Choi couldn't shake him off. And it's not only that. Sugiyama committed treason. He purposefully wounded certain prisoners so that they wouldn't be chosen for medical treatment. Like Hiranuma. After Sugiyama died, we made sure Hiranuma was selected for medical treatment.'

It was just as I'd suspected. I now truly began to understand why Midori believed Sugiyama wasn't evil. 'Is that why you killed Sugiyama?'

He shook his head. 'I did use Sugiyama's death, but I didn't kill him. He disobeyed orders and he was a traitor, but he was still a war hero. He was valuable to me.'

'Then who?'

His burning gaze seared through my skill as the amorphous pieces of truth began to find their places at last.

I burst out of the warden's office, screaming.

I ran into Director Morioka's office. He was getting off the phone. 'Yuichi,' he greeted me with his ever-pleasant demeanour. 'The warden just called. He said you had a question for me.' His voice was silky.

I glared at him, my eyes bloodshot. 'I need your cooperation in the investigation of Sugiyama Dozan's murder.'

'Are you still on that case? Wasn't the perpetrator caught and the investigation concluded? Don't you have better things to do?' Morioka looked at me sympathetically.

I spat out my rising rage. 'The criminal was caught, but the incident wasn't concluded. Because Choi wasn't the murderer. Someone else killed Sugiyama.'

'Who killed him?'

I took in a deep breath. 'He's in the infirmary.'

Morioka's voice turned syrupy, trying to disarm me. 'How did you end up believing such nonsense, Yuichi?'

I had to goad him into anger. 'Sugiyama's lips were sewn with surgical thread. Seeing that the killer used a surgical needle and thread, it's clear that the son-of-a-bitch was a doctor. But he was sloppy.'

'And you have proof?'

'I saw the corpse. The stitches were crooked. He was probably shaking so violently, so frightened, that he ran off without even making a knot.' I was lying through my teeth: the sutures were precise and immaculate. But I was trying my best to confuse him.

The corners of his eyes trembled slightly. He smiled. 'Don't go running your mouth off when you don't know anything. Why would a Kyushu Imperial University doctor kill a trifling guard?' He looked at me with a benevolent expression, but I could detect an edge to his warm smile.

I swallowed hard. 'Sugiyama knew what was going on in the infirmary. He stood up to those murderers. He beat certain prisoners so they wouldn't be included in the experiments. His only fault was that he had a heart.'

Morioka gave me a pitying smile and pushed his glasses up his nose. 'You're partly right, but mostly wrong. He was a traitor who needed to be eliminated. His lips had to be sealed.'

'A traitor?'

'As a guard, Sugiyama had pledged to give his life to the Empire. But he forgot who he was. I talked to him several times, but he wouldn't listen. He was once a great soldier for the Empire, but he became a turncoat. Let me assure you, he was a problem that needed to be removed.'

I didn't know what to do.

He continued gently, 'Yuichi, I do hope Sugiyama didn't

infect you. You're too young and good to be marred with the ideology of treason.'

'The problem isn't Sugiyama, it's the rest of us!' I cried.

'I know it's hard for you to accept it, what with your youth. But our nation is at war! As a soldier, you must be cognizant of that!'

'I'm not the one who started this war! Those who started this war killed thousands of people, and they did this just to grab more power. They'll pay for it. They have to pay for it!' I knew I was going too far, but I couldn't stop now.

Morioka kept his expression gentle. 'You're a smart young man who has a brilliant future ahead of you. You're not foolish and brutish like Sugiyama. I believe in you.'

I wasn't brave enough to risk death. I wanted to live. As Choi told me to, as Dong-ju requested, I wanted to survive.

Watching me grappling with this dilemma, Morioka's face bloomed into a smile. 'Sugiyama's dead. That's an irreversible fact. We must make sure his death wasn't for naught. We'll pray for him to go to a better place. Although he was a terrible man, his death could still be valuable to us.'

I felt violently sick. I covered my mouth and ran towards the wall. He followed me and rubbed my back as I heaved. 'See? You act tough, but you're actually quite gentle. This is life – disgusting. But you'll find your way. I'm sure you'll forget everything you heard in this office today, right?'

I ran out. I couldn't do anything to stop this. I was overwhelmed by this immense conspiracy. I wanted to tell someone, but I didn't have anyone to tell. Even if I did, nobody would believe me. Nobody, I was sure, could do anything about any of it.

# ANOTHER LINE OF CONFESSION

In July, damp ocean air drifted over the prison walls. Bluish-black mould bloomed on the walls of the censor's office. Air raids continued. The bomb shelter was like the inside of a dark grave. I stared at the darkness. I thought of faces – those of the dead and those of the living. I was one of the survivors, but that made me ashamed.

By August, high humidity permeated the prison. The bluish mould in the censor's office had spread to the pillars. The voices on the radio were becoming more heated and indignant, as the air raids grew ever more intense, death tolls climbed, and cities became mass graves. And yet I lived on. That in itself made me feel as though I'd committed a crime. I closed my eyes, submitted to easy lies and lived with evil. The truth could only live inside me. The war kept dragging on.

On 7 and 9 August, Hiroshima and Nagasaki were bombed. Everything burned and vanished. The war ended on 15 August. When I heard the news, I counted on my fingers to work out the number of days I'd spent without Dong-ju – just one day shy of six months. He'd died only six months before the independence of his country. I was too exhausted to be glad. And that was how I fled from that filthy era.

# EPILOGUE

TRANSCRIPT OF JAPANESE WAR CRIMINAL
INTERROGATION

DATE: 29 October 1946
LOCATION: Fukuoka Prison
INTERROGATOR: Captain Mark Haley, War Criminal Investigator,
   Judicial Department, Pacific Ocean Areas Command
WAR CRIMINAL: D29745 Watanabe Yuichi
INTERPRETER: Nakashima Kyotaro

HALEY: We finished reviewing the lengthy document you
wrote during your year of imprisonment. Is that all you
have to say?

WATANABE: Yes.

HALEY: If this testimony is accurate, you may not be able to
avoid being sentenced as a war criminal. Do you understand?

WATANABE: I do. I didn't write this to defend myself. This
is just a record of what I witnessed during the war.

HALEY: Is this the truth? Or is it fiction?

WATANABE: It's both. My writing is the truth, but there are
some fictional elements.

HALEY: Is the human experimentation by the Kyushu Imperial
University medical team based on facts?

WATANABE: Yes.

HALEY: Do you know about the American B-29 bomber that

was forced to make an emergency landing in Kyushu in May 1945?

WATANABE: No.

HALEY: Do you know anything about the eleven men who were on that plane?

WATANABE: No.

HALEY: The Western Military Headquarters overseeing Kyushu sentenced Lieutenant William Fredericks and eight men to death without a trial. Do you know about that?

WATANABE: No.

HALEY: From our investigation, it has been revealed that the Kyushu Imperial University medical team brought the captives to the infirmary at Fukuoka Prison. Do you know about that?

WATANABE: No.

HALEY: The prison records do not mention the medical treatments you wrote about.

WATANABE: We were ordered to burn all the records when the war was over. I was the censor and was in charge of the incineration of documents. I took all the records from the guard office, the censor's office and the warden's office and burned them.

HALEY: Why did you write about something that nobody else has talked about?

WATANABE: Because someone has to know. I can't let the things I saw vanish into oblivion.

HALEY: Why didn't you just record the facts? Why did you write it in the form of a novel?

WATANABE: Sometimes fiction can reveal more truth than the bare facts. I wanted to speak the truth, but I couldn't record the truth as I saw it.

HALEY: Do you believe you are innocent?

WATANABE: No, I'm guilty. I didn't act.

HALEY: Is there anything else you want to say?

WATANABE: Can you open the window? Dong-ju would have loved looking at the sky tonight.

# ABOUT YUN DONG-JU

At the end of the nineteenth century many Koreans began to move to Manchuria to avoid the deepening famine in northern Korea. Dong-ju's great-grandfather moved his family to Manchuria around 1886. On 30 December 1917 Dong-ju, the eldest son of Yun Yeong-seok and Kim Yong, was born in Mingdong village, Helong Prefecture, Jiandao Province, Manchuria.

As a child, Dong-ju showed talent in poetry. In 1935 he transferred to Sungsil Middle School in Pyongyang, which was closed down the following year for its refusal to worship at a Japanese Shinto shrine. Dong-ju returned to Manchuria to finish middle school and began to publish poems in magazines. In 1938 he enrolled in Yonhi College (now Yonsei University) in Seoul. He began to immerse himself in Korean literature, history and the nationalist movement. In 1940 he attended Hyupsung Church and Bible study on the campus of Ewha Woman's College while continuing to write and publish poems.

In 1941 Dong-ju graduated from Yonhi College. In celebration of that occasion, he gathered nineteen poems into his first volume of poetry, entitled *The Sky, the Wind, the Stars and Poetry*. However, three of the poems, 'Cross', 'Sad Tribe' and 'Another Home', were censored. Concerned for Dong-ju's safety, his professor urged him to give up. Dong-ju entrusted his professor, and his friend Jeong Byeong-uk, with copies of the manuscript for safekeeping.

At the end of 1941 his family changed its surname to Hiranuma to assist in Dong-ju's application to study abroad in Japan. The following year Dong-ju moved to Tokyo and enrolled in the English Literature department at Rikkyo University. He visited his home town for the last time that summer. In the autumn Dong-ju transferred to Doshisha University in Kyoto.

In July 1943 Dong-ju was arrested as a political offender and all of his writings were confiscated. In 1944 he was indicted and sentenced to two years at Fukuoka Prison for the violation of Clause V of the Maintenance of Public Order Act.

On 18 February 1945 Dong-ju's family received a telegram notifying them of his death. At Fukuoka Prison, Dong-ju's father and cousin witnessed fifty-odd Korean men standing in front of the infirmary, waiting for infusions. Prison officials told them that Dong-ju died at 3.36 in the morning on 16 February. A young Japanese guard approached them and said, 'Right before he died, Dong-ju shouted something loudly.' His body was cremated and brought home, and the family buried him in a church cemetery. 'Self-Portrait' and 'New Path' were recited at his funeral.

In May 1945 the Yun family erected a tombstone inscribed 'The Grave of Poet Yun Dong-ju'. On 15 August 1945 Japan was defeated, and Korea became newly independent. In 1947 'Easily Composed Poem' was published for the first time in the newspaper *Kyunghyang Sinmun*, and in 1948 Dong-ju's friend Jeong Byeong-uk published the thirty-one poems that the poet had entrusted to him, under the title *The Sky, the Wind, the Stars and Poetry*.

In 1977 the top-secret document 'Monthly Report of the Special Higher Police', published during the Japanese occupation, was obtained, and Dong-ju's interrogation records were released. Two years later another document was declassified, confirming Dong-ju's sentence and his participation in the independence movement. In 1982, thirty-seven years after Dong-ju's death, a copy of the verdict was released. In 1985 a Professor Omura, of Waseda University in Japan, and officials in Yanbian discovered Dong-ju's grave and tombstone in Longjing, China.

Yun Dong-ju is one of the most well-known and well-respected poets in Korea. His poetry continues to be taught in schools nationwide.

# AUTHOR'S NOTE

This is a work of fiction. I consulted a variety of records for an accurate description of the times. The poems by Yun Dong-ju are from Dong-ju's only published book of poetry. The characters' personalities and actions are entirely fictional; I ask for the understanding of their descendants.

I would not have been able to write this novel without the books about Yun Dong-ju and his body of work, such as *The Complete Collection of Yun Dong-ju's Poetry*, ed. Hong Jang-hak (Munhakgwa Jisongsa), *Night Counting Stars*, ed. Lee Nam-ho (Minumsa World Poetry) and the writings and research materials of countless scholars whose names are too numerous to include, such as *The Critical Biography of Yun Dong-ju* by Song U-hye (Purun Yeoksa), *Yun Dong-ju – 1 Study of Korean Modern Poet* by Lee Geon-cheong (Munhak Segyesa) and *If Spring Comes to My Star – Yun Dong-ju's Life and Literature* by Go Un-gi (Sanha).

# LIST OF SOURCES

'Good Night' by Wilhelm Müller: www.recmusic.org/lieder/ get_text.html?TextId =11830. Translation compiled by Arthur Rishi

*Selected Poems of Francis Jammes*, trans. Barry Gifford and Bettina Dickie (Utah State University Press), 1976

'Day in Autumn' by Rainer Maria Rilke, trans. Mary Kinzie, *Poetry* magazine, April 2008

*German Love: From the Papers of an Alien* by Friedrich Max Müller, trans. Susanna Winkworth (Chapman and Hall), 1858

'Va, pensiero' lyrics by Giuseppe Verdi: http://en.wikipedia.org/ wiki/Va,-pensiero

*The Notebooks of Malte Laurids Brigge*, trans. Burton Pike (Dalkey Archive Press), 2008

Vincent van Gogh in a letter to his brother Theo van Gogh, Arles, Monday 9 or Tuesday 10 July 1888 [638]. Vincent Van Gogh – *The Letters*, 2009, web edition: Van Gogh Museum and Huygens ING, www.vangoghletters.org/vg/letters/let638/letter. html

*Crime and Punishment* by Fyodor Dostoevsky, trans. Constance Garnett, Introduction by Ernest J. Simmons (Dell Publishing), 1959

*The Sorrows of Young Werther* by Johann Wolfgang von Goethe, trans. R.D. Boylan (Norilana Books), 2008

extracts reading groups
competitions books new
discounts extracts
competitions
books new
events books
new extracts
new reading groups
interviews
discounts
new books events
events new
discounts extracts discounts
www.panmacmillan.com
extracts events reading groups
competitions books extracts new